CW00833284

# Fierce
# Thunder

## Courtney Silberberg &
## Jacquelyn Kinkade Silberberg

PNl

First Published in 2015 by:
Pneuma Springs Publishing

**Fierce Thunder**
**Copyright © 2015   Courtney Silberberg & Jacquelyn Kinkade Silberberg**

ISBN13: 9781782283966

Courtney Silberberg and Jacquelyn Kinkade Silberberg have asserted their right under the Copyright, Designs and Patents Act, 1988, to be identified as Authors of this Work

British Library Cataloguing in Publication Data. A catalogue record for this book is available from the British Library.

Pneuma Springs Publishing
A Subsidiary of Pneuma Springs Ltd.
7 Groveherst Road, Dartford Kent, DA1 5JD.
E: admin@pneumasprings.co.uk
W: www.pneumasprings.co.uk

We would like to dedicate FIERCE THUNDER,

our first novel,

to our parents:

Richard Alan and Tissie Silberberg and

CMDR Martin J. and Bette Kinkade.

# Contents

| | | |
|---|---|---|
| Chapter 1 | Sommers |
| Chapter 2 | Enrique |
| Chapter 3 | Turbulence |
| Chapter 4 | Kevin |
| Chapter 5 | Celia |
| Chapter 6 | Cargo |
| Chapter 7 | Rebels |
| Chapter 8 | Robbie |
| Chapter 9 | Where's Lorenzo? |
| Chapter 10 | Elena |
| Chapter 11 | Last Call |
| Chapter 12 | Cracking The Eggs |
| Chapter 13 | Lupe |
| Chapter 14 | Ramon |
| Chapter 15 | Jorge |
| Chapter 16 | The System |
| Chapter 17 | The Mountain |
| Chapter 18 | Hunting |
| Chapter 19 | Survival Of The Fittest |
| Chapter 20 | Texas |
| Chapter 21 | Paradise |
| Chapter 22 | Campfire |
| Chapter 23 | Storms |
| Chapter 24 | The Boar |
| Chapter 25 | The Grand Morass |
| Chapter 26 | Lieutenant Rosa |
| Chapter 27 | The Race |
| Chapter 28 | The Locket |
| Chapter 29 | Go To Ground |
| Chapter 30 | Choices |
| Chapter 31 | Turning Tables |

| Chapter 32 | Accusations |
| Chapter 33 | Hide And Seek |
| Chapter 34 | Ambushed |
| Chapter 35 | Unfriendly Jungle |
| Chapter 36 | Massacre |
| Chapter 37 | Mama |
| Chapter 38 | The Well |
| Chapter 39 | The Chamber |
| Chapter 40 | Passages |
| Chapter 41 | The One |
| Chapter 42 | Game Changer |
| Chapter 43 | Greed |
| Chapter 44 | Spared |
| Chapter 45 | Broken Trail |
| Chapter 46 | Salvation |
| Chapter 47 | Wrong Guide |
| Chapter 48 | A Chance |
| Chapter 49 | Liar's Poker |
| Chapter 50 | Pushing Pedals |
| Chapter 51 | The Pilot |
| Chapter 52 | Jungle Music |
| Chapter 53 | Mules |
| Chapter 54 | Keeping It Together |
| Chapter 55 | Masks |
| Chapter 56 | Violations |
| Chapter 57 | Negotiations |
| Chapter 58 | So Go The Spoils |
| Chapter 59 | Tracks |
| Chapter 60 | Coke Bottles |
| Chapter 61 | Just Press Play |
| Chapter 62 | Raging Legs |
| Chapter 63 | Unfinished Business |

*Chapter 64*        *Big Dog Barks*

*Chapter 65*        *Simple Plan*

*Chapter 66*        *Necklace*

*Chapter 67*        *Pale Riders*

*Chapter 68*        *Treasure Lost*

*Chapter 69*        *The Apothecary*

*Chapter 70*        *Ghosts*

*Chapter 71*        *Maps*

*Chapter 72*        *Valley Of The Lost Souls*

*Chapter 73*        *Death Leads*

*Chapter 74*        *The Marapa*

*Chapter 75*        *Swimmers*

*Chapter 76*        *The Oath*

*Chapter 77*        *Found*

*Chapter 78*        *Tourists*

*Chapter 79*        *Doctor Sommers*

*Chapter 80*        *In Plain Sight*

*Epilogue*

# 1

## SOMMERS

Mountain biking at the Big Bear Ski Resort, high above the Los Angeles basin in the middle of summer, was like being on a different planet. The once crowded, manicured ski runs where virgin powder once lay were now unpatrolled, barren, mountain bike trails. An accountant, who was also an extreme sports enthusiast at the corporate offices, had realized a ski resort could run basically year round, hence, greater revenues and stronger balance sheets.

Chairlifts carried both bikes and bikers up to the top, where lodges that fed hundreds during the winter months, now worked with a skeleton staff, parading in bikinis and shorts. It was in sharp contrast to the congested, smoggy metropolitan area below, as it was pure up there, the air and water clean. The crisp blue sky canopied any danger for the rough and tumble adrenaline junkies the trails attracted, making for an exhilarating place to go, as it was supposed to be fun.

It probably wasn't fair. At least that's how Dr. Brad Sommers saw it in that glimpse of time and space that passed before he was forced to react. Of course "fair" wasn't one of his favorite words at the moment.

An athlete, the twenty-nine year old Sommers was riding hard, too hard, stressing the mountain bike to its limits, pointing down a narrow, winding chute. The gravel and sand rooster-tailed up from the trail as his rear, knobby tire found grooves and then hopped between them, inches from peril.

Sommers tightened the muscles in his strong arms, gingerly maintaining and sensing his precious balance... shifting, leaning. He was a good biker, instinctive, but it was almost futile, as this downhill ride was equivalent to gliding over shiny black ice, and going down or catching an edge here meant falling off the mountain. But Sommers didn't care about that. He was on a mission, trying to forget, cope maybe; with the odd hand fate had dealt him.

The phones kept ringing in his head and cryptic messages about appeal decisions, court dates and where his case was headed if he didn't respond bounced around in his brain like his tires skirting between the ruts for precious traction.

*His case.*

Those two words pierced him. He was being sued, embroiled in what he thought was a frivolous legal battle for just doing his job. Frivolous or not, a career, his career and professional life, was on the line for, of all things... helping.

He was a third year resident on the internal medicine fast track. Being a professional, a physician, now made him a target. Over analyzing, he thought it perverse to stay buried in books in dank libraries or labs, work double shifts in a thankless environment in order to find some light at the end of the tunnel, to ultimately become vulnerable and twist in the wind in this unique profession that ultimately saved lives.

But that was the system. His hand.

Sommers had paid his dues and kept paying them, spending a fortune garnered from different crap jobs, a small trust fund and many, many high interest student loans. So where was the light?

"Sommers," bellowed the beleaguered voice of his attorney, friend and novice mountain biker, David Wethers. He had heard the voice earlier, but kept riding, plunging down the trail... cerebral wheels racing. Seeing Wethers, overweight and whale-like, awkwardly wrestle the high-tech two-wheeler would have been comical on any other day, but Sommers had brought him to the ski resort to get away, to escape the turmoil that was crippling him, and perhaps find a solution.

Sommers twisted his bike into a perfect power slide and skidded to a halt. Moments later, the pudgy Wethers wobbled down the narrow trail. Upon spotting Sommers, he panicked and turned the bike into the hill, riding up a few feet before promptly falling over in a heap. Coughing up a lung full of dirt, he ripped off his helmet and wheezed for air.

"Why are you trying to kill me, Sommers?"

"The hill will do that without my help. Here, have some water."

Staggering up, Wethers almost lunged for the water. "Why did you bring me up here? How much farther to the bottom?"

"Three, maybe four--"

"MILES?"

"Yes, miles. You're on top of the world here. Look around. Enjoy it."

"Right," Wethers whined sarcastically, gulping more of the quenching fluid, a trickle dripping on his chin and shirt. "We need to talk."

"I didn't bring you here to--"

"Yes, you did." Wethers took on a serious tone. "The Medical Board isn't backing you."

"Bunch of hypocrites--"

"Be that as it may, your appeal, and how and when it's filed, is all you have. That is, if you still want to be a doctor in this country."

"Forget 'em. I didn't do anything wrong. Nothing!"

"Ethically and morally, no. Believe me; any attorney can put a defense together. But these guys have momentum. It's high profile. My suggestion is we cop to a lesser charge. Go the probation route and in, say, six months--"

"I'm not copping to anything. I did my job."

"And someone died." Wethers didn't like ramming the point home, but he knew his friend was in trouble, career trouble. A cautionary fine line needed to be delicately walked. "Look, it's not your fault it was a Senator's daughter. Wrong place, wrong time."

Sommers adjusted his chin strap. "I suppose her alcoholic, ex step-mom, whose blood alcohol was three times the legal limit, driving a hundred and five down Pacific Coast Highway into oncoming traffic was my fault too."

"Sommers--"

"I'm not taking the fall. You didn't see her face, Wethers. You didn't see--"   At a loss and disgusted, Sommers swung his bike around.

"Sommers... Sommers," came Wethers' pleas to no avail. "We have to file the appeal-- and I'd cancel your vacation--"

Wethers' voice became an echo, as Sommers pedaled quickly away. The angry tires bit and spewed, and Sommers' focused mind raced into another state, another time.

The police report read like a bad headline from a second rate newspaper.  "Traveling at a high rate of speed, the singular car drove into the oncoming traffic lane and made no attempts to correct direction. The Mercedes clipped a swerving car head on; then was propelled upside down for approximately sixty feet, where a nine year old girl was thrown from said vehicle into the sand, sustaining fatal head, neck and spinal injuries. Female driver was killed instantly. Autopsy later found her to be intoxicated from alcohol and three different prescription sedatives."

Sommers didn't care about the bimbo driver or the gory details. If the old Senator wanted to shack-up with Bambi and party every day in Malibu, so be it. The problem, his problem, was when Bambi decided to take her act on the road.

In order to cover his sins, the Senator launched a full-out campaign against Sommers in particular and the medical profession in general, gaining sympathy mileage from his young and innocent, dead daughter. Sommers thought it diabolical how quickly the political spin machines went into action to save the politician's fading career.

All Sommers wanted to do that day was bike to the beach through one of the trailed canyons that dot the Pacific Coast Highway landscape. It was late spring, everything was blooming and he had a new bike.

About a mile from the beach, he heard sirens and wailing horns. Continuing, he spied a plume of black smoke billowing above the trees. Reaching the highway, he encountered total chaos.

A fire truck was spraying an upside down, burning car. One occupant was obviously dead, still inside, hanging from the seatbelt. There was a group huddled on the sand seeming to give aid to another.

Sommers dropped his bike and serpentined through the makeshift police barriers shouting, "I'm a doctor; I'm a doctor." The exhausted firemen, though medically trained, were definitely relieved to see him.

Sommers went to work on the child's body, but could never get her to respond. The firemen watched, as he did all he could, but Sommers wouldn't quit. Not quitting doesn't carry much weight in legal briefs. Nothing was enough in Sommers' mind, as he repeated CPR, trying to breathe life back into the child.

Somehow through the trauma, she had an angelic face that was at peace, even though he pounded, massaged, willed and called upon everything he knew about medicine to revive her. After thirty-three minutes, the firemen pulled him off. He had lost himself on that beach in that half hour. He knew it wasn't his fault and so did everyone else, but in his mind… he had failed. The little girl was dead. The doctor was out.

Then it started. There was an investigation, accusations, proceedings, legal wrangling and the lawsuit, which threatened to break him financially and spiritually, and prevent him from ever practicing medicine. The grieving Senator wasn't backing down. He wanted someone to blame, a fall guy to deflect upon and rallied support from key people on the Medical Board. Their view was that, yes, it was a terrible tragedy and Bambi shouldn't have been driving. She was under psychological care, medicated and after all, a third year resident couldn't possibly know what he was doing, as he wasn't a fully licensed practitioner. Why should the Senator's pretty young friend be responsible? She was just out for a drive.

It was disgusting to him, as it was all muck and mire, shadows and mirrors within a cruel machine. But if Sommers didn't fight, he would be at its mercy… their mercy and his life, as he knew it, would be over.

He was so fed up at the machinations and the possible, unthinkable outcome that he withdrew into himself. He lived at the beach, hermit-like and there were evenings and mornings when he could be found sitting on his bike in the foot deep surf, gazing at the sea. Staring. Thinking… the grand morass.

The mountain bike trail suddenly hair-pinned downward into a tight, grooved turn, propelling Sommers back into the moment. A simple maneuver of setting the back tire and shifting his weight would slide the speedy bike through the apex, and he would quickly emerge with quite a rush.

Sommers set his tire, but aimed the sleek machine into a flat area off the trail. Vegetation grew thicker here on an untouched part of the mountain, leading nowhere... cliffside.

Determined and balanced, he pedaled, gaining speed toward the edge... the end of the world. It was him now, no medical boards, schedules, lawsuits or lives. Sommers and the bike... flying.

The grass ended and the mineral geology of the cliff began. Gravel, rocks and surprisingly, no sound... Sommers and the bike.

There is a point of no return one reaches. Speed magnifies it and proximity defines it. Sommers passed it; then something went off inside him. Perhaps it was a subconscious voice or some primal instinct. Maybe it was the dead girl's face, her eyes opening, but somewhere, synapses fired... collided, changing his thoughts, causing him to drastically shift his weight and lay down his bike, hard.

Sommers wasn't ready to quit; to die.

The bike's back end whipped around and Sommers' body landed with a rifling, rolling thud, scraping flesh, banging bone. The bike fought to free itself from his grasp and Sommers released. His choice.

The beautiful, fiber composite machine flew gracefully off the cliff's edge into breezy space, soaring, spinning. He remembered it glistening, thinking it would make a great YouTube video. He lost sight of the bike, as it started its descent, disappearing over the edge.

Sommers' hands clawed the earth to stop his deadly momentum. Dust rammed into his mouth, eyes and nostrils, burning on every membrane. The pain meant he was alive, but was that good or bad? He didn't know.

Lying there alone, the reality of what transpired hit him. He was angry at life and himself. Ashamed. Now he was in the same place and circumstances, except he'd trashed and lost a two thousand dollar bike. He needed some stitches and would ache for days. He had no idea what he would tell Wethers.

# 2

# ENRIQUE

The mountains on the eastern seaboard of Mexico are riddled with villages and small farms with families, who have struggled and barely survived for generations. The economy and government had always thwarted a middle class presence and the offspring who didn't escape to the cities have been doomed to a minimal existence, surviving not too far above hand-to-mouth. History has shown the Mexican poor that it's been a lose-lose situation without much incentive or upside.

In the poverty stricken, third world economies, barter and trade emerged as the grease that lubed the wheels of commerce. The Mexican Peso, extremely devalued and completely unstable because of the whims of a corrupt government, took a back seat to the almighty U.S. dollar. The Mexicans might dislike "gringos" but they love "greenbacks." Nature of the beast. Supply and demand. Reliability.

In a bartering economic system, rules and unwritten codes are established. Cartels are formed and the players are forced to heed them. On the flip side, in any financial universe, there's an unsavory element, playing both sides of the fence. Legal or not, everything is fair game, because ultimately, where the money is and who controls it, is all that matters.

Enrique Salerno, a burly fifty year old with strong features, was a known trader with ties to the government, black marketers, cartels, local militia and rebels. Mexico had morphed into a mule state, a transporter of contraband, whether it was goods, arms, people or drugs, on a river of greenbacks. If one could use the local players for services, one could develop an advantage in his business plan. Enrique knew this and wasn't shy about exploiting anything or anyone, as long as it benefited him. Conflict requires at least two opposing sides and Enrique could play them both.

Born in Mexico City, he was shuffled at an early age between relatives in the city and country. He had rebelled, joining the army, as soon as he was able. He then quit, as soon as he could, realizing there was no payoff being a lemming in the Mexican military. Instead, he turned his energies to learn the ins-and-outs of life. "Follow the money," was his mantra. It didn't matter what the deal was, as long as there was a profit in it for him and the risk fit the reward.

After he had pulled the trigger and tasted blood, Enrique soared into the big leagues of black market commerce. He was fearless and his "colleagues" knew and respected this. Enrique had come into his own, his way, and after three decades he was a force to be reckoned with.

Based near Vera Cruz, he had relationships with the local constables and a new faction spreading across the country, the loosely knit bands of rebels. Tired of the two-faced, corrupt government and relegated to a lower economic class, the rebels wanted their place, their moment in the sun to change things. On the surface, it sounded good, positive. In reality, it was violent and bloody, and there was a strong case that the rebel movement hindered any type of progress.

Enrique couldn't care less. If there was a way to do business, that fattened his wallet, he was in. If the rebels needed guns, he would deliver. If the militia needed information, he was there. The devil can play both sides of the fence; creating the illusion both sides needed him. Enrique was a master at this.

On this day, south of Vera Cruz in the foothills, it was raining. Weather was nothing when conducting business and Enrique's Range Rover had no difficulty maneuvering up a narrow, muddy pass.

He was on his way to meet with an acquaintance, whom in public was anonymous, but in private was a respected rebel leader. They had met numerous times before, for many different undertakings. Today was no different. There was a shipment to transport and a percentage to split. Business.

Enrique rounded a corner into a small village. He exited the Range Rover and walked into town. Twenty-five yards from his destination, he was joined by an escort and they guided him down the main road, past adobe type huts and a few tents.

Enrique wasn't surprised or afraid. Lupe Ferrar, the rebel leader, had his protectors and protocol. Everyone knew there wouldn't be any trouble. No one needed that.

Outside a pavilion type structure with no windows, Enrique was searched and then allowed to enter. Lupe had half a dozen men with him at a table. They were sipping beer and waiting on food. Lupe was glad to see Enrique.

"Hola, Amigo," erupted Lupe's greeting.

"Hola," Enrique responded, hugging Lupe and sitting close.

"You braved the unpredictable weather?"

"Of course. We have business, Lupe."

"Yes, business. A beer for Enrique," he snapped. "Always business with you. Can't you enjoy the rain, my friend?"

"Of course, but my time is money and I don't want to muddy my pants."

Lupe laughed, "So be it then."

"I was thinking of the meadow camp for the exchange."

"Yes, the facilities are adequate. What are we getting?" Lupe eagerly asked.

The food arrived and Enrique buttered a tortilla. "The usual goods, but a large shipment. My clients have also promised a bonus and I am assured it will be profitable."

Lupe smiled, relaxing. "All right then. How many men?"

"A dozen. Men that can move quickly on short notice."

"Of course, Enrique. And when will be the payoff?"

"Three, maybe four days. Sooner rather than later."

Lupe laughed at the remark and began eating, slathering beans on his tortilla. He had what he wanted, a commitment from someone he had done business with before. He believed the demons known were better than the ones unknown. To him, Enrique's word about business was enough. "We have a deal."

"Good," Enrique responded. "Then I think I would like some frijoles too."

# 3

# TURBULENCE

The plane rumbled over the Mexican desert through a slight head wind, causing occasional turbulence. Sommers didn't mind the small commuter plane; he had both tray tables and the seats next to him filled with legal papers. A tequila drink sat on one file, condensating and dripping. He didn't care. He actually hoped all the ink would run and this mess would just dissolve.

Against Wethers' advice, he went on his vacation, a mountain biking excursion in the wilds of Mexico, near Vera Cruz. Planned for months, it was supposed to be the capper to his last year of medical school. A celebration. It wasn't. It was an escape, a "just get me away from anything connected to my world" trip. Maybe the tequila would work.

He peered out into the infinite night. Stars speckled the sky, but no moon. There was jungle down there somewhere with fantastic trails and vistas. Freedom. At least that's what the brochure that sat on top of the legal briefs promised. Certainly, the brochures wouldn't exaggerate and anything sounded better than, "party of the first part--"

Normally he would have slept, but he was too anxious. He wanted to get there, be where he could ride and relax. Joining a small group of bikers he'd never met for a few days in the wilderness, in complete anonymity, suited him just fine. No explaining required.

"Excuse me, but are you Dr. Sommers?" the voice probed, startling Sommers so much he bumped his tequila drink, drenching all his papers. "Whoa, I'm sorry… let me help you," came the voice again. It belonged to Kevin Black, a lanky, bearded American with long hair in a ponytail.

"That's okay; I've got it," Sommers replied, wiping the ice and alcohol to the floor.

"The travel agency said there would be other 'gringos' on the flight. I'm Kevin Black," he offered, extending his hand.

Sommers was taken aback. So much for anonymity. "Brad Sommers."

Kevin sat on the aisle seat arm. "It's going to be great. I've heard everything is custom-- small group, great food-- did you bring your own bike?"

"Kevin is it? I'm sorry... I was kind of in the middle of something."

"Oh right. Sure. Sure. Just wanted to say, hi."

There was an awkward moment, as Sommers didn't respond. He didn't want to say anything, except maybe, '*Go away Kevin.*'

"Okay, right. I'll see you on the ground," Kevin assured, reluctantly retreating up the aisle.

Sommers straightened the wet papers, and then decided to shove them all into his backpack. *Just forget it,* he mused; Kevin probably wasn't that bad of a guy, he just wasn't in the mood to meet and greet. If he could have had his way, Sommers would be taking the trip by himself, but there wouldn't be that luxury.

He produced another little airline bottle of tequila and downed it in two gulps, letting the elixir burn his throat. The prop engines droned and he lay back gazing at the infinite galaxy. He slept the rest of the way to Vera Cruz.

# *4*

# KEVIN

Kevin Black wasn't put off by Sommers' coldness. He probably wouldn't have liked it either if some stranger had approached him unannounced on an airplane, but he at least would make the effort to be polite... manners were free.

Kevin had biked recreationally for years, mainly on road bikes. He was a fan of the mountain bike, but only from a cursory point of view, as it was a different animal. Kevin enjoyed the wind in his hair more than worrying about the weight of hi-tech, titanium frames, suspension, mono-shocks or shifter gear ratios. He rode strictly for pleasure, and this holiday to the Mexican jungle for a few days, seemed perfect.

He needed a break, a change... a new life direction.

Kevin had been embroiled in a family corporate fight, pitting brother against brother in an ugly takeover battle. They were in the "rag trade" or garment industry, and had been for fifty years. His two younger brothers, both sporting MBAs and book smart capital goodwill, felt it was time to expand, sell out in order to conquer the world.

Kevin didn't want to go that route and was finding himself without supporters. It sickened him that control of the family business would ultimately fall into the hands of impersonal shareholders and a Board of Directors. Granted, he would make a windfall, as he already had, but the fact that he would be losing something his father and grandfather had literally built from nothing troubled him deeply. He felt a stewardship... responsibility. *What would they have done?* was the haunting question.

With allies both in the family and out, Kevin's attorney had devised a plan where he could buy out his brothers and the

20

company would be solely his. It was complicated, expensive and he'd been advised to "lay low" or "disappear" during this intricate announcement period, or what he called 'the dark side of the moon' time. So a week furlough in Mexico sounded perfect to him.

On the personal front, his life was experiencing as much turbulence as the plane. Kevin was in a custody battle for his two children. If his brothers weren't after him for birthright, his ex-wife was dragging their children into the ring, upping the ante.

He was sick of it and had delegated the responsibilities to lawyers and aides. He needed this time to reflect and regroup, and hopefully reemerge as a victor. He loved being a father and all the ex-Mrs. Black wanted was money. Forget the expense, his team would fix it.

At his seat, Kevin produced a prescription pill bottle and popped a Xanax. About to put the vial back, he took another. *Whatever*, he thought. *I'm on vacation.*

# 5

## CELIA

Upon landing in Mexico, all incoming passengers are directed to the customs stations. Officials randomly search the incoming tourists, which is usually more of an annoyance than a precaution to smuggling something inside the country. They loved throwing their weight around; reminding the tourists they weren't in the United States anymore.

Celia Dane, a petite forty, who looked younger, was one of those randomly searched. A good attorney, who had clawed her way up her metropolitan based firm's ladder, she should have been glimpsing a future partnership on the horizon. The Grail. Celia had worked hard, endured the wrath of less competent associates and it was finally going to pay off for her… or so she had thought.

Her husband had presented her with divorce papers just yesterday.

Even though the golden corporate carrot was dangling within reach, her personal life was a mess. This trip was supposed to be an adventure, a ten year anniversary present. She just didn't realize her husband wanted to take it with someone else. The thought of him with another woman sickened her, especially someone younger… more attractive.

The cancer scare had been too much for him. The surgery, chemo, radiation and the ultimate scarring consequences of her body left him cold. Physical perfection was of the utmost importance and he wanted children. The other cruel joke the muses were enjoying at her expense was that having a baby wasn't going to happen for them… her.

These unhappy thoughts consumed her. Seething, she absconded with the tickets, cashed one of them in and boarded the plane. The trip's brochures looked beautiful and the tickets had been bought... on her husband's corporate card. Money wasn't the issue, but it would make him mad. Tough. It wasn't her fault all her hair had fallen out and her hormones had imploded. Ah, life.

*Let it go,* she kept saying to herself, focusing. *I can bike... I do bike. It's supposed to be fun. This will be FUN.*

Arriving intact, her anxious adrenaline in check, she was stopped for no reason at the Vera Cruz customs station by an overweight guard and his machine gun carrying lackey. Celia was the only person stopped that day, maybe that week.

"Hola, Señorita," the guard began, pointing at her bags. "Abre la caja." This meant, open your bags.

"Excuse me," Celia retorted, trying to maintain her composure. "It's biking gear. I'm on vacation."

"Pronto." He kept pointing, jabbing the bags. "Abre, Abre."

Celia didn't like her person or her belongings to be touched. She immediately grabbed them back, with a honed attitude of "I protect what I have... I'm from the city."

The machine gun clad lackey was startled. He hadn't expected any kind of resistance, especially from such a small female tourist.

"Señorita... la caja. Abre la caja!"

"It's biking gear," she retorted, raising her voice, now pedaling with her hands. "Look, I'm not breaking everything down and opening everything up."

"I'd do as they say," the sharp, American voice of Sommers commanded.

"Look, Pal," Celia began, "I'm an attorney--"

"Who's not in the States. Just let them see what you have and we can all get out of here. You're holding up the line."

Celia glared at Sommers and his piercing eyes, then at the imposing guards. "Fine. Open it up. Open up everything."

She stood back, arms folded. The guards unzipped one bag, then zipped it up and motioned her to pass. Celia was more angry than shocked. "What... you wanted them open. Open them."

The guard motioned to the lackey to wave her through and then in perfect English said, "Move along."

"About time," Sommers blurted, brushing past her with his luggage.

Rattled, Celia picked up her bag, then dropped it. The zipper broke open and a biking helmet, gloves and shoes toppled to the worn linoleum. "Now look--" she muttered to the guard, sweat beading on her forehead. "This is your fault-- your fault."

A hand reached down to help; picking up a rolling can of deodorant. "Hi. I'm Kevin, fellow biker I believe."

"Celia Dane. Thanks. I can't believe this," she stammered, trying to stuff everything back inside the broken bag. "This would only happen to me."

"Happens to everyone. Don't sweat it. I saw you met the other Yankee in our group."

"Oh... great, that jerk's with you?"

"Well, I had to pay extra." Kevin grinned.

"Then you got taken." Celia laughed and picked up her bag. She mischievously smiled at the guards, stuck out her tongue at them and hurried away with Kevin.

# 6

# CARGO

Enrique expertly piloted his Beechcraft King Air through the familiar southern Mexican mountain passes far below any radar or satellite detection. He had flown these routes, evading the authorities for years, and had no difficulty maneuvering the high mountains and tricky topography.

About a hundred miles west of Villahermosa, with the sun melting on the horizon, he touched down on a secluded airstrip high in the mountains and parked at the opposite end of the runway. He kept the engines running. He monitored his short wave radio, GPS transponder and radar to see if anyone had tracked him. No one had. At this point, he was just an innocent, lone pilot in a plane... waiting.

After fifteen minutes, he spotted two quick bursts of light far down the runway. He responded in kind with his landing lights, hid a cocked pistol in each pant leg and climbed out of the plane.

A second-hand, military Jeep made its way toward the plane, carrying two men. Stopping short of Enrique, they jumped out and walked the last few feet.

"Enrique," the first began, extending his hand, "long time."

"Yes, too long. Do you have the goods that were contracted?"

"Ah, straight to business with you." That man chuckled, as the other, Paulo, moved closer.

Enrique knew the speaker as Lorenzo, but did not know the other. He had a suspicious feeling, but was not alarmed.

"Enrique, my friend, we do not have the goods. Our Guatemalan contact did not make his delivery."

Enrique's mood changed. "Why was I not informed of this in the air? I left hours ago!"

"Because to take your plane, we needed you on the ground."

In a quick, blind-siding blow to the jaw, and another between the eyes, Paulo knocked Enrique to the runway. Enrique dropped hard, face down. Paulo cautiously checked Enrique for a pulse, slowly grinning at his accomplishment. "He is dead, Lorenzo... without firing a shot!"

"A stupid, stupid man," Lorenzo chided. "Coming here alone."

The two quickly approached the idling plane and checked it over. Lorenzo feathered the engines and tested the radio. Paulo opened the small cargo bay. He pulled off a tarp and began transferring wrapped packages from the Jeep into the plane, their attention consumed by loading the bales.

On the ground, there was a small, irritating pebble between the rough tarmac and Enrique's cheek. The gritty silica point dug into Enrique's flesh, causing a sharp pain that countered the numbness from the facial blows.

He awakened.

Enrique opened his eye closest to the ground and watched the two exuberant men work in blurry tandem. They assumed they were safe. Occasionally, Lorenzo would glance at Enrique's lifeless body, but continued working, packing.

In their haste, they overlooked the fact they were dealing with someone devious and smart... much like the devil.

After eagerly loading the last package and securing the cargo hatch, they both turned and found Enrique's body gone, the tarmac empty.

Before Paulo could ready his gun, Lorenzo had a forty-five caliber, snub-nosed revolver shoved into his temple.

"Your associate was mistaken about my demise," Enrique growled. "Now, how do you suppose that makes a stranger feel?"

"Enrique, I--"

"Quiet. Your lies do not interest me."

Enrique drew his eyes to Paulo, who now had his shaking gun trained on Enrique's head.

"So this is what the gringo's call a Mexican standoff, no?" Enrique questioned, smiling at the unfolding strategy.

"My friend… let him go."

"Your friend would have sold you out long ago, Amigo. For just one bag on the plane, your body would be rotting under the vultures' wings."

"That's not true," Lorenzo hissed. "Shoot him, Paulo."

"Ah, tactics. Yes, Paulo, by all means, take the infamous shot. Surely you could hit my fat head from such a short distance."

Paulo was rattled. Enrique could see the muzzle vibrating an erratic two inches.

"Paulo, aim high," Enrique coached. "That way you'll pierce my temple and not hit your friend here…"

"The shot… take the shot--!" demanded Lorenzo.

Paulo, by nature, was easily confused. His cognitive function was designed for simple things, not multi-tasking combined with newly introduced adrenaline filled variables.  He was freezing up and Enrique knew how to tighten the screws.

In the tense standoff moments, unbeknownst to either of his enemies, Enrique had reached into his trouser pocket, put his fingers through a slit and grabbed his second pistol.

With Paulo's gun wavering and sweat forming on his brow, Enrique aimed the second gun. "I can't wait any more, Paulo. Unfortunately, time is costly."

Enrique fired, dropping Paulo. He then backed away from Lorenzo. "Enrique, please--"

"Yes, I will make it quick." He killed Lorenzo, firing both guns at once.  Lorenzo fell into a heap on top of Paulo.

Enrique pocketed his guns, found a canteen in their Jeep and poured water over his head and hair. The stress from the event drained from his body. The water and breeze cooled him and he started for his plane.

Loaded with the cargo he had come for, he looked to the bright side. The two had saved him sweat and money, and their dead presence would certainly send a statement.

Throttling the engines, he rolled down the desolate runway and flew off into the night.

# 7

## REBELS

Sommers, Kevin and Celia rendezvoused with a driver sent from the resort where they were staying. Children, looking for tips, scurried to carry their bags and gear to an old, tightly packed van. They were the only passengers and as they exited the baggage claim area for the first part of their journey, the balmy heat hit them all like the inside of an oven at Thanksgiving. Brutal. Burning heat.

Sommers had forgotten how poor the country was. He'd been to Mexico City and a few of the beach resorts when he was a teenager, but hadn't ventured this far south since beginning medical school.

As the van moved away from the main tourist areas and maneuvered onto the local roads, Sommers was reminded the residents here were either extremely wealthy or extremely poor, with not much in between. He had never been a hundred percent comfortable in Mexico and had always stayed around the tourist areas. Safe. Until this trip, he had no interest in seeing the "real Mexico," as the culture and people never interested him.

Sommers knew Americans weren't always popular, yet were needed because of the money and trade they brought into a thirsty economy. To the natives it was a love/hate relationship and a necessary evil in order to survive the asset rich, cash poor homeland.

The bike trip itself was unique, a kind of resort-adventure with knowledgeable guides... the best of both worlds. He hoped the brochures were accurate, as they portrayed a world within a world. There would be trails, yet it was jungle, way off the beaten path. Seclusion was what Sommers yearned for. It called for experienced riders, able to take the heat, terrain and distances. It also boasted gourmet food and various surprises designed to "heighten the enjoyment of the ride." Sommers just wanted a good time and to be basically left alone.

The roads were terrible and the driver seemed to purposely hit every pothole or rut, as the pavement changed from asphalt to dirt, to mud.

Sommers' musings were interrupted by Kevin calling from the back, "So do you think Rodriquez here knows the exhaust fumes are coming through the floorboards?"

"No se, no se," came the reply.

"I think he knows everything," Sommers shared. "Habla English?"

"No se. Es mi prima dia en el autobus para resort."

"That means yes, I think," Celia said. "Can't he slow down? We're not catching a train."

"No se, no se," came the driver's reply.

Sommers caught the driver grinning and knew he understood. You can't carry hundreds of "gringos" and not pick up something. The ride was part of the show. Functioning in a state of implied ignorance was what made the world go around in Sommers' mind, in Mexico, as well as in the realm of legalese.

He couldn't prevent his grey matter from returning to his case, but he was determined to focus on this vacation in paradise. It really was a unique, if not a once in a lifetime opportunity and he vowed to make the most of it. Kevin and Celia seemed okay, although he doubted their riding ability. He chuckled to himself to lighten up; reminding himself this wasn't the Tour De France.

"Hey, who are those guys?" Celia challenged, breaking the moment.

Sommers watched the driver's face turn serious. His grin tensed and his lips pursed closed.

Sommers peered ahead and saw a roadblock of sorts with about a half dozen armed soldiers standing in the middle of the road. There were three men in fatigues, but not uniforms, sitting on the ground, hands bound with their backs to each other.

The soldiers' guns trained on the van.

"Uh-oh," uttered a nervous Kevin. "What do they want?"

29

"Hey, Driver," Sommers interjected. "Who are these guys?"

The driver slammed on the brakes, causing the luggage to be thrown forward. An overnight case glanced off Kevin's head and he moaned in angry pain. "Ow... What's going on?" he asked. "Why are we stopping?"

"They have guns," Celia whispered.

"No problemo, no problemo. Please keep quiet. It is only soldiers on patrol."

"Soldiers? You do speak English," Sommers stammered. "What are they doing out here?"

"Rebel patrol. Please. Tourists are always safe, but I must speak."

The driver then reached down to the floorboard. Sommers saw him shove a small handgun underneath the seat.

"What do you need a gun for? Hey, what is going on?"

The driver kept focused on the soldiers and stopped for the officer in charge. A soldier dropped his rifle across the hood and the other soldiers gathered ominously around the van.

"Hey, they're surrounding us," Kevin blurted out, obviously afraid and confused.

"It will be fine," the driver retorted. "Quiet."

"Do you think it's because I wouldn't open my bag?" a timid Celia asked. "I bet the airport guys called ahead."

Before Sommers could respond, the driver engaged in a rapid conversation with the young lead soldier. Sommers guessed him to be early twenties with a fair degree of power.

They didn't argue, but harsh words were exchanged and voices raised. Finally, the driver turned to them sheepishly and announced, "The Sergeant is requesting we stand outside. It is all right. Please do as he says."

"Out there?" Kevin grimaced. "Maybe this would help."

Kevin produced a wad of cash, as the van door quickly opened and two rifle muzzles were inserted inside.

"No, please," the driver stated. "They just want an inspection of my van."

"You know we're Americans," Sommers calmly reminded him, opening the front door and getting out.

Celia and Kevin reluctantly exited as well, as the sergeant opened the back cargo door. "Here we go again," an upset Celia mouthed. "Let's just open up everything."

"Quiet," the sergeant ordered, moving closer to all of them. "We could open, search and take whatever we want, Señorita. We don't know if you're really tourists, smugglers or terrorists."

The soldierly ranks chuckled at his remarks. His perfunctory English was definitely striking a cautionary nerve with Sommers, Celia and Kevin.

"Look, Sir... I'm a doctor and we're here on a biking trip."

"Yes, we have caught many smugglers and criminals on these trips, posing as professionals. They are a bastion for crime."

"We're not criminals," Kevin chimed in.

"Silencio."

The soldiers pulled out Celia's suitcase and began opening it.

"Wait, wait," Celia cried, running to the back, grabbing the bag on the ground.

"You have something to tell us?" the sergeant imposingly questioned, hoping to strike gold.

"They're my cameras, all right? Here." Celia opened the bag revealing two smaller cases. Digital memory chips, rolls of film and video equipment were secured to the lining. "I want to document the ride."

The sergeant brushed past Celia and scooped up the still camera. He inspected the lenses and mount, and without warning, opened the case, exposing the roll.

"Wait--"

"Silencio," he retorted, exercising his ego and muscle, ripping out the film.

"We're on vacation," Sommers protested. "They're pictures. No wonder this place is in such a mess."

The leader smirked, dropped the roll of film and tossed the camera to Celia. He exchanged some more words with the driver, who seemed agitated as well.

"Come, come, back in the van!" he exclaimed.

The group wasn't happy. Celia was rattled and Kevin helped her put her bag back together. Sommers lent them a hand. "Come on. Let's get to the resort."

The soldiers formed up behind their leader, went to the three bound men on the ground, and yanked at them. They awkwardly stood up and the soldiers started marching them away.

Sommers helped Celia and Kevin get into the back, then slid the van door shut. He locked eyes with the sergeant and hopped back into his seat. With everyone loaded, the driver pulled away on the dirt road.

"Did you see those machine guns?" Kevin was heard asking, as he shakily popped a Xanax. "Fifty caliber, I bet."

"Power play," Sommers exhaled, leaning back, putting his foot on the dash. "They just want to piss us off."

"The soldiers meant no harm. They are just looking for the rebels."

"Is that who they were marching away?" Kevin asked.

"Sí, always looking for rebels. American tourists are safe," the driver volunteered, trying to retrieve the light mood they had had before.

"Define safe," Celia said, trying to load and pack her camera. "That was a brand new black and white roll. You can't get that here. I guess they've never heard of a warrant."

"What were they going to do? Can you imagine the press if they would have done something?" Sommers asked. "I can see it now. Armed soldiers kill three Americans on vacation. Film at eleven."

"It's not funny," Kevin stated. "A lot of weird stuff goes on down here. They would get away with it. Look at the borders. No one cares anymore."

"Kevin, that idiot knew we're on a bike tour. He knows we're biking from the mountains back to the ocean. We're not coming from some South American drug capital. Give me a break." Sommers looked at the driver. "You might not love us, but you better not mess with us either."

"Sí," responded the driver, not liking it, but knowing there was truth in the statement. "We will be there soon."

# 8

## ROBBIE

The Vera Cruz Beach Club Resort was from another time. Built by expatriate U.S. citizens in the twenties, it was one of the largest and most respected resorts on the eastern coast of Mexico. Only the vacation spots of Cancun or Cozumel could rival the facilities boasted by the Beach Club.

In recent years, attempting to keep pace with the aging baby boomers and vying to attract their dollars, the Club expanded into sanctioned events and tours that were geared for more exotic tastes. One of them was a guided mountain biking tour, which was based at the hotel. They started in the mountains and wound their way through the jungle, from one to five nights, ending at the ocean, returning to the resort.

Sommers, Kevin and Celia had chosen the five-night trip, which traversed a hundred and fifty miles inland. Similar in scope to a rafting trip through the Grand Canyon, the tour would have gourmet food, exotic sights and a chance to witness what few locals even saw, thousand year old ruins high in the mountains. It was an eclectic trip for the adventurous at heart. At least that's what the travel agents and slick brochures had guaranteed.

Upon arriving at the lush resort, the scenery changed. The enclosed grounds were beautifully manicured and aged palm trees lined the cobblestone driveway.

Colorful, scented flowers were everywhere. It was certainly first class and a pleasant respite from what the group had just experienced on their way from the airport.

The driver wheeled the van to the front entrance and was glad his part was completed. Four young bellboys attacked the van at every door, welcoming, helping, and carting away the luggage.

Sommers, Kevin, and Celia were glad to be in civilization again with a margarita tinge. They might have wanted to enjoy the wilds for various reasons, but a hot meal, cold drinks and a clean bed didn't sound bad.

"Hotel California," Sommers mumbled, glad to be exiting the van.

"It's beautiful," Celia happily offered. "See, it'll be worth it."

"Maybe," Kevin muttered, hitting his head on the van roof. "Ouch."

Smelling the ocean breeze, they all seemed to breathe a calming sigh of relief, as the hotel manager, Franco, walked up and greeted them.

"Ah, Doctor Sommers, Mr. Black and Mrs. Dane. Welcome to Vera Cruz and our beach resort."

They all shook his hand, happy at the English and some sort of familiarity. "Your rooms are ready and tomorrow you will be introduced to your guide."

"Thanks," Sommers offered up. "I'm glad we made it."

"It will be so exciting. We never have any complaints, only that the ride is too short. Please come inside."

Franco ushered them under the awning covered entrance. The mood and tone lightened, until the booming voice of Robbie Roberts startled them all.

"Hey, hey, fellow biker gringos," Robbie barked, getting their attention, as he strolled from the lobby. "There's no babes, but the Corona's cold!"

Robbie, another American, an old, mileage heavy thirty, was tall, fifty pounds overweight and wore Bermuda shorts with a ratty T-shirt. A cigarette dangled from his lips and he held four icy bottles of Corona beer.

"Andele, andele," he shouted at the passing bell boys, struggling with the luggage. "Pay 'em and they'll do anything."

The group was taken aback, but Kevin finally extended his hand. "Hi, Kevin Black."

"Blackie, nice to meet you. Here, have a beer."

"Right. It's Kevin."

Robbie fumbled with the slippery bottles, but handed one to each of them. "Sure, sure. Man, am I glad to see you guys. It's hotter than the head cheerleader on prom night and nobody speaks English."

"They just pretend not to. Brad Sommers." He swigged his beer, watching to see if all the gear was unloaded.

"Hi, I'm Celia. Have you been here long?"

"Couple of days. I took an early flight. Thought I'd check out the Señoritas and hang at the pool, except the Jacuzzi's been drained. Can you believe they're cleaning the sucker? Nice of management to tell me."

"So you're on the bike trip too?" Kevin asked, hoping there was a mix-up.

"Oh, yeah. Wouldn't miss it," Robbie said, chugging the last of his beer. "Hey, let's get another round."

"Mr. Roberts," echoed Franco's voice. "There's a call from the United States for you."

"For me? Must be the contest people."

"Contest?" Kevin asked, surprised.

"Yeah. The casino where I play cards had a drawing and this was the prize. I've never won anything and whammo... my name gets called and next thing I know I'm on a plane down Mexico way, baby."

Robbie did a little dance, slapped Franco on the back and disappeared inside. The others looked warily at each other, a bit lost in the activity, and ventured into the lobby.

# 9

## WHERE'S LORENZO?

The short radio call Lorenzo had made from the cockpit of Enrique's plane before his demise, was perceived as a mistake. The recipient, a captain in the Mexican army was confused and angry. If things had unfolded to plan, the plane and shipment would have arrived at the strip near Vera Cruz hours ago. There was no plane and no Lorenzo.

What they did have, and were dutifully tracking, was a GPS blip, heading northwest into the mountains. This was extremely odd, as the army had no men or posts in that region.

The captain attempted raising Lorenzo for hours on different frequencies to no avail. He came to two conclusions: one was that Lorenzo, a privateer himself with affiliations to criminal elements had turned and betrayed him, or two, Enrique Salerno was still alive and completing his journey and transaction as scheduled.

Watching the GPS blip edge farther away and feeling Lorenzo would rather retain the captain and army as allies, he surmised Enrique had somehow gotten away. It actually didn't surprise him. He knew Enrique was like the ocean; you couldn't turn your back on him.

Reaching for the phone, the captain reluctantly called his superior and ordered a unit of men into the mountain area where there were known landing strips.

"We'll get you, Enrique," the captain promised, lightly touching the computer screen. "Sooner, rather than later."

# *10*

## ELENA

The Vera Cruz Resort lobby was decorated in a typical Mexican motif with artwork from local artists positioned everywhere. Muzak was piped throughout the ground floor and Robbie wished they would turn it off, as he picked up a house phone in an alcove off the front desk.

He knew who the call was from, whom it had to be from, and he treaded lightly when he spoke.

"Yeah, it's me--" he began, before getting interrupted. "Look, I know we have an arrangement-- yes, I understand the terms-- you'll get it, all right--? Of course I'm not stupid-- hello? Hello? Forget you too, Buddy."

Robbie slammed down the receiver, stood up slowly and started to light another cigarette, but something, or rather someone, caught his eye across the lobby.

For his large size, Robbie could move quickly. Sometimes he could even hear his old college football defense coach yelling directions to "move his butt," and he happily obliged.

College was something else Robbie didn't finish. He'd gone to play ball, drink beer and see how many sorority houses he could get kicked out of. After three years and a blown out shoulder, he gave it up and decided to try bookkeeping. Not the kind the IRS tracks.

Deregulation of the gaming industry brought casinos to almost every state and on most nights, Robbie could be found playing cards. The problem was he wasn't very good, but that was the story of his life... a day-to-day existence of missed starts, eternally hoping for a lucky break.

The woman who had attracted Robbie from across the way was of Mexican descent with obvious upbringing and background. She was in her twenties, dressed conservatively in a sun dress and sandals. Lithe and incredibly attractive with long, dark hair, her skin was creamy smooth. Her eyes radiated wholesomeness from within. In short, she was perfect.

Robbie saw her admiring jewelry in the lobby store's window and approached from behind. Seeing an ornate bracelet on her arm, he suddenly blurted, "Wow. Great shape."

It caught her off guard, as this wasn't a normal greeting for the traditional Mexican protocol. Usually, one had to be introduced with references.

She looked at Robbie's hulking mass and regained her composure, eyes searching his... no chemistry.

"Perdoneme."

"The bracelets. Like yours-- great shape."

"Thank you," she began. "Mine was a regalo, a gift. Excuse me."

Without another acknowledgment, she turned and left, leaving Robbie and his cigarette in front of the window.

"Cold," he muttered. Then he was face to face with a video camera, being operated by Celia.

"It's on video, Robbie. Wave for me. Smile for everyone at home."

"Get that thing out of my face."

Celia slowly lowered the camera. "Sorry. I was just getting some coverage for the trip. I want to document everything, you know?"

"Then document this." Robbie put his face up to the lens, bared his teeth and walked away. Celia turned off the video. "I didn't mean anything," she called after him.

"Tough day?" asked the questioning voice of Kevin, arriving next to her.

"Well, it beats armed soldiers I guess. Maybe they shot at him. He's a real jerk."

"Look at the bright side. We only have to spend the next five or six days with him and Sommers, marooned in the wilds of a foreign country."

"Great... can't wait."

"I was heading for the bar," Kevin informed her. "You want a drink?"

"I like to drink," Celia joked, grabbing Kevin's arm.

They headed for the lounge.

# *11*

## LAST CALL

Sommers' room was small, but clean.  He unpacked what he needed and rearranged his gear for the following day.  His bike and some hardware had already been routed to the bike tour's shop, so all he had to worry about was having dinner that evening and getting a good night's sleep. He ordered a sandwich from room service, then took a quick shower. Cleaned up, he reluctantly decided to grab a drink at the bar, then maybe take a late walk.

Entering the lobby, Sommers tried using his cell phone, but there was no signal. He guided himself to the lounge where he saw Celia and Kevin drinking. Accepting the fact he was going to be with them for the next few days, he ambled over to their table.

"Hola," he said.

"Hey, Doc," Kevin greeted. "Pull up a chair."

"Missed you at dinner. We were just discussing how many mixed nuts big Robbie could eat in the next five minutes," Celia volunteered.

"He's here, too?" a wary Sommers asked.

"Oh, yeah. That boy can pound them. Already on his fourth round," Kevin answered.

"Great.  B D D," Sommers declared.

"What?" asked Celia innocently.

"Big, dumb and drunk."

Celia and Kevin laughed so hard everyone in the bar looked over at their table. Sommers even smirked, starting to relax.

"Sommers..." the tipsy Robbie yelled, arriving with a bowl of peanuts and popcorn. "Hey, you didn't get the score of the Knicks game did you? They have ESPN in the rooms."

"No, missed it. Sorry."

"That's all right, all right. Can you believe I had to explain to Manuel over there at the bar what pretzels are? I mean how much English do you have to know, to know what-- "

Robbie stopped in mid-sentence eyeing the bar. "Oh man, a lone lass, the perfectly shaped lone lass has arrived."

"What are you talking about?"Kevin asked, everyone now turning to see.

"That girl over yonder wants me."

"Here goes round two," Celia exclaimed, cueing her video camera.

Summoning courage and ego, Robbie downed his drink. "Celia, I bet you have a ton of other uses for the batteries in that thing." He winked and started for the bar.

"Cocktus Erectus on the prowl," Sommers sarcastically added, watching Robbie wobble over to the bar.

The woman was seated at the bar and had just ordered. There were men on her left, but the chair on her right was empty. Robbie sidled up and tried to continue from where he had left off earlier.

"Hello, hello. Remember me?" Robbie slurred, sliding a knee upon the empty chair.

She turned. Her eyes radiated a seductive beauty, yet when she saw who he was, they became cold.

"Bet you're a Scorpio," Robbie barked. "Have to be. I'm Robbie Roberts... I-- we just got here. My friends, over at that table."

She gazed over the room, seeing the tables, then... Sommers. Their eyes met and locked in a fleeting moment.

"Would you like to join us?" Robbie pushed, now sitting.

Her drink arrived and she fumbled with the straw. "Where are you all from?"

"The states. El Norte." He chuckled, obviously thinking he was making headway.

"She's not interested," rasped a man's voice.

Robbie looked up and saw the face of Ramon Garcia, a handsomely chiseled Mexican in his forties. His eyes, tone and

41

manner emanated street smarts and sophistication. "Not interested, my friend."

"I know this is a friendly country, but I didn't know we were friends. Besides, I'm just trying to buy the nice chick a drink. You can have one too."

Ramon stood up.

"Please, Ramon, don't," the woman requested.

"Who do you have to talk to around here to get some service? So are you with Raymond head?"

The woman suppressed a laugh, but Robbie found his ribs being poked by Ramon, who had moved in behind him.

"Ow, hey watch it!" Robbie complained.

"Maybe my English, it's not clear, Boy--"

From across the room, Sommers, Celia and Kevin watched the budding confrontation. "He's not doing what I think he's doing is he?" Sommers questioned.

"I think so," Kevin replied.

"Ramon, please." The woman was now pleading.

The imposing Robbie stood. "Who are you calling, Boy?"

"He is only kidding, Ramon."

"Stay out of this, Elena."

"Hey, hey... be cool. This is a happy bar," Kevin announced, appearing with Sommers and Celia.

"Come on, Robbie, let's have one of those mango margaritas," Celia urged, hoping to calm everything down.

"Hey, that's cool," Robbie retorted. "Sure, let the Mexican pay for it."

Ramon grabbed Robbie, but he broke free, then lost his balance, falling into Kevin, knocking them both down.

"Enough," Elena commanded. "Stop!" Fed up, she stormed out.

Ramon stood over them and announced, "By the way... Boy. She's with me." He brushed past Sommers and left.

"Nice going, Ace," Sommers huffed angrily.

"Hey, I had him."

"I got it on video," Celia gleefully pronounced. "We can go for assault."

"Blind siding-- I'll-- "

Sommers gingerly helped Kevin up. "You're not doing anything. You're drunk. We'll be lucky if we all don't end up in jail."

"Oh, back off," Robbie spit, awkwardly standing.

"Fine, just leave us out of your stupid escapades."

"Forget you, Doctor." Robbie knocked over a stool, leaving the three to watch him stumble to the elevator.

Kevin wiped his brow with a glass of ice, then toasted, "It's good to make new friends."

# *12*

## CRACKING THE EGGS

Sommers awakened early the following morning after a restless night. He didn't like attracting attention and felt the incident at the bar was a complete fiasco. The last thing he wanted was to be worrying about the volatile behavior of someone in the group he didn't even know.

At dawn, he took a walk around the resort, which was impressive. The pool was huge and being prepped for the day's vacationers and families. There were different themed restaurants and a number of bars, so the weary traveler wouldn't have to go off-site for entertainment. Sommers felt if he wasn't biking and if things were different, it would be a great place to vacation himself, find some Señorita and disappear.

He found Kevin and Celia breakfasting at the patio coffee shop and they waved him over. They looked tired, and for a fleeting moment, Sommers wondered if they had slept together.

"Ah, the infamous Dr. Sommers," Kevin began. "Sleep well?"

"Not really. The whole thing seemed a little off last night."

"A little?" Celia asked, between bites. "Look, maybe big boy won't show. How does someone that big expect to ride in the mountains anyway?"

"Hey, I go to the gym," boomed Robbie's voice, startling the others into wondering how much he'd overheard. "Hola, hola, Coca-Cola."

Robbie wore the same outfit from the previous night, except he had added dark glasses. "What's the big deal about riding downhill anyway? You just mount the thing. The rest is second nature."

"It's not all downhill," Sommers retorted. "There'll be jungle, terrain, mountains."

"Folks, I'm feeling a very distinct energy shift. Hey, I'm sorry about last night, but that guy crossed the line."

"And you didn't?" Sommers pressed.

"I'm not getting into an opinion contest with you, Doc, over some skirt and her boyfriend. I just wanna enjoy my vacation, same as you. Now, can we start fresh and forget it, or not?" Robbie extended his hand, putting the onus on Sommers.

He didn't want to be a baby-sitter, but he didn't want trouble either. "Fine," Sommers reluctantly agreed. "It's forgotten."

"Excellente; now how about a big greasy omelet and some of those fine mangoes? Man, it's good to be alive. Any day above ground, you know."

Robbie shuffled over to the buffet. Kevin and Celia both smiled at Sommers. "You did the right thing," Kevin acknowledged.

"I guess."

"So, good or bad, we're stuck with him," Celia volunteered, making the best of it.

"I didn't come down here to be stuck," Sommers argued. "And neither did you."

"It's not 'survivor castaway'," Kevin chimed in. "We can't vote him out-- off the ride."

Sommers watched Robbie fill his plate and balance two cups of juice in one hand and his plate in the other. He was intrigued such a large person could move so fast, almost gracefully through tight places. "Yeah, I know. There was a note under my door from Franco. We're supposed to be at the bike shed at nine."

"I received the same thing," Kevin said.

"Me too," added Celia. "I've got my cameras locked and loaded."

"Celia," Robbie chimed in, then sitting down. "Hey, if you want to film me, go ahead. No charge. Was just having a bad hair day."

"All right. Thanks."

"No problemo," Robbie replied, mouth full. "No problemo. Hey, pass me the Tabasco."

# *13*

## LUPE

Lupe Ferrar expressed concern over Enrique's perilous journey and flight. This of course was after his men had transferred the shipment from the plane to a four-wheel drive Jeep.

"I find it odd, their ambush," Lupe told Enrique with a chuckle. "I guess we can no longer trust clients."

"Enemies would suit the scum better. We had done numerous deals from Columbia and San Salvador with them. This transaction will affect many things to come," Enrique shared, sipping a cup of coffee. "We must always be looking to the future."

"How do you think they'll respond?"

"How would you? They know they weren't paid for their goods and that two of their men are dead. I would expect reprisals, but they must find and catch us, and they are not in the tracking business."

Lupe looked concerned. He was fighting for a cause and had enough problems with the army and government politicos. He had been lucky with Enrique, skirting the authorities and financing his band of rebels. Lupe didn't need to be running from shadows and ghosts, being afraid at every turn.

"Who do you think the mule contacted on the radio?" Lupe blurted out bluntly.

Enrique knew the question would be asked and for most of the flight there, he had pondered the same thing. "In my mind, he called his superiors or the people with whom he had made his new alliance. The plane and shipment were quite valuable, Lupe. For someone like Lorenzo, it could have been the score of a lifetime."

"You are very fortunate to be alive my friend."

"I would consider being lucky versus skilled any day."

"That too."

"I want to delay the delivery dates. If there were concerns on the front end, I want to make sure of the commitments on the back end."

"Not a problem, Enrique, but this will change our terms."

"Meaning?"

"Our risk has increased, so our share should as well. For my services, on this extended contract, I want double."

Enrique wasn't happy, but didn't show his disdain... *the demons you know...* "That is quite an increase, for doing the same task as before."

"But the elements--"

"No. All that has changed is the time. I'll increase your share by half."

Inwardly, Lupe was pleased. He knew he wouldn't get double, but didn't think he would get this much. Outwardly, he frowned, hissed at his men, and then, after he had milked it, agreed to terms.

The two shook hands, both feeling they had come out on top. Lupe had more money and Enrique had the precious commodity of time.

"Then off to the meadow, Lupe."

"Yes."

"I think it would be wise to have security prepared at a higher level. No chances."

"Consider it done, my friend."

They hugged and Enrique walked Lupe to the Jeep, where the cargo was tarped and secure.

"We will come out of this for the better," Enrique reassured.

"I know we will," Lupe confirmed, nodding to his driver and leaving. "I trust you."

# *14*

## RAMON

Sommers, Kevin, Celia and Robbie were shuttled to a corner of the resort near the jungle and hills, which bordered the west side of the property. The driver told them to follow a path and the bike shed would be just over a small rise. Grabbing their packs and gear, Sommers led the way.

Approaching, they could hear work being done and an air compressor kicking in. Sommers hoped his bike had arrived in one piece, the bike personnel were qualified and the shop was stocked with spare parts.

He saw someone working on a machine, adjusting the shifter of a bike on a rack. Sommers made note the place was clean and orderly, as about a dozen bikes were in various states of readiness. He watched, as the Mexican technician put the shifter through its paces and listened to the whirring gear mechanism.

Sommers was much more at ease until the technician turned around… it was Ramon Garcia from the bar.

Ramon grinned at them, stopping the group in their tracks. Today, he was dressed in biking shorts and tank top. He was definitely in great shape for his age, with toned muscles and tanned skin. Confident.

"The biking group has finally arrived," he chirped, putting down his tools and wiping his hands.

"Do you believe this?! I don't believe this!" came Kevin's wanton remark.

"Look, we don't want any trouble. Maybe there's been a mistake," Sommers intoned, trying to make sense, the previous evening's events flashing through his brain.

"No, I don't think so. No mistake." Ramon laughed. "Biking gringos on vacation... whom I owe an apology."

Ramon trotted over, extending his hand. "I am sorry. Last night was not good... too much tequila, too little time and a swelled head."

He shook each of their hands. "Sometimes things can get crazy down here. I am your biking guide, Ramon Garcia. I promise you an exciting journey and lots of fun. You will be glad you did not go to your Disneyland." He smiled at Robbie, shaking his hand.

"Hey, I'm sorry too. No hard feelings," Robbie said.

"None... you are bigger than me."

The group laughed at his wit. Ramon certainly had them at a disadvantage, but didn't play down to them. Sommers thought he came off sincere, genuine.

"Doctor Sommers, I hope you are ready to put your magnificent machine through its paces."

"Oh yeah. Definitely."

"It looks brand new. Your frame is a wonderful creation, but I'm concerned your rims may be too delicate, and your tires-- "

"They're a hybrid," Sommers defended. "I use them all the time."

Before Ramon could respond, a voice shouted his name from the shed. A female voice.

"Ramon... what about these?"

The woman from the bar the night before emerged from the shed, carrying two large handguns. "Did you want these packed as well, or not?" she asked before seeing the group.

"Uh-oh," Celia muttered.

"The hits just keep on coming," Kevin mumbled under his breath.

Ramon happily went over to her and took the guns. "Please, please," he began. "May I introduce my little sister and better half, and future Olympian biker, Elena."

Sommers noticed she was even more attractive in the sunlight. He was drawn to her and the youthful innocence she projected.

She was drop-dead gorgeous. "Hi, I'm Sommers. It's nice to meet you."

"Elena. Yes, I remember... from the bar."

"I'm Celia and this is Kevin."

"Robbie Roberts," Robbie exclaimed, intruding on the moment. "This is a pleasure and I hope a bonus."

"Don't mind him," Celia advised. "His breath is worse than his bite."

Elena didn't take Robbie's hand, and instead, inched closer to Sommers. Chemistry.

Robbie fixed on the handguns. "Those are nice pieces, Chief. Can I see one?"

Ramon deftly removed the clip and emptied the chamber from one of the guns and handed it to Robbie. He cocked it, eyeing the inside of the barrel. "These are sweet."

"For the trip," Ramon stated, gingerly taking it back. "Only a precaution. Now, I am glad you all are here. We are going to have a wonderful time and adventure. I have assembled your bike, Dr. Sommers and have fitted everyone else's according to their weight and height. Here, come with me."

Ramon led them to the other side of the shed where four, hi-tech mountain bikes stood ready. They were shiny and tuned.

"All right," Robbie began. "You even have one big enough for me?"

"Yes, of course... for the big, happy gringo," replied Ramon.

Each of them sat on their bicycle checking, adjusting and fitting. They felt comfortable and rode around the shed area.

"Hey, mine only has two wheels," Kevin uttered, catching an edge and falling.

"Yes, and it helps if you keep the rubber side of the tires on the ground." Elena laughed, helping him up.

"Please get used to them, feel them out. They will be your home for the next few days. Tell me of your special requirements, adjustments you want, before we leave for the hills," Ramon stressed. He watched each of them, trying to discern their level of riding ability. "This is the best place to discover any trouble."

Sommers powered his bike off into the brush away from the group, landing on the sandy shore. He shifted through the gears, absorbing the feel of his new bike, riding on the hard packed sand of the beach. The suspension flowed smoothly and he felt the balance of his body versus the machine. Ramon had done a good job, putting it together well and Sommers felt more comfortable with him than he did twelve hours ago.

He stopped at the water's edge, looking at the ocean. The water was crystal blue and a slight breeze blew. He felt good... like he could ride across the water if he wanted. A bikini clad girl walked past and smiled at him.

Returning, Ramon and Elena were going over specifics of the trip and divvying up gear. Ramon had each of them lay out everything they were bringing near their machines, then cherry picked necessities and made them leave one third behind.

"We're in the mountains, jungle," he explained. "And we have to be mobile... moving all the time."

Grumbling, but understanding the parameters and the need, each of them relinquished clothing and items that weren't deemed absolutely necessary. Ramon had a plan, had done this all before and wasn't sympathetic to the whinings of American tourists.

This wasn't a bike trip in Napa Valley with a chase van and lodgings at different inns each night to enjoy wine tastings. They would be out in the wilderness, a foreign country's wilderness. Ultimately, all they would have would be each other.

"What about stuff in my pockets?" asked an already tired-of-the-discipline Robbie.

"If you think it's important, but forget the candy bars and sugar," answered Ramon.

Robbie shoved four little airplane liquor bottles into his fanny pack. "There's sugar, then there's sugar."

Kevin didn't have a problem with too many things. He'd brought a pair of shorts, an extra pair of socks and two shirts. He liked the idea of roughing it and thought traveling light was better.

Celia had the hardest time of all. Packing and covertly getting away at the last minute, she over-packed everything. She arrived at the shed with two full backpacks, swearing she needed everything inside. Ramon immediately forced her to unload and only take the essentials. After arguing and fighting for every item, Ramon convinced her to take one pack. Fretting at the enormity of the eventual undertaking, she had a little anxiety attack and wondered if she should stay behind. Sommers took her aside, away from everyone, and she started crying.

"I shouldn't go; I shouldn't go," she began in earnest. "I'll just hold you up."

"No, you won't. Come on, Celia. It'll be fun."

"But we're out there. I've never been in a place like this, at least not without my husband. I get paranoid in traffic."

"Even more reason you should just throw on that pack and start pedaling."

She laughed at Sommers' candor. He wiped her cheek. "Come on. Give it a go."

"Okay. Thanks, Sommers."

They started walking back and Sommers saw a bell boy from the hotel running up the path. He ran to Ramon, who then pointed at Sommers.

"Dr. Sommers, Dr. Sommers-- Franco told me to bring this to you."

He handed Sommers a folded piece of paper.

"Thanks," Sommers said, opening it. A scribbled phone number was all that was there. He knew who it was from.

"It's probably your bill," Robbie blurted.

"I wish." Sommers tried his cell phone to no avail. "Why isn't there signal?"

"Some work, some don't here," Ramon said.

"Ramon, I have to make a call. You'll wait for me, right?"

"I wouldn't have it any other way, Doctor. Go talk to your girlfriend before we disappear into the jungle."

Sommers started away, following the bellboy. "It's not my girlfriend. It's my attorney."

# 15

## JORGE

The sixteen year old boy was uncomfortable on the horse he was riding alone, so far up into the jungle. He'd been on the sweating animal close to six hours and was concerned the crude map he'd been given wasn't correct. It was brutally hot and every turn, every hill, seemed strange and foreboding. He felt as if he was lost in an alien world.

His name was Jorge De Aguilar and his parents owned a street bar in the town of Puerto Villa, near Vera Cruz. His father was a rebel sympathizer, a politico with contacts and connections among the locals. He knew Lupe and what he stood for, and had helped him over the years. Nothing illegal, but Jorge's family was working poor and native Mexican. There were loyalties and if Lupe could make things better, so be it.

A few days earlier the captain, who had disseminated the radio call from his contact, was speaking in hushed tones at the Aguilar's bar with other militia. The father thought it strange and knew the men whom were being discussed. One of them was Lupe Ferrar.

Not attracting attention, he sent Jorge to find Lupe and tell him to be on guard, something was amiss and he could be in danger. The soldiers spoke of the mountains and camps, and had specifics. It would be up to Jorge to warn him.

The father knew the general vicinity of Lupe's whereabouts, but not the actual location, as shadowed men like him usually slept in different places every night. However, he felt if Jorge could get far enough into the mountains, he could make some kind of contact. He was right.

Riding along a stream, four rebels suddenly appeared in front of Jorge, startling his horse. They grabbed the reins and pulled him off the saddle to the ground. Firing questions in Spanish, Jorge tried explaining why he was there, but the rebels were extremely suspicious. *Why would a boy come this far? Who was he? What was he really there for? Who was with him?*

The questions kept coming, but Jorge stood his ground, stating he could only speak with Lupe, whom the rebels denied even existed.

After an hour, and realizing they weren't getting anywhere, the rebels put a hood on Jorge and drove around for two more hours through the jungle to a temporary camp. Stripping him, they bound Jorge's hands and led him to Lupe, who was bathing in a stream, under a waterfall.

Lupe was upset Jorge had to go through such a rigorous interrogation, but he couldn't take any chances. Lupe was a wanted man with a price on his head. He could trust no one.

"Amigo," he began. "How are your father and mother?"

Jorge rubbed his wrists and smiled. "They are fine and send you their respects, Lupe."

"I have dined and drank many times in your father's bar. I only wish I could go there more. Better times, you know."

"Yes, I understand."

"Why were you sent all the way up here to find me?"

Jorge told Lupe everything he knew and why his father was concerned.

Lupe toweled off and had one question. His tone turned serious. "Do you believe you were followed, young one?"

"No, Lupe. There were no soldiers in town and I often go riding. There's no one."

Lupe looked to one of his lieutenants, who nodded in agreement.

"If this is the case, I owe you and your family much. How do you think I should repay my debt?"

Jorge smiled ear to ear. "I want to go with you, Lupe. I want to carry the cause through the whole country. My father says it's our time."

Lupe happily laughed and ran his hand through Jorge's thick black hair. "He is a wise, honorable man and has instilled those traits in you. Very well then. But before we change the world, I think we should eat. You must be hungry from your journey."

"Yes, I have eaten nothing today."

"Then tonight, you'll eat like a king." Lupe barked an order to his lieutenant about keeping a sharper eye and tighter security, then walked with Jorge into the main camp.

# *16*

## THE SYSTEM

Sommers wasn't happy he had to hike back to the resort's lobby to take the call from Wethers. *If he could have held out fifteen more minutes...*

"Hey Wethers, it's me. What wonderful news do you have that couldn't wait a week?"

"Your buddy the Senator was on the *Today Show* this morning. He's taking the whole thing national and my phone's been ringing off the hook," Wethers responded, exasperated.

"That's your job... to field offers."

"It's not funny, Sommers. I'm not used to this. He's bringing in the heavy guns and you're not doing anything about it."

Sommers was disgusted. That calm beach with the clear blue water and bikini girl, flashed in his mind when he was on the bike in the resort surf. "What's the medical board saying?" he asked sheepishly.

"Nothing; no comment. Standard say nothing 'til they have to. You have to file the appeal and fight this thing. Why won't you get in the fray?!"

"Because I didn't do anything... the law is supposed to protect the innocent!"

"The system's all we have, Sommers, and you know it. What do you want to do?"

Sommers held the phone to his forehead, then spoke. "Nothing."

"You can't be serious. How can I protect you?! Let me file, let me--"

"If they come after me, then it's on their heads. The creepy old Senator and medical board know that."

"But-- all right. I'll stall them, wait to hear from you."

Sommers felt the exasperation in Wethers' voice. They didn't say anything else and hung up. In Sommers' mind, it might not have been the smartest decision, but it's the only one he could make at the moment.

He left through the lobby, waved at Franco checking in some guests and headed back to the bike shed.

# 17

## THE MOUNTAIN

The skies held white, puffy clouds of lyrical shapes and sizes which touched the beautiful mountains rising above Vera Cruz. It was a typical coastal day where the fog engulfed this little part of the world in the morning and burned off by noon.

Gaining altitude, in a Viet Nam era, American Army, Huey helicopter, the group huddled in back. They wore oversize, intercom headphones and were tightly strapped in. Because their gear was secured outside, both doors were open and the wind pounded through the cabin. To say the least, they were uncomfortable and the choppy ride wasn't for the faint hearted.

A heated inversion layer stifled the air at one thousand feet causing turbulence and the craft to drop, then climb in an endless washing machine type cycle. It was a horrifying, bumpy flight with the lush and severe terrain seemingly just inches below. The av-gas exhaust fumes weren't helping either.

"Oh, I hate this," Celia spurted through gritted teeth, hanging on tighter than anyone else. "Ow. When do we land?!"

"Man, I'm surprised something this old can even get off the ground." Robbie chuckled. "Hey, where's your video cam? Let me shoot you puking."

"Be cool," Kevin stated. "It's okay, Celia. These old things are horses. We'll be there soon."

"Yeah. Dog food horses," Robbie grinned.

The craft lurched downward and Sommers saw Celia was turning a faint shade of green and clutching her side. "You okay?"

"Yeah. Old surgery scar."

"Here," he offered, opening a small flask. "Makes it go faster. Helps with the pain."

"I hear that," Robbie agreed, drinking from his own mini, airline bottle.

Celia accepted the flask, taking a big swig. "Thanks, Sommers. I don't care what everybody else says, you're all right."

The joke brought a laugh, easing the tension. Ramon was heard directing instructions to the pilot and Sommers felt Ramon knew exactly what he was doing. He took a drink from the flask and looked at the lush jungle below and thought about Wethers and what was at stake. He just couldn't escape. The era of Big Brother was here and turning the screws tighter.

He knew he needed to give Wethers an answer, needed to act, but was in the wrong state of mind. A bad state that was a complicated funk with everything riding on the line. If he could have, he would've taken his bike at that moment and jumped from the Huey, riding and disappearing into that infinite jungle. *Forget'em,* he thought. *I'll deal with it when I deal with it.*

"Sommers..." Elena began. "You look as if you're a million miles away. Is there someplace else you want to be?"

He hesitated before he answered, catching her eyes. They were deep in color with something going on behind them. Maybe it was her youth or her appearance, or just that she was a fresh face in the middle of nowhere. Regardless, he was attracted to her. If nothing else Elena was a distraction that allowed his racing brain to turn off. "No... Sorry. I want to be right here. Have you ridden much in the mountains?"

Ramon's voice interrupted... the silent and unseen guard. The real Big Brother. "Elena has ridden in races and the mountains strengthen her legs for the Olympics."

"Must be working," intoned Robbie, who sat next to Elena on purpose, eyeing her long, firm legs.

"I train hard. It burns fat," she said directly to Robbie. "How about you, Sommers?"

"Well, I'm not going to the Olympics, but you can't do a ride like this without working out. I usually ride in the Malibu hills... sometimes go up to Big Bear or Mammoth."

"The ski trails," Elena blurted happily. "I have never done that. I would love to see them. I hear they're... radical."

Her face radiated and Sommers wanted to get lost in there, be absorbed by it... by her.

"Sounds like a date to me," Kevin quipped. "I can certainly dispense sage advice on the subject. Let me start by having a drink from your flask, Sommers."

Sommers smiled, tossing him the engraved container. Kevin read it out loud. "For long days in the lab and late nights in the operating room."

"My dad gave it to me."

Kevin downed a large gulp. "Ah... breakfast of champions. Of course Xanax helps too." He popped another pill.

"You have a relationship that's gone bad?" Robbie probed.

"That's putting it mildly," Kevin responded. "Let's just say putting my head in the Huey's rotor blade would be more pleasant than what faces me when I get back."

"Women--," Robbie started.

"I'd be careful," Celia warned. "You're on thin ice."

"Okay, okay. I was just defending Kevin."

"Where's your girlfriend, Sommers?" Elena asked.

Deep down Sommers liked her questions because it meant she was interested. He didn't have one. Sommers hadn't had a girlfriend since the beginning of medical school, which, at the moment, seemed like another lifetime ago. After her first year, she quit and returned home to the east coast and their long distance affair faded. "I haven't really had time... you know with school, residency and everything," he answered.

"Sounds like a cop out to me," Robbie blurted. "A man can always make time for that."

"What?" Elena asked, confused, looking again at Robbie.

"Yeah... you know--"

"No, I don't think she does, Robbie," Kevin joked, getting a laugh from everyone else.

"I don't understand," Elena said earnestly.

"Robbie's saying I should spend less timing riding bikes and saving lives, and more time dating," Sommers confirmed.

"Or playing cards. Get a life, Sommers. You're going to wake up one morning and it'll all be over."

"Yeah, I'll work on it."

The radio cackled and Ramon interrupted. "We're almost there. See the ridge in the distance?"

The group craned their necks to see a flat, barren plain, high in the mountains.

"That's it?" Celia eagerly asked.

"If we make it," Robbie sarcastically joked. "I didn't know this model of chopper could get this high."

Celia sneered at him, as the Huey jerked downward, buffeting the mountain wind.

"Hang on, everyone," Ramon ordered. "We will swoop down like angry eagles from the clouds."

"Let's just land the thing," Celia murmured.

The pilot leveled off and made his approach. The antiquated big bird angled and swung around, and he landed like a feather on a grassy plain.

"Whoo... what a ride," Robbie yelled, jumping out... "I'm on the Koo Fong plain-- roger that Charley. Let's do it again. Attack, attack!"

"Let's not," Celia blurted, happy to be on the ground and in one piece.

The others began the tedious process of breaking out their luggage. Ramon eyed each piece of gear and checked each bike, as the wheels, pedals and cables were adjusted and secured. Sommers again felt Ramon was seasoned, knew what he was doing.

"I smell rain," Ramon announced at the now clear blue sky.

"I smell helicopter exhaust," Robbie surmised. "Smells like the Detroit airport."

Sommers wondered how much time Robbie had spent at places like the Detroit airport, shining some bar stool with his polyester pants. For some reason, he wondered about Robbie and his life, and what he was doing there. Not in an ulterior way, but more of an observation about how the hand of fate deals the cards and how life forces one to sit at the game.

"Okay, okay," Celia shouted, fumbling with enough camera gear to weigh down any mortal. "I want proof. We have to capture this."

She was right. The helicopter and the high meadow were majestic and a money shot. Looking at the enormity of the world from where they stood, they all felt small, insignificant. That may or may not have been the point, but it was true. The breeze whipping at them and the peaks in the distance confirmed they were just temporary guests in a permanent world.

Celia arranged them all in a row, sitting on their bikes. They looked fresh, new, to the vast world that was their friend. She handed off the still camera to the pilot, who snapped a couple of pictures.

Sommers stood in the middle, next to Elena. He enjoyed a faint hint of her perfume. It made him smile and he immediately thought the picture would look good on his end table overlooking the ocean. He realized in that moment, he didn't want to be anyplace else and was ready to ride. His world, so far away, to be forgotten.

"How far do we go today," Kevin asked, replacing his seat with one with more padding.

"Twenty or twenty-five kilometers. Tomorrow, maybe forty," Ramon advised. "We'll see what the mountains and trails have in store for us. Most of all, enjoy."

"I want to enjoy that," Robbie whispered to Sommers, as he watched Elena riding past. "Man, she is worth the whole trip."

"Doctor Sommers, are you sure you want to dirty up that sleek, new machine?" Ramon asked.

"I'll risk it."

"A beautiful and sturdy one. Expensive, no?"

"Expensive, yes. I love it, though."

"All right... everyone has food, supplies and spare parts in their packs. I'll carry the radio."

"So, we're not completely isolated?" Kevin asked meekly.

"Mr. Black, we are in the wilds with limited contact, but we will mostly be in touch. The technology of the world has even invaded poor old Mexico," Ramon stated. "Come now, time to ride."

The group mounted, getting the feel of their bikes. "It's fun," came the squealing shout of Elena, riding ahead.

"We will head east toward the ocean and follow the earth, around those mountains and through streams," Ramon called to everyone. "Take your time, make your own pace. It's your vacation."

Robbie fell in behind Elena, then Kevin. Celia fumbled with her camera gear and took a panoramic shot before hopping on the trail.

Sommers held back with Ramon and watched the chopper lift off, its backwash almost knocking them over. The *thwack-thwack* of the engine faded in the distance and the meadow became silent.

"I guess we're in it now," Sommers admitted.

"Oh yes," Ramon happily agreed. "This is the top of the world. I think you will receive your money's worth. Best of all, leave your troubles behind."

Ramon joined the others on the trail. Sommers looked at the sky and jungle. The sun felt good on his face and he was primed. For that moment, he was completely alone and he felt pure, absolved in a way. He wished time would stop and he could stay forever on that mountain, in that meadow. *This is the secret of the universe,* a little voice told him. *Nothing else matters. Nothing.*

For the first time in months Sommers felt happy. Grinning, he headed his bike down the path to catch the others.

# *18*

## HUNTING

The small unit of Mexican army militia surrounded the adobe structure, cordoning off the adjoining dirt streets of Puerto Villa. The captain wanted no mistakes in his calculated pre-dawn raid and made sure all sides and exits were covered.

Juan and Maria De Aguilar were sleeping soundly, holding each other, when both the front and rear doors were demolished by the raiding and screaming soldiers.

Juan had barely awakened. When he sat up, he was confronted by the angry captain. A half dozen armed soldiers pointed their weapons at him and his wife.

"Your son..." barked the captain. "Where is he?"

Juan's face went pale... *how could he know?*

Maria began crying and Juan held her tightly.

"He went riding yesterday. Up into the mountains," Juan explained. "He rides his horse there often."

"And does he often stay the night?"

"Yes. Many times. He fishes, hunts--"

"Stop lying," the captain ordered. "We know you sent him to join Lupe Ferrar. We know you've had contact with Lupe Ferrar."

"That is not true. My son is hunting in the mountains."

"Yes, hunting a wanted, murderous rebel leader. This is a criminal action."

The captain snapped his finger and his lieutenant brought him a pouch. Opening it, he produced a photograph of Enrique.

"I'm only going to ask you this once," the captain began. "Do you know this man?"

Juan studied the picture. He felt there was some familiarity, but in all honesty he didn't know Enrique. "No, I do not know him."

The captain probed Juan's eyes for the truth. Maria was too hysterical to be of any use. "Very well. You are under arrest and are to remain in custody at the armory until the truth is revealed."

He nodded and four soldiers manhandled the couple from their bed.

"I'm telling you the truth," Juan protested, rising up. "My son is hunting."

"Yes," the captain angrily replied. "So are we."

# *19*

## SURVIVAL OF THE FITTEST

The terrain and ride were indescribable. Sommers' tires floated through a constant, gentle grade on a narrow trail that wound its way through multiple kinds of topography. He was in his element, enjoying every nanosecond. It was a slice of heaven in an untouched world… and it was his.

Sommers' mind was clear, just subconsciously focusing on keeping the bike in the groove and following the others. Relaxed and absorbing any undulations, he rode with a calm, wandering eye, taking in this magnificent world for the first time.

Topping a rise, he stopped. He could hear the whoops and hollers of the group, as they disappeared into the lush terrain.

Below him was the vast jungle. Somewhere, intermixed among nature, was a ribbon of trail that eventually would return him to civilization. He wanted to stay there, absorb and live it, never having any of it change.

Kevin rode past, a fire in his eyes, adrenaline pumping. "Where's that bed and breakfast?" he yelled.

"Napa Valley ride," Sommers hollered back.

Bringing up the rear, Sommers saw and learned how each of them rode. Ramon and Elena were extremely proficient, able to set the rear tires and maneuver through anything easily. Celia and Kevin were competent, but were weekend riders at best, out for passive enjoyment. Robbie seemed to have the most trouble, fighting the machine and trails, at times even catching edges laying his bike down.

Sommers surmised Robbie hadn't ridden much at all. If he was caught on the wrong trail at the wrong time, he could be in trouble quickly, similar to an inexperienced skier on a slope that was too steep.

Being the "doctor," Sommers was always making mental notes and observing. *A curse,* he thought, snippets of useless information, stored forever in his gray matter, just in case. Of course, after a few hours pedaling the machines, he did have things sized up and knew more of what to expect. Practicing medicine or not, that seemed to be his job.

"Sommers--," came the shouts of the others up ahead. "Come here. Hurry."

"Yes, hurry," Ramon reiterated. "You'll want to see this."

Ramon had brought them to a small ridge plateau, overlooking a large grassy plain. As Sommers arrived they were watching a herd of antelope running in formation. Hundreds of them charged, galloping gracefully in one direction, and then spontaneously turning in unison.

"Watch now--" Ramon captured their attention.

The herd leapt in synch when unforeseen, a mountain lion bolted from the grass, chasing down a much slower, younger animal.

The kill was slow, gruesome, as the dying antelope tried in vain to escape and survive the mangling claws and teeth.

"Oh my-- ," Celia gasped, looking away.

"Catch that on video, Celia," Robbie snickered.

"You're sick. That's awful. That poor animal."

"Survival of the fittest," Sommers chimed in, watching the drama intently.

"Hunters and prey. Survival here is more than being strong and fast. It takes muscles of wit... how you say... tenacity."

"And I thought the corporate world was brutal," Kevin quipped, turning away.

"It is life my friends, as it has been for millions of years," Ramon preached, standing. "Come now, a bit further and we will make camp and eat soon. Enough excitement for one day."

They followed Ramon back to their bikes, except for Sommers. He watched the mountain lion, gorging on the fresh, bloody kill. As vile and violent as it was, Sommers saw a purity only nature could provide. He knew Ramon was right. The process life had enforced and unfolded for a million years, would be the same for a million more. Man was nothing, but a temporary intruder at best.

Watching the placated mountain lion skulk into the jungle, Sommers joined the group.

# 20

## TEXAS

Enrique rolled off the Houston, Texas, prostitute, lit a cigar and walked out on the balcony of his hotel room. The city was muggy and smoggy, more so he thought than his native Mexico.

He loved the United States, *Los Estados Unidos,* and traveled there frequently for business and of course, pleasure. That's what he thought of when he thought of America... pleasure. At some point in his life, he knew he would live in the States, maybe in that exact room with the cheap art and spectacular view. He wanted that... to work and live in the United States, engulfing the American offerings on a daily basis.

This trip had hastily been put together, an end product of the business he was conducting with Lupe Ferrar. *Ah Lupe,* he devilishly thought. *You should see this... experience this. A completely different kind of jungle.*

Enrique met with a Texas importer. The state's black market economy thrived and had long rivaled the Florida and California contraband pipelines.

The Texans were friendly, more low-key than the Floridians and more dependable than the Californians. Of course to Enrique, all that mattered was the end product of the deal. Money. It was just business.

He'd met with two men the previous evening. They had wined and dined him, and provided the charming entertainment that was asleep in his bed. The dealings had gone well and Enrique had what he flew in for... a confirmed delivery date and a cash down payment. American cash. With those two elements in place, he could confirm the shipping status with Lupe and complete the deal.

Simple and successful.

Enrique enjoyed Anglo, blonde women and this one didn't disappoint him. She had even offered to bring a friend, but it was late when the festivities broke up and he decided she would suit his purposes.

As he heard her awaken and watched her move from the bed across the room, he felt lucky. *Yes, luck versus skill.* He had everything and could accomplish anything at that precise moment.

He saw her casually move to the dresser and retrieve his cell phone, which was going off. "Hey," she said, half awake and in a stupor. "Looks like somebody wants you."

She held it out, taunting him with the device. As he was about to take it, she pulled back, forcing them together. "I wish mine had this ring tone."

Enrique took the iPhone, not letting go. "We can take care of that later." He grinned.

Fumbling with his iPhone and balancing her toward the bed, he stopped, as they tumbled onto the sheets.

"What's the matter, Baby?" she cooed.

Enrique studied the number on his iPhone, his mind torn and racing. "I have to handle this."

"What about me?" She nestled the sheets with one of her long, inviting legs. Her eyes and body wanted him. "I'm yours for the day."

*So go the spoils,* he thought.

Enrique grabbed up his cell phone and emerged onto the balcony, quickly dialing. A man answered and Enrique proceeded in Spanish. "Are you sure?" was all he said.

The man rambled a moment, trying to convey everything he knew about the De Aguilar's arrest and their son's trip into the mountains. He knew nothing of Lupe Ferrar or his location.

Enrique knew immediately he would have to return to Mexico, and find Lupe before the militia did. Much more was at stake than just a delivery. If discovered, this event would topple an underground network that had taken decades to build. His lucrative livelihood was at stake, in possible jeopardy, and it had to be protected at any cost.

He scanned his accommodations. There was that fleeting moment when he thought about staying... about having lunch with Miss Houston, then a salmon salad and iced tea, and an afternoon in the sun drenched pool. It was what he yearned for and it was there for his taking. He could let Lupe fend for himself in that jungle. It was just another deal... business.

But that's what drove him. Delivering.

Houston would be here. The salmon salad and pool would be here, and so would she... in one form or another.

Enrique strode into the room and looked at the seductive and willing prostitute. "Shower with me," he commanded. "I want to feel your skin, so I can remember this."

"Sure, Baby. If that's what my Mexican man wants, then that's what he gets." She hopped out of bed, sliding up next to him. "You know if you have to leave, you can call me anytime. If the price is right, I mean... you know... I can go anywhere."

She kissed him hard on the mouth, which he knew was rare. Her words and tanned smooth skin resonated in Enrique's mind for the rest of the day.

# 21

## PARADISE

Sommers had a feel for his bike and the terrain. On the difficulty meter, it wasn't hard and he could certainly ride faster than the rest if he wanted, but he held back, savoring every moment.

The jungle was alive and he was part of it. Unlike Kevin, Robbie and Celia, the heat and different types of trails didn't bother him. He challenged whatever it threw at him and relished it all.

Bringing up the rear, he rode to the base of a hill, a dead end of sorts. Celia was trudging up its side, carrying her bike in the sweltering heat.

"Can you believe it?" Robbie asked. "Nobody said anything about walking."

"That's part of it," Sommers retorted, stripping off his helmet.

"Well, nobody told me. It must be a hundred and ten here. Why do we have to climb this sucker anyway?"

"Look, he wouldn't have brought us here if he didn't know where he was," Kevin stated. "Just go with it."

"I would've stayed in Margaritaville if I knew this was coming." Robbie swatted at a fly on his neck. "And these flies... do you believe-- ?"

"We're all tired," Sommers began. "It can't be that much-- "

Elena's piercing screams radiated through jungle, scaring them. It caught them off-guard and was the last thing they expected. All turning at once in the scream's direction, they shockingly felt alone. They were. In that instant, the jungle had turned, become darker, less friendly.

"Come on," Sommers commanded, dropping his bike and charging up the hill.

"What the-- ?"Robbie questioned, but Kevin brushed past. Robbie reluctantly followed, slipping, unable to get any footing. "Wait up, wait up," he awkwardly yelled to no avail.

Sommers was on a mission and blew through the jungle foliage like a tornado. There were other screams; then what seemed liked whoops of laughter, all echoing in his mind. He had to be closer, the top had to be nearer.

Emerging at the crest, he found Celia, peering over an edge. She was at first startled to see him flying out of the jungle, but her angst became a smile.

"What's going on, what is it?" Sommers questioned, out of breath.

"Take a look."

Sommers peered down on a breathtaking, clear pool, fed by a waterfall. Ramon and Elena were happily swimming and playing... frolicking in something wonderful nature had created eons ago. In Sommers' mind, it was just for them.

"Come on, come on," came the delicious squeals of Elena, being dunked by her brother.

"Yes, yes, gringos. Come and join us."

Kevin arrived, out of breath. "Do you believe him?! I thought they were in trouble."

"Me too."

"I've never seen-- "

"I know," Sommers acknowledged. "But he's found the end of the rainbow."

Celia stripped down to her panties and bra. Not hesitating, she jumped in with the words, "You guys are wimps..."

"Fearless," Kevin joked.

"Yeah, but still the whitest white person ever created."

They both laughed, enjoying, as Robbie arrived. "All right... nobody said anything about Elena getting wet."

Robbie dove straight in, clothes and all. He belly-flopped so hard, water sprayed twenty feet.

"Paradise," Sommers mumbled to Kevin. "Looks like you're next."

"Think I'll take a pass. The view's better from up here," Kevin replied, kneeling for a closer look.

"How do you explain this? I bet we're the only people who get to-- "

"No--!" The ground shifted beneath Kevin and flipped him forward with nothing to grasp. Sommers reached, but was too late, as Kevin, almost in slow motion, tumbled over the edge headfirst into the clear pond.

Sommers watched his flailing body hit hard, a ball of flesh and bone. Panicked, Kevin found leverage and shot up from the water, mouth wide open. Yelling for help, he swallowed liquid and gagged.

"Get him," Sommers shouted, flinging off his shoes and jumping in. The others, seeing the emergency, immediately went to Kevin's aid.

"Get his head up, his head. He's drowning," Ramon yelled.

Each one grabbed a piece of the coughing Kevin and helped haul him to shore.

The magical moment was over.

# 22

## CAMPFIRE

After Kevin's accident, Ramon made camp near the pond. There was a flat area, surrounded by jungle and foliage, but enough room to pitch tents and store gear.

He broke out the wine and prepared a gourmet trail meal of fish and vegetables. In the outdoors, it was a heavenly scent... burning wood and perfect cuisine.

They sat around the large cooking fire, its reflection glistening off the now still pond. Sommers was amazed and happy at how quiet it was. For whatever reason, there weren't any insect or animal sounds, just the crackling fire and scant conversations. The group was transfixed, letting the fire and nature do the talking. None of them had broached Kevin's accident, until he brought it up.

"I've never liked the water, so I never learned how to swim," a weary Kevin announced out of the blue.

"That's crazy. Everyone knows how. You learn at two," spit Robbie.

"Not me. Gave my ex the house because of the pool. Let her clean it."

"Didn't anything go right in your marriage?" Celia asked.

"What does that mean?"

"Nothing... you're just so bitter. Do you ever wonder if maybe some of it was your fault?"

"She and her attorney will say it's all my fault. Now, I have a question. Why does every attorney feel they're in some kind of position to judge?"

"No, I'm... sorry," Celia exclaimed, backtracking. "I'd just like to know. There's nothing ulterior... I just got served with divorce papers three days ago. The day before I left to come down here."

She took a long drink and stared into the fire. They all looked at her, wondering… not really knowing what to say. "Was it my fault? Should I have seen it coming? Who knows? I had a cancer scare, so instead of uniting us, coming closer, little 'ol hubby couldn't deal and found someone else. Life in the fast lane, huh?"

"Celia-- I'm sorry." Kevin meant it.

She took a gulp of wine, "It's okay. She's got time for him. Lots of plastic surgery too. I mean-- I don't know what I mean! We were supposed to do this ride together, his great vacation. He thinks I'm afraid of adventures. You want an adventure, go through chemo. When I said I didn't really want to go on this trip, he said, 'no problem, I'll take Misty.' I thought he was kidding."

She impulsively stood, raising her glass. "To Misty. What kind of name is Misty anyway?!" They watched her down her drink.

"Is that Misty with a 'Y' or an 'I'?" Sommers asked the glaring Celia.

He slowly grinned and so did she. Then she started giggling and broke down laughing through her tears, realizing maybe Sommers was okay and he was only trying to make her feel better.

"What am I missing here?" Kevin asked.

"Yeah, I don't get it," Robbie blurted, swigging more wine.

"Nothing means nothing," Sommers enunciated. "Nothing matters."

"Hey, we need names," the laughing Celia announced, falling to her knees, not spilling a drop. "Mexican biking names."

"Big Dog," Robbie shouted, then howled at the moon. "That's mine."

Kevin lurched forward, a serious look on his face. "His Lordship."

"On the right track there," Robbie smirked.

Ramon joined in. "Panties… panties man, I think will be mine."

Sommers leaned over to Kevin and whispered, looking right at Celia.

"What--?"

At the same time, Sommers and Kevin blurted, "Brainiac," then fell backward into the sand laughing.

Elena giggled at the spectacle. Sitting up, Sommers asked her, "what's your name, o great riding goddess?"

"Mine will be Raging Legs."

Sommers absorbed the name, knowing it was right on the mark. "The gods would approve."

"Speaking of gods, what's yours, Doctor Harvard?" Celia asked.

Sommers took another drink and stared at the sand. Raising his head, the shadows eerily danced on his face. "And when the fourth seal was broken I saw a pale horse... and his rider's name was... Death."

As if on cue there was a thunderclap in the distance.

"There's a mood changer," Robbie exclaimed, standing. "I gotta go take a leak."

Small droplets began to fall and Ramon jumped up. "Elena, help me with the gear. I would advise we end tonight's festivities and button up."

"I'm out of here," Celia sighed. "I hate the rain."

"Me too," Kevin agreed. "Pools and rain. It's that water thing."

Sommers watched Kevin and Celia scurry to their tents. He was alone. The fire allowed him to see the rain falling and he raised his face into the tropical shower. The pelting felt good, cleansing. "To Raging Legs," he toasted, raising his glass. "And everything else that matters... whatever it is."

# 23

## STORMS

Enrique was annoyed with the uncooperative weather. A hurricane in the Gulf had come ashore and its remnants were creating thunderstorms from Texas, all the way down the eastern coastline of Mexico.

His flight had been delayed twice and by the time he arrived in Vera Cruz, he was behind schedule. The cautionary call he had received in his Houston hotel room alarmed him; Lupe Ferrar was in danger, his operation in jeopardy.

Regarding any type of information, he knew one must consider the source. The informant here was a Vera Cruz associate of Enrique's with no vested interest. A pre-favor of sorts, where Enrique might remember him down the line for future lucrative ventures.

In a perverse way it made sense, the military absconding with everything, never to be heard from again. That of course was the risk at face value. Still, Enrique did not want this to be the case, for it to go that far.

He and Lupe had a long history, one that demanded going the extra mile for protection. Like the men at the abandoned airstrip wanted, the acquisition of these goods by an outside force would be quite a take.

Enrique wasn't surprised, shocked or moved at the rumor the military might be involved. Emotion played no role at this point. It was business.

To meet with Lupe this time he would prepare differently. He wouldn't go alone. In fact, going at all was putting him at risk, but he had to know if the goods were safe, deliverable.

After landing, Enrique proceeded downtown. There was a place off the square, a local spot where he could find a few men for a quick job. They would travel by air, Jeep, then finally on foot.

The new hires had certain skills. They were not afraid to use weaponry and definitely not to be trusted. It was an odd trade off, as Enrique, again, would be watching his back. This of course was nothing new, strangers and liabilities were part of his lot in life. The process wouldn't take too long and he hoped to be on the road by nightfall. A long day, but a necessary one.

*The demons...* he had to know.

# 24

## THE BOAR

Sommers was dreaming. The light rain tapping on his tent, combined with the alcohol and altitude, had put him right to sleep. He was floating, somewhere above the world in the clouds. It was a good dream, one with no stress and no worry. *Maybe it was heaven,* he thought. *Could it really exist?*

Floating, in REM state, he hoped it did. Unlike the jungle he was in, no harm could come to him there. He was shielded, unlike this wilderness, where he saw, heard and felt everything. Sleeping soundly was such a distant concept that when a shadow moved stealth-like next to his tent, Sommers was oblivious.

The apparition glided along the perimeter to the opening of the tent. An arm reached inside and its hand covered Sommers' mouth and nose. The dreamy clouds hissed, then faded to black and Sommers awakened with a start, to the face of Ramon, who murmured, "Quiet. Come with me."

"What--?"

"Shh--"

Awakening, Sommers' adrenaline kicked in and he leapt from the sleeping bag. He was in his clothes and slid into his shoes.

Ramon hovered outside. "Wake the others," came his hoarse whisper.

Sommers went quietly to each tent, he now becoming the floating shadow. Kevin and Celia appeared, half awake. Robbie, unable to sleep, met them near the fire. Elena stood by Ramon.

"Do you know what time it is? What is this?!" Robbie angrily asked.

"Something you will like," Ramon answered. "Time to go."

Ramon started for the edge of the jungle and the group obediently followed.

The jungle and terrain were pitch black. Except for Ramon's wavering penlight, there was nothing but a weak moon and stars.

Celia stumbled, tripping over a vine. She exclaimed, "It's still dark."

A loud "Shh...," from Ramon. He led them like the pied piper and Sommers could only hope the beautiful jungle that was there in the afternoon was still their friend in the pre-dawn blackness.

Ramon abruptly stopped and knelt. In the next instant, Kevin saw him retrieve his handgun, but before he could say anything, there was a rustling, then a loud squeal. Some kind of animal, or beast, or monster, lunged from the night at their feet and disappeared.

Ramon leapt up and yelled, "The hunt, the hunt... come amigos... run!"

He charged after the squealing beast, leading the rest, who followed blindly. Their world was rocks, branches, and infinite darkness. Yelping and screeching echoed.

Kevin rounded a boulder and tripped. Rising up, he was alone and a sense of fear engulfed him. "Sommers... Celia..." he called out. "Hey, where are you guys?"

There was nothing, no one. The hair on the back of his neck stood up. He didn't want to be there. This was a bad place and he started running in the direction he thought would lead him back to camp. He was lost. "Hey, where is everybody? Come on-- "

Out of breath, his mind raced, filling with horrible thoughts about life and death. Every sound radiated and magnified his fear. His heart pounding and body spinning around, trying to find anything familiar, a hand grabbed his shoulders, scaring him.

"We're right here," came Sommers reassuring voice. "Don't panic."

"Sommers-- what is this? What's he doing?!"

"I don't know. Just go with it. Come on."

Kevin watched Sommers jog off and followed, trying to keep him in sight. Sommers stopped on a small rise and Kevin joined him, breathing hard. There was nothing; silence. No one.

Then something in front of them rustled the brush. In the dim light, they could see a huge mass, advancing.

"Sommers..."

A wailing animal began to take form. As it was about to lunge at them, shots rang out. Sommers and Kevin both retreated, falling backward, as the dying animal dropped near their feet.

Stunned and shocked, they watched the snorting, wheezing boar fight for its life. Every muscle twitched, not giving up.

Ramon appeared, pistol drawn, with Robbie, Celia and Elena following. They stared at the animal, the gory mess, trying to make sense, sort out what was happening.

Ramon fired twice more into the animal's torso. The concussion startled them, as blood oozed from its wounds.

"What is going on?! What is this?" an angry Sommers asked, regaining his footing.

"This --," Ramon replied, "is dinner."

"This is crazy. You're nuts," Kevin stammered.

"I am hunting for survival... not games." Ramon reiterated, kneeling next to the boar.

"Man, that was something. It went right over you guys," Robbie eagerly stated, stepping closer, examining the animal's head. "What a brute."

In one last gasp for life, the boar reared, knocking Robbie down. Its eyes fiery red, as if on fire. The beast's whole front torso went for Robbie, who scampered backward.

"Watch out!" Sommers yelled.

"Kill it-- Shoot it!" Robbie screeched.

Ramon fired into the back of the boar's head, dropping him.

"Worthless pig," Robbie sneered, scrambling to his feet.

"You know I'm not used to being shot at," Sommers exclaimed to Ramon.

"You were never in any danger, Doctor."

"That's not the point."

Ramon grinned, studying the boar and speaking. "The point is that there are no warnings here. You kill your prey or it kills you. A simple concept that should be heeded."

"What prey?" Kevin interjected. "This is a bike tour. A vacation!"

Ramon softened a bit, rubbing his hand on the boar's coarse hide. "All of you must understand to share in this world's rewards, you must experience its secrets, its risks. To outwit is to survive."

"Does that mean each other too?" Celia asked.

Ramon didn't answer. Instead, he produced his knife and slit the boar's throat, side to side. The group, although leery, watched transfixed.

Ramon then produced a cup and positioned it near the incision. As he massaged the neck, blood trickled and filled the cup. "There are passages in life," Ramon began. "This is one of them-- to bond and become one in the continuing journey."

He sipped the blood. Afterward, he dipped two fingers inside the cup and streaked the red liquid across his cheek. Light reflected off his face and the viscous liquid sparkled. The group became mesmerized, entranced, as he passed the cup to Sommers.

"What about trichinosis-- ?" Kevin whispered to Celia.

Sommers cradled the cup, knowing he was at a crossroads. "It's still warm," he quietly stressed, forcing a smile.

Focused, he hesitated, absorbing the surroundings, the moment. He glanced to Ramon for assurance, then brought the cup to his lips, closed his eyes and swallowed. Sommers' eyes immediately popped open... *the spoils*. The blood burned his throat, but he smiled at the odd accomplishment and then streaked his face. He felt a guilty empowerment, like he had stolen a magical gift, taken something that was not his, not earned, yet it felt right.

Then it was Kevin's turn. "Seriously?" was all Kevin could muster.

Sommers nodded. Their eyes locked and Kevin knew he was part of something. He took a deep breath, sipped from the cup and streaked his face. He handed the cup to Celia.

"I don't know about this, guys," she reluctantly said, staring at the red liquid.

"It's okay," Sommers reassured.

"I know, I know, I know-- " She couldn't raise the cup to her lips. Robbie snickered, watching everything unfold.

"Take your time. Think of it as Kool-Aid," Kevin encouraged.

"Save the commentary, please."

Sommers moved next to her. "Come on, Celia. You're here. One of the adventurous guys." He lifted the cup and held it up to her face. "I bet your husband wouldn't do it."

Celia looked at him, Kevin and Ramon. Without hesitating, she guided the cup to her lips and gulped the liquid. In the next instant she streaked her cheek.

"All right," she gasped, holding up the cup. "Elena."

"I always wondered what the boys did out here." Elena took the cup and quickly drank. As she dipped her fingers in the thick liquid, she spoke. "I believe you're up, Robbie."

As Elena extended the cup to Robbie, he abruptly stood up and knocked it onto Elena, splattering her with blood. Elena yelped, "Robbie--!"

"You guys are nuts. It's pig blood. I'm not drinking anything close to that." Robbie stormed off.

"Robbie--" Sommers started, but was stopped by Ramon.

"Let him go."

"Angry little tyke," Kevin joked.

"He doesn't get it," Sommers offered, helping Elena wipe up the bloody mess.

"And you do?" Kevin asked.

Sommers stopped, as everyone looked at him, contemplating the answer. "Maybe."

Ramon interrupted. "Come now. It's time to ride. Big day today. Sommers, Kevin, help me with the meat."

# 25

## THE GRAND MORASS

The sun broke the eastern horizon half an hour before the group began riding. A light haze burned off and the heat seemed to increase exponentially with the intolerable humidity. The jungle had teeth today.

The scenery from various ridges and switchbacks was magnificent, with the terrain seeming to change into a myriad of topographies after every few miles. There would be flat areas, meadow-like, then thick jungle in which they would have to maneuver. Their riding skills were called upon and put to the test. At times, the trails vanished or became narrow and rocky... treacherous in their own way. There were moments when even Sommers had to work, focus and stay alert.

Problems on this day were two fold. The humidity produced a myriad of jungle insects. Gnats and mosquitoes swarmed, especially if they were near any kind of water. The other concern, and that was constant, was their bodies ached. The cycling, time zone changes, weather and stress... were all catching up with them. None of them, except for Ramon and Elena, were in as good shape as they thought.

Still, the "buzz" of being there and riding through a wild wilderness hadn't worn off. If there were ebbs in the group's energy, adrenaline would kick in, much like a caffeine fix in the morning.

At a watering hole, some scrawny cattle drank peacefully until they heard the bikes and shifting gears. Robbie rode to the water's edge and stopped, swatting at the buzzing insects. Kevin and Sommers joined him.

"He's pushing us today," Robbie complained. "And these flies are horrible."

"At least you didn't have to pay for them," Kevin chimed in. "How about some water, Sommers? I'm thirsty."

Robbie interrupted. "I think I'd rather be paying for drinks with ice at the pool. Getting sunburned and chasing some young señoritas." He jumped on his bike and pressed on.

Sommers tossed Kevin a water bag. He glared at the jungle, absorbing the hazy sunlight, maybe even enjoying it. "Do you ever think about life, Kevin?"

"Day to day, my taxes or the big picture?"

"No. Your purpose in this grand morass. All the questions."

"Sure. I suppose so. Why?"

Sommers swigged some water, letting it trickle onto his chin and neck. "Because it can change in a second and what you think you have, you don't. Who you think you are, you aren't."

Kevin chuckled. "That's way too deep for me this time of day, Sommers. However, right now I'm thinking I don't feel so hot."

Sommers saw Kevin was perspiring through his clothes and he had sweat beads on his forehead. It wasn't uncommon, especially in the humidity, and of course it depended on what kind of shape an individual was in, how they reacted to a given environment. "I could be a jerk and say you don't look so hot, but don't worry about it. We're all sweating. We'll eat soon. Come on, let's catch up."

Kevin rode ahead and Sommers secured the water bag. Afterward, he wiped his brow, checked his shirt and noticed he wasn't perspiring half as much.

# 26

## LIEUTENANT ROSA

Lieutenant Marco Rosa had been assigned the heroic and often dubious task of locating Lupe Ferrar's camp in the mountains. A native of Vera Cruz he was familiar with local customs and the local players. His family had farmed in the area and he had firsthand experience of much of the region.

Combining his local knowledge and scant military intelligence, he surmised Lupe could only be so many places if he was in the mountains. Geography and topography only provides freedom within parameters.

Lieutenant Rosa had been involved with other raids of secret camps and had varying successes and failures. The bad guys had gotten smarter, but so had the military. The Estados Unidos could be thanked for that.

Usually a few days old, if not more, U.S. Intelligence had provided satellite information of the specific requested sector to the Mexican government. At least it was something, a starting point utilizing his past experience. Using profiling and intuitiveness, Rosa had a very good hunch of the proximity that needed to be combed.

Under the captain's orders, Rosa headed into the hills without apprehension, his mission clear. Lupe had been a thorn in the army's side for a long time and he was to retrieve him, hopefully alive. However, if force needed to be implemented, he would not hesitate. In the army's opinion, Lupe was a problem and problems got solved.

Rosa didn't push his men. He had enough supplies for two weeks and more could be shipped to various points. This was his show; with his twenty, hand-picked soldiers. In his mind, if it took six days or six months in the mountains, it would be a small price for success. For once, he believed he had an upper hand and this time he felt much more confident. This time he had something more than satellite intelligence. This time he had a bloodhound.

The captain had requested some of Jorge De Aguilar's clothes. Given the scent, the dog would follow his horse's trail from the village to whatever point in the mountains. If the weather held, Rosa expected contact within a few days. The boy's own energy would be his and Lupe's downfall.

Following in a Jeep, then on foot, the four-legged canine lumbered through the jungle without hesitation, conscience or remorse. It might have been Rosa's show, but it was the dog's mission in the spotlight. The target would be found.

# 27

## THE RACE

The Vera Cruz hills and mountains are a treasure-trove of historical ruins, dating back thousands of years. Ramon had visited many of these sites on and off the beaten path. Because of vandals and tourists, the Mexican government had begun limiting visitation to sanctioned tours. The adventures of a bike tour allowed one to travel high in the mountains and encounter many places that were still untouched, maybe even undiscovered.

As a light, warm mist fell, Ramon topped a hill and dropped down to an area of abandoned foundations made of rocks and shaved stones. It still amazed him how a culture, a civilization, could penetrate this far into the jungle and create a functioning city with nothing more than their bare hands and backs. It impressed him to no end and he was glad he saw it every few weeks. It invigorated him, reminded him of the power of man's spirit. He also wondered to no end, how it abruptly ended.

Looking back to the rise, he saw Robbie, Celia and Kevin spurt down the hill. "Where are Sommers and Elena?" he asked, somewhat concerned.

"Just wait," Celia cautioned, looking back up the trail.

In the next instant, two mountain bikes crested the top and flew down the trail toward them. Celia began rooting for Elena. Kevin and Robbie cheered for Sommers.

The bikes were neck and neck, wheel to wheel, both riders giving it their all; their tires fighting for every inch of trail. Smiling broadly, Elena crossed the finish line a half bike's length ahead of Sommers. They both power slid to a halt past the applauding group.

"I got you, Sommers," Elena chided, happily patting him on the back, catching her breath.

Courtney & Jacquelyn Silberberg

"That was great! You almost had her," encouraged Kevin.

"Yeah, yeah," Sommers puffed.

"Next time I'll give you a head start," Elena teased.

Happy at the friendly competition, Sommers smiled. "I'll take it."

The group cycled to them, enjoying the moment.

"You can ride, Elena," Kevin said.

"Thank you."

"I don't think her nickname was an accident," Celia shared, snapping a picture. "Your legs... they never stopped pedaling."

"I hear that," Robbie gloated, taking a swig of vodka.

"Yes, my baby sister is very fast," Ramon agreed. "She never ceases to surprise me."

Sommers sensed an edge in Ramon's voice, but didn't push it. "Well, she beat me," he volunteered. "Of course I don't know if I'd brag about it. Oh, and I will take that head start next time."

Elena playfully knocked his shoulder. "You got it."

Robbie finished off the little airline bottle, then noticed his surroundings. "Wow, where are we anyway, Chief?"

"I wondered when someone would ask," answered Ramon.

They were standing near more ruins of temples and pyramids that had obviously been abandoned for hundreds, if not thousands of years. They belonged to the jungle now, the unique and sacred structures, reclaimed by foliage, weathering and time.

"Do you forgive me for the hunt?" Ramon asked, gleefully full of himself. "Are you getting your money's worth my friends?"

Sommers knew the spectacle was magnificent. "It's like out of a book, Ramon. Guess the tour buses don't make it up this far."

"Only a special few see this, Doctor. As you would say, legally, it is protected. We can't actually enter what was the township, but the view should suffice."

"Smile everyone," spouted Celia, filming with her video camera.

Ramon laid down his bike and stood on some stones. "This is history, a book of life that was. Imagine hundreds living and

90

flourishing here, a thousand years ago. A barbaric and merciless civilization... unique unto itself."

"No casinos, huh?" Robbie exclaimed, breaking the moment, then looking skyward at a flash of lightening. "Hey, hey, hey... that's close."

A downpour began, drenching them, with loud thunderclaps all around. The group instinctively took shelter under a canopied tree.

"No, no; we must retreat off this ridge into the jungle. Hurry now," Ramon instructed.

They mounted their bikes and followed Ramon. It was muddy and soaking wet; and something none of them had really planned for. The bikes slid and fish tailed. Eventually, the difficult trail fed into lush cover and the group quickly congregated.

"I think we stay here for awhile," said Ramon. "We can eat, then make our way off this ridge. The weather comes in cycles."

"So, this is the wet cycle," a coughing Kevin stated.

"Yes. Elena, let's heat some water and break out the soup."

Sommers watched Ramon and Elena start on lunch. He went to Kevin, who was pale, his face puffy. "How do you feel now?"

"Besides being soaked to the bone and these short shorts riding up, not great."

"We'll get some fluid in you. You'll feel better."

"Right. I'm freezing, then burning up."

"Yeah, maybe it was the boar blood."

"Hey, whatever the group does, I do." Kevin's eyes sparkled, but Sommers knew he was uncomfortable.

Celia huddled over. "What's wrong?"

"Our boy has a touch of fever, some chills."

"I'm okay," Kevin chirped, mustering courage.

"Here," Ramon offered, handing Kevin a metal cup of steaming soup.

"Is this all there is?" Robbie wanted to know, spitting out his ration. "This tastes terrible. What did you put in here, bugs?"

"At least it's hot," Kevin grinned, sipping the liquid.

"What do you think is wrong with Mr. Black, Doctor?" Ramon asked, sitting beside them.

"Probably a bug or a virus. It came on suddenly... I don't really know. We've all eaten the same things."

"And you call yourself a doctor... a practitioner of medicine," Kevin joked, not realizing the subtext. "You're not going to bill me are you?"

"Just eat. We need a shelter where we can light a fire, dry out, Ramon."

"Yes. At the bottom of the ravine... in a couple of kilometers there will be better cover. The storm will break at some point." Ramon tried to sound encouraging.

There was more thunder and the rain pelted, becoming a hard, fine mist. Droplets fell through the jungle canopy.

"Let's hit it then," Sommers suggested. "Kevin, ride my bike, it's lighter. It'll be easier."

"Super. Thank you for lunch, Elena. I want that recipe, even if I puke."

# 28

## THE LOCKET

Lupe Ferrar arrived at the mountain meadow a few hours before this latest of downpours. The trip had been a perilous one, and one he had a bad feeling about. There was just something, at least in his mind, that wasn't right.

He was troubled Enrique had been ambushed and also that the De Aguilar boy had appeared from the village with a warning. One of the rules Lupe lived by was if it didn't feel right, get out. Why take an unnecessary chance? This simple fundamental had saved him many times over the years. It was the little voice only he heard and he had been hearing it more lately and pondered why.

He liked Enrique, but really couldn't call him a friend. Lupe didn't have "friends." No, he knew the only way to survive was to have minimal contact with outsiders. No emotional attachment. Trust no one.

Lupe had worked quickly and was ready to depart. He sat, wanting to enjoy the meadow, this special place of ruins that at one time housed an entire civilization. Intricate rock foundations were spread out for miles and he knew Mexico harbored over two thousand known ruins' locations. All were different and well fortified. He sometimes wondered why it had all disappeared, vanished in time, like dust on the wind. He knew about the contracted diseases and how the Spaniards appeared one day, forcing their culture and religion on the natives, but complete extinction puzzled him.

Looking at the deteriorating foundations, Lupe contemplated how he had arrived at this point in his life. Surely there had been safer choices, alternatives. He was an educated man, a man of principles, yet here he was hiding illegal contraband for money and being hunted by the Mexican army. That made him laugh.

93

He looked at young De Aguilar, a poor boy from a poor family with not much future. Maybe that's why he was there, slogging through the mountains, causing disruptions in a corrupt government to draw attention to the Jorges of his world. There had to be something better, something above perennial poverty. He hoped he was making some kind of difference.

Lupe was different from Enrique in that regard. He wasn't just doing this for the money and a lucrative deal. His share of proceeds would go to a cause. Whether it was to finance a political movement or buy some milk for children, it would do more than lay in a numbered bank account or buy junk bonds.

"Lupe." Jorge ran over, sliding on some gravel to stop and plopping down next to him. "The men say everything is ready and secure."

"Did they say both those words, Jorge?" It was a test. Lupe watched Jorge struggle with the exactness of the question.

"They said... they said that--"

"Always remember, Jorge, that words are all we have. Be precise, specific. Do things right the first time, even if it takes longer. Comprende?"

"Yes."

"What is that locket around your neck? It is very pretty."

"My mother. She gave it to me on my last birthday. Look."

Jorge removed the locket and opened it carefully. Inside was a picture of his mother, smiling proudly.

"This is beautiful," Lupe agreed, handing it back. "She is very proud of you."

Lupe tasseled Jorge's hair, then was startled, as one of his men came running from the meadow.

"Lupe, Lupe... come quickly. They're here... intruders!"

Without hesitation, Lupe lifted Jorge to his feet and started running for the meadow.

# 29

## GO TO GROUND

Lieutenant Rosa and his men slogged through the jungle rain, irritated at the turn of events. The bloodhound seemed out of sorts, unfocused, and his men, lethargic. Still, Rosa's intuition told him they were close. The terrain had changed and there were indications of foundations and ruins lurking beneath the vegetation.

"Stay alert," he ordered, leading his men up a trail, then stopping. He thought he heard rustling or saw movement ahead. Slowly, he unholstered his pistol and knelt, motioning his men to do the same.

Crawling on all fours, he serpentined through the brush at root level, until he could just glimpse into a clearing.

Carefully peering out, he didn't know if the gun he heard being cocked was one of his men's, or someone else's.

# *30*

## CHOICES

Sommers rode the front point and carried one of Kevin's packs. The trail was muddy and difficult in the misting rain and he couldn't keep his wrap-around glasses clean. He knew they needed to find shelter soon and not just for Kevin. The ride and weather was taking a toll on everyone, himself included. Some of the fun was wearing off.

The path meandered down around a ridge and Sommers likened it to a fire break at Big Bear. He could hear the others lagging behind him and didn't want to create too large a gap between them. He would pedal to keep pace and get off the hill. It wasn't a race and that's why what Kevin did next surprised him.

Sommers heard the whine of his derailer shifting gears. He knew that unique, high pitched sound, because he'd special ordered it and waited a week while it was on back order.

Turning his head, Sommers caught Kevin on the edge of his peripheral vision, pedaling, pumping and standing up. The corners of his mouth turned up, as he saw Kevin pass everyone with the wet wind in his hair and a fiery look in his eyes. Sommers knew and understood that look, that feeling. It was the pure freedom and the rush mountain biking rewards those who push their limits. Kevin was testing his, maybe releasing all the angst and frustration that had built up, consumed him over the months. Sommers envied that... that ability to let go.

As Kevin passed him, Sommers wanted to yell and join him, but in that next instant his euphoria changed to fear, then to terror, as he heard the distinct "pop" of a tire.

To any above average rider, the sudden change in balance and speed of a deflating tire can be controlled. To Kevin, in his current state of illness, and only very average riding skills, it spelled doom.

Kevin immediately overcorrected his steering, as his front tire plugged into the soft mud. He crushed the sensitive brakes and all of his weight crammed forward… as the laws of physics always win. His rear tire lifted off the ground, the entire bike wanting to flip over completely.

Kevin had no time or more importantly, no ability, to alter what happened next. In slow motion, Sommers and the others gawked at Kevin, catapulting into the air and down a ravine. His limp body tumbled hard, rolled over and over, through brush and rocks, finally coming to a stop in a shallow stream about fifteen feet below the trail.

"Kevin--!" came the hysterical shouts and calls of the others, who were throwing down their bikes, trying to navigate down the steep drop.

Kevin lay still on his stomach, both arms pinned beneath him. The broken bike was a few yards away, both tires bent and spinning pointlessly.

Sommers was the first one to arrive, watching his friend's breath kick up sand granules. "Take it easy, Kevin. Take it easy."

"Shoulder… my shoulder… Ahhh…"

The others clamored close by, amazed, shocked… afraid. Ramon bent down, close to Kevin. "Okay, Boy. Elena, the first aid kit and a blanket from my pack. Quickly. Help her, Robbie."

Kevin grimaced in pain, his body releasing adrenaline. His moans were guttural, frightening, as his bruised and broken body writhed. There was a bleeding gash on his forehead and blood trickled on his face. His temple and cheek were scraped and he convulsed.

"Hurry. Do something, Sommers," blurted Celia's panicked request.

"Assist me, Sommers," Ramon demanded, positioning himself to move Kevin.

Sommers didn't respond. Obviously withdrawn, he stood still, not even assessing the situation, but staring coldly. He was frozen, unable to move, to administer.

"Sommers, are you helping or not?" Celia interrogated.

He backed farther away, not wanting any part of this moment. *It wouldn't be his fault again,* he thought. *No, let's let it unfold-- play it safe, Baby.*

"Sommers!"

Celia helped Ramon roll the moaning Kevin over. Ramon calmly ran his hands over Kevin's chest and head. As his fingers approached Kevin's right shoulder, he cried out.

Robbie and Elena returned with the kit and blanket.

"His shoulder. There is a separation. We will put him on the blanket and move him out of here. Celia, apply pressure with this gauze to his forehead."

"He's burning up," Celia retorted.

"Will he be all right?" Elena asked, looking at Sommers. "Shouldn't you be helping? Are we doing the right thing? Sommers, what should we do?!"

Ramon eyed Sommers warily. "Everyone grab a corner. We need to get him out of this water. Onto flat ground," he ordered. "On three." They all grabbed the blanket, "One, two, three, go." They slowly lifted the helpless Kevin and carried him to level ground.

Sommers lagged behind and Ramon confronted him. "What kind of doctor are you? Help your friend."

The group weighed Sommers, confused and glaring at his lack of involvement. "I-- I'm in a lawsuit. They're saying because of me, a little girl died."

Celia shook her head. "Is that what this is about?! Some lawsuit? Getting sued is part of the profession-- any profession. It doesn't mean anything. Hire an attorney. You're a doctor!"

"She's right," Ramon reiterated. "You can really help him."

Sommers saw their faces and the grimacing Kevin. His stomach turned... fight or flight. "She was my first."

"What are you talking about?" Celia asked, her voice rising.

"She was the first one I lost, all right? I did everything I was supposed to, right by the book. Boom. Boom. Boom. Like I was trained. And it didn't work. She died. I did everything-- they had to pull me off."

A sobering moment. The group looked at each other before Ramon spoke. "You are the only one who can help him."

Kevin clenched his teeth from pain. "It wasn't your fault Sommers. And I'm not dying. Just feels like it." Kevin grimaced, his pale face etched in agony. "Maybe this is your purpose in life-- that grand morass-- ahhh!"

Elena touched Kevin's shoulder and tried calming him, then looked up. "Please, Sommers. Help him!"

Sommers knelt facing his ultimate demon. In all the wrangling and haranguing, he'd never contemplated not helping someone in trouble. Someone who was hurt. Someone who needed him and his abilities... the moment of getting back on the snarling horse.

He dove in. "Ramon, what kind of painkillers do you have? Percocet? Demerol?"

"Morphine."

"Kevin... can you hear me?" Sommers gingerly asked. "Are you allergic to anything? Anything I need to know about?"

Saliva drooled from Kevin's mouth, as he muttered, "penicillin-- I don't know!"

"Give me the kit," Sommers ordered. He assembled the syringe and prepped the needle, measuring a dose of morphine.

"That thing's huge! I hate needles that big," Robbie announced, walking away, lighting a cigarette.

Sommers prepared the injection and stuck Kevin's arm, then handed the syringe to Ramon. "Okay, we need to get this set into place. Kevin, I'm going to massage it and try to slip it back. Just go with me. Everyone, hold him."

Sommers placed his hands on key points of the shoulder joint. He leveraged with the collarbone and kept feeling for something near the crown of the bone. He remembered the little girl and put her face out of his mind... searching. The bone and tissue were there... small, swollen ripples... *just finesse it and get to the house.*

Then he stopped. He found a pressure point, a vacuum in a sea of bone, blood and muscle. He knew that's where the joint needed to be and it wasn't. "This isn't going to feel good, Kevin. But only for a second. You ready?"

"Just do it."

Sommers admired his persistence. "Okay, here we go. Maybe we'll get real lucky here." He kept massaging, feeling for something in the soft tissue. "There it is... okay easy now-- you know, Kevin, you handled my bike pretty well."

"I did? Looks busted to me--"

Sommers suddenly yanked Kevin's arm. They heard a light "thud" and in an instant, it was back in place.

Kevin's eyes popped open. "Whoa... did you--?"

"Yeah, she's in. Just lay still a second."

Ramon patted Sommers on the back, looking at him with a new perspective. "Very well done. That was textbook. It's back in perfectly."

"Well, it fits," Sommers said, playing it down. "That morphine should be kicking in."

"Don't even feel it. That's a horrible sound though," Kevin volunteered.

"It's going to be tender. I'll set a sling so the shoulder can't move."

Ramon stood, surveying the riverbed and campsite. "We'll stay here by the stream and I will radio the helicopter. We can rendezvous at the lower meadows, fly out later--"

"No," Kevin begged, trying to form sentences in the morphine haze. "I'll be okay."

"That's the drug talking. You need to be sipping margaritas at the pool."

"Sounds good to me," Robbie yelped, swatting at a mosquito. "I've had enough drama out here. Maybe I can get some ball scores at the hotel, play some cards. This roughing it is getting old. My cell phone isn't worth anything out here."

The group huddled around Kevin, ignoring Robbie. Elena dabbed his brow, Celia held his good hand and Sommers checked to make sure nothing else was broken or needed attending. "You're bruised up pretty good, but the separation wasn't too severe. We'll watch your fever. Good thing you're tough."

"And divorced..." Kevin joked, then finally passing out, grinning at all of them.

# *31*

## TURNING TABLES

Lieutenant Rosa crawled silently to the perimeter of a meadow surrounded by ruins. Rock foundations supplanted foliage and grass. At one time families congregated near the remains of a water well and lived nearby. Rosa knew there were thousands of such ruins throughout his country. Some were extremely famous tourist attractions and more were discovered every year. He wondered, however, how many were used to hide illegal contraband for insurgent rebel forces. That idea made him chuckle. The ingenuity, the simplicity and the nerve. He smiled until he felt the muzzle of a machine gun at his temple.

"Hola," Lupe's coarse voice whispered. "I'm surprised they only sent a lieutenant. I thought I would at least rate a Colonel or General. Stand up."

At the time of his capture, Lupe's men had spread out and flanked Rosa's militia. They were all captured in the brush, surprised and duped. The rebels had perfectly executed what they did best, mobilize in secrecy, then execute their given task. All of them were brought into the camp.

"What is your name, lieutenant?" Lupe asked, lighting a cigar.

"Lieutenant Rosa."

"Don't you realize the jungle is dangerous? Even for well trained soldiers. There are bad men lurking everywhere."

This brought a laugh from Lupe's men. At the moment, they carried the obvious advantage. Still, Rosa sensed something. He did a mental head count of his men and it didn't total. Some of his men, his armed men, had yet to be captured.

"I have come to arrest you and return you to Vera Cruz under military guard," Rosa uttered adamantly. This brought another chorus of laughter.

"I can see that, lieutenant. You've made great strides in that effort."

Rosa took the chiding, the almost silly censure, because he knew he still had a chance. He carefully glanced to the perimeter... searching for any movement-- his men. "If you come with me peacefully, I'm sure the courts will consider leniency on you, Lupe Ferrar."

"Lieutenant, your banter amuses me. Young Jorge, come over here and see this."

The sixteen year old leapt at the opportunity to stand next to his hero, especially with prisoners. "Jorge," Lupe began. "This is the reason you are here and fighting with us. Look hard at our inept military forces. Is this where our tax dollars go after the corrupt officials empty our treasury? I don't think they could find water in a lake."

Laughter. "We found you," came Rosa's brisk reply.

Lupe had the boy step aside and moved closer to Rosa. "Are you not aware of who holds whom at this moment, lieutenant?"

In that instant, Rosa saw a glimmer of a weapon, low on the perimeter. He knew what was coming next and he grinned. All the cards hadn't been played yet. In fact, the game was just about to begin. "Moments change, my friend," Rosa said. "Life and moments change."

# 32

## ACCUSATIONS

They had made camp, a quick makeshift with one tent and a couple of tarps. Everything was different now, shaded and shadowed, with concerns from Kevin and the bikes, to the uncooperative weather.

Sommers was agitated. The day's events had once again forced him to relive the moments of the accident. They kept resonating in his brain, bouncing around like one of those old pinball machines that just took your money. *Some vacation.*

Ramon was repairing Sommers' damaged bike, or trying to, and not cutting any slack to Sommers on two fronts. The first was his hybrid tires, which bothered Ramon from the start, and then the lack and confusion of medical attention when Kevin first fell. That bothered Sommers as well, a prickly demon only he understood, and one that could crop up when least expected or wanted.

Not facing Sommers, tooling the bike, Ramon spoke. "I warned you about your tires. That is why he fell."

Before Sommers could mount his defense, Celia interrupted. "Kevin hit a rut. He's sick and not the best rider. That's why he fell. Sommers and his tires had nothing to do with it."

"Americans. Always looking for some excuse, then believing it. Here, look at this."

Ramon held up the blown tire tube and squeezed air from its rubber soul. They heard hissing.

"Fine, blame it on me. We might look for excuses, but you certainly pass quick judgment."

"I look at the facts, Señor."

Sommers dropped his tools, angry. "You know, Ramon, in the real world it doesn't matter who's fault it is anyway. It's how they spin it."

He strode away, thinking even in the jungle, in the middle of nowhere, you're vulnerable.

They had placed Kevin near a tree with some netting over him. Sommers thought it ironic that even though he was in the worst shape, he was probably the most comfortable at the moment.

"Hola," the hazy Kevin offered up, as Sommers approached.

"How are you feeling?"

"Like a truck hit me. You know you did good back there. You're a good doctor."

"There's about a thousand people who beg to differ, Mr. Black. Want to call them?"

"No way. Don't even want to give them the chance."

They both smiled. The sun was trying to break out somewhere in the clouds, but the sky still spit rain.

They watched Elena about forty yards away. She was with Robbie, who kept nipping at his airline bottles of liquor. It looked like they were playing chase, horseplay in paradise.

"Ramon's a jerk," Kevin stated. "I have two brothers that could give him a run for his money though."

"Do you find that everything you do or want is some kind of battle?"

"Sure. Didn't they tell you that in school? That's what they should teach... 'How to prevent getting taken advantage of.' And, 'What to do when you are,' because we all get taken in the end."

"I guess."

"Sommers, I've made a fortune in the market and real estate, and sure I inherited a bunch, but not one dime, not one, could've helped me back there. To tell you the truth, it really scared me."

Sommers listened to him, contrasting his voice with Elena's high-pitched laughing. She and Robbie were chasing each other through the meadow, but Elena had the advantage. She would allow Robbie only to get so close, then dart away. It was comical... her ability to control him.

"Money's just a head trip," Sommers quietly stated, watching Robbie fall over himself, trying to push his weight and body to places simple physics would not allow. "I became a doctor to help people. Now my whole world is on the line because I did what I'm trained to do-- try and save a life. Then today I almost didn't help you because of what could have happened. How's that for ironic... or is it moronic?"

"It's the irony that gets you. Thanks by the way. Really."

Kevin offered up his hand and grinned. "Now go save Elena. Doggy Boy's on the hunt and I think she'd rather play chase with you."

Sommers shook Kevin's hand. He knew he'd done the right thing regarding the shoulder. He was a doctor and somewhere in his subconscious, he also knew he'd done right by the little girl.

# 33

## HIDE AND SEEK

Elena lightly stepped over rocks and plotted strategy in the high grass. She could hear Robbie panting in the near distance, but knew he couldn't catch her. He was too big, too slow and becoming drunk. That made her laugh.

Robbie anxiously kept traversing the uneven terrain, a large blob removed from his element of low rent bars and smoky casinos. Too tired to continue, he stopped, finishing one more little bottle of vodka. He opened another, as his sense of taste was heightened in the outdoor weather. So was his testosterone.

"Elena… Elena, I'm going to get you," he playfully chided, swigging back the bottle. "Come on out. Uncle Robbie's here and ready to play."

A dollop of mud hit Robbie, splattering his chest. Elena innocently appeared. "Oops," she giggled.

"You're mine now," Robbie happily exclaimed, lunging a handful of mud at her and missing.

"You have to have better aim than that," she laughingly retorted.

"I was aiming for your head…" Robbie followed her upstream, half-angry, half-eager at her gag. He wished he'd hit her or at least splashed some water on her, as that would have gotten her top wet.

Elena stealthily moved beneath the cover of the moist grass. She could hear him, but not see him. Crouched, she wanted to laugh so hard, but held back. *The look on his face when the mud hit…*

She burrowed deeper into the jungle, following the little stream. It was pretty and clear, fresh and clean.

Coming to a rock tower, she needed to figure out her next move. Robbie was behind her, trotting upstream... advancing closer.

Spotting his large figure and ducking for cover, Elena suppressed another snicker, hoping he didn't hear her. About to stand and run away, she saw something, a shiny object in the brook. A uniformly round, bright object, that had no business being there.

Curious about something so out of place, she reached into the crisp water and tentatively pulled it out. Securely nestled in the palm of her hand was a gold coin the size of a U.S. half-dollar. Flipping it over, it appeared brand new, sparkling, but the date was--

"Got you!" blurted Robbie's commanding, forceful voice. He grabbed her from behind, lifting her. Elena shrieked at the surprise, remembering the game, dropping the coin. Her legs flailed, as Robbie hung on, probably too tightly. "Knew I'd get you."

"Okay, okay. Put me down, Robbie."

"I will, just hang on a second. I didn't come all the way out here for nothing."

"Robbie-- I found--"

"The big doggie scores! Woof!" Robbie squeezed tighter, inhaling her.

"Stop it, Robbie. I mean it. Put me down now."

But he didn't. The alcohol and testosterone had taken hold. He shoved her back against a tree, not letting go.

"You're drunk, Robbie."

He froze. There was a moment, when it was still a game. *Horseplay in the Mexican jungle.*

He had her pinned against the damp bark, her soft skin against his. Craning her neck, she caught a glimpse of his eyes and the blackness behind them. Robbie wasn't going to stop.

"Robbie--!"

He shoved her hard into the tree, hitting her head. Dazed and panicked, Elena's adrenaline kicked in. Using all her might, she kicked-- flailed. Yelping, she bit him.

Robbie recoiled in pain, as Elena shoved him and they tumbled to the ground. She scrambled, trying to get away, but Robbie held her firmly, even as her bracelet accidentally scratched his face. He wiped blood from his cheek, grinning and breathing on her neck. "You little tease."

He forced her down, pinning and covering her writhing body with his own on the wet leaves and mud. He kissed her lithe form, bending her arms over her head. Then in the distance--

"Elena? Robbie? Hey, where are you guys?" broached Sommers' echoing voice. "Yo, we're eating soon. Are you out here?"

Robbie covered Elena's mouth and scanned the area. He could only hear Sommers, but knew he was coming.

"Hey... are you here? Hello?"

"Okay," Robbie whispered. "Just be a good girl. We were just playing around. You know it and I know it. Okay?"

Feigning agreement, she bit his hand and Robbie squealed, as he finally let go. In his confusion, she kicked Robbie in the groin, then rolled away. He lay there, an angry, beached whale.

Sommers appeared, arriving only moments after they separated. "Hey, looks like Kevin's going to make it. Ramon and Celia are--"

He saw Elena's torn shirt. "Hey, what's up?"

"Nothing's up, Sommers," Robbie bellowed, slowly trying to stand through the searing pain in his groin. Sommers sensed the moment, glared at Robbie. "What's going on--? What did you do, Robbie?"

"None of your business-- Nothing. We were playing around, that's all. Tell him!"

Elena moved closer to Sommers. He saw the fear in her eyes.

"Tell him nothing happened," Robbie ordered.

"You're pathetic," Sommers angrily growled, diving for Robbie full force, landing a couple of quick blows.

"Stop it, stop... " Elena pleaded.

Taking advantage with his size, Robbie rolled Sommers over and hit him in the face. "Nothing happened that she didn't ask for."

More agile, Sommers held his own, punching Robbie. He could have hit him again, but didn't. Robbie had to catch his breath and Elena helped up Sommers.

"You make me sick," Sommers coughed, spitting a little blood.

"I'm all right, Sommers. Really," Elena confided. "He is just a stupid drunk."

"Get out of here, Robbie. Now."

Robbie stood up slowly, dazed. "It's the booze-- all right? I was just playing around. It got out of hand."

"That's an understatement."

"I mean it. Really. I'll keep away from her. Please, it won't happen again-- just don't hate me…"

"Hate you?" Sommers questioned. "What's that supposed to mean? This isn't some popularity contest. Just stay away from us."

"Don't tell the others. Please."

"Robbie--" Sommers began, but was cut off by a popping sound that if they didn't know better, sounded like machine gun fire. The popping repeated; coming in short bursts.

"What is that?!" Robbie asked for all of them.

# 34

## AMBUSHED

A thick, acrid gray haze settled over the lush meadow, hanging at eye level. The once beautiful, historic ruins of a thriving civilization, now lay wasted in a sea of bodies, spent bullets and blood.

Lieutenant Rosa's men, the ones who weren't captured, made their surprise move, and for a few moments had the advantage. The chaos allowed Rosa to escape his immediate bonds, as bodies fell and died around him in unrelenting hails of explosive gunfire.

He maneuvered, took a gun from one of Lupe's men and joined the fight. Because of the element of surprise, the beginning of the battle was even, but each side kept losing men until fewer and fewer stood fighting. There were no cowards.

Lupe was gunned down advancing to a Jeep near the well. He took cover by the American made vehicle, but its thin metal was no match for the Mexican Militia's high caliber weaponry. Bullets ripped through the Jeep's quarter panels, and into Lupe, killing him instantly.

Upon seeing their leader fall, the rebels began to retreat and the militia made their final assault. However, it was futile and too little, too late. The last of the rebels fired until they were out of ammunition and the dying militia took their final shots. Both sides were valiantly massacred. No one was unscathed.

Jorge was shot in the stomach and shoulder. His sixteen year old body fell against a tree and his adolescent eyes watched the finality of the ambush. As his sinewy blood covered his clothes and ran into the dirt, he probably suffered the most, seeing the skirmish first hand, as the cause of each group unfolded and unraveled.

It was ugly and horrific, something he had never even dreamed about. *This was surreal, a movie or a story… it had to be,* he thought. Nothing in his short life was like this, real life and death, with moments where one was here and then not. It made him sick, but he was too weak to vomit.

Then he thought if this was life, he didn't want any part of it. No, if this was an example, a taste outside of his world, then so be it. No cause is worth this. *I will just leave now,* he thought… leave and maybe return as something else, something that would never have any part of either side.

He craved sleep and water, and he tasted the stagnant haze of wasted gunpowder and death. He thought he heard something along the perimeter, but was too weak to look… to care. Maybe it was an animal, or maybe someone on his side had survived. He hoped that to be true, to tell of this. Maybe tell the truth… that in this game, there was no winner. There never would be.

# 35

## UNFRIENDLY JUNGLE

More staccato pops echoed off the jungle like concentric circles. Sommers, Elena and Robbie huddled, backs to each other, forgetting what had just happened.

Then it hit them. "The others at camp..." Sommers murmured. They faced each other, fear filling them. "Come on."

Like a bad dream, each of them suddenly felt helpless. For some reason, their brains wouldn't transmit running signals fast enough to their legs. Even though they started running full out, it felt like they weren't moving at all, like they were caught inside those concentric circles, their legs crumbling beneath; getting nowhere.

"I can't keep up," Robbie anxiously admitted, not wanting to be left behind.

"Keep moving."

Sommers helped Elena, but Robbie was on his own. They didn't know if they were moving toward the gunfire or away from it. Sommers was confused, lost. There was the stream, which now seemed foreign, the tall grass and endless jungle.

*Which way? What do you do now?* Sommers' gray matter spurted, asking all the questions for the unexpected. Then more gunfire, maybe a little bit closer. *Why was there gunfire?!* Sommers kept moving, pushing them forward to--

The terrain changed and Sommers recognized the riverbed. Then he saw Kevin's netting and the bikes. He had never been so happy to see those muddy bikes... until his eyes riveted on the gun pointed at him.

Hearing a rustling in the nearby brush, Ramon had pivoted toward the sound. He deftly aimed one of his handguns at the charging Sommers.

"It's us... it's us. Don't shoot!" Sommers exclaimed.

"You... thank God," Ramon blurted. "Are you all right? Elena...?"

"Yes," Sommers answered. "What is going on?"

If the exchanging gunfire wasn't closer because of proximity, it was faintly louder at the camp.

"Is it the soldiers? Do you think it's the soldiers?" Celia anxiously asked, obviously scared.

There was more gunfire, which grabbed their attention, but it was accompanied with angry shouts.

"I don't know," Ramon offered, confused as the others.

"Let's get on the bikes and ride out of here-- now!" Kevin exclaimed, half dazed from the fall and the drugs.

Ramon began speaking quickly in Spanish to Elena, who stood frozen, scared. "Speak English," Sommers demanded. "We're in this together."

Gunfire exploded with excruciating volleys, then anonymous yelling. The group huddled together, the thunderous sound pulling their focus to an area above them. "I think it comes from over the hill," Ramon surmised, looking beyond the jungle.

Hearing scuffling in the bushes, Ramon aimed his gun again. It was Robbie, panting and sweating. "Can you believe this? That is a ton of firepower... what do we do?"

Gunfire erupted again. "Do you think they are coming this way?" Elena asked, as a thunderclap made them all jump.

"Take these," Ramon ordered, handing guns to Sommers and Robbie. "We can protect ourselves."

Sommers examined the ammunition clip and safety. "We should check it out."

"Do you have a death wish?" Robbie asked. "They're shooting."

"What if they come here? We need to see what's going on first, so we can deal with it. What do you think?"

"I think you're crazy. We need to get out of here," Kevin stated. "Those bullets are real."

"I'm with Kevin," Celia said.

"Yeah, she's right," Robbie agreed. "Way too much tension around."

"Ramon...?" Sommers persisted.

Holding his gun, Ramon was genuinely interested, his curiosity piqued at what was over the hill. He looked at Sommers and determination filled his eyes.

# 36

## MASSACRE

They struggled up the hill, trying to be quiet. Every time they took a step, a twig or something snapped. It was the jungle, it wasn't supposed to be quiet, conducive to something covert or friendly. The errant sounds only magnified in their fear.

Ramon led cautiously. This was new territory and he was out of his element, but not as much as everyone else. He thought he had some idea of what to expect. He'd never been close to a conflict or a battle, but had heard recounts of the militia and rebels, seen photographs. He'd never fought in any war. His was a simple life... take care of Elena, stay on the fringes, get by.

Sommers helped the unwilling Kevin along. He was probably right, yet Sommers was too. They needed to know what was out of sight, what could hurt them. Sommers knew if you were running, you needed to know what you were running from. Then maybe you had a chance.

"I have a bad feeling," Kevin kept repeating. "We should go back."

There were more sticks breaking, but that was the only sound. The gunfire and melee had silenced or scared the animals. It was just them and the imposing, now suspect jungle.

Sommers crawled the last bit, separating the grass and maneuvering through foliage. He scurried ahead of Ramon and arrived at the edge of a clearing. Peering out from the protective cover of the jungle, he couldn't comprehend what his eyes saw.

It was a ragged campsite, nestled in some historical Mayan ruins. But what Sommers had difficulty digesting, was the more than a dozen, bullet riddled bodies and dead men, strewn under an ominous fog-like haze. It was sickening, even to someone trained medically and more accustomed to death.

The others sidled next to Sommers, slowly bringing into focus what they were witnessing. It was a slaughter with no victor. A small fire burned near the Jeep and a stockpile of guns, ammunition filled boxes and supplies sat unopened. The men who came to this party didn't leave.

"Do you see that?" Robbie whispered. "Look at that!"

"What is-- ?" Celia gawked. "What happened?"

"I don't know," Sommers answered, glad he didn't know the details. This carnage was incomprehensible. "Ramon?"

Ramon peered at the decimation, searching for any clues. "The bodies over there are Army militia-- the others-- rebels maybe, Cartel, I'm not sure. Something is wrong."

"No kidding," Robbie chided.

"It's a drug deal," Celia exclaimed. "Has to be a drug deal gone bad."

"Can we just leave?" Kevin pleaded. "I'm going to be sick. Let's go get help."

All eyes focused on Kevin, when unexpectedly a sound from the camp grabbed their attention... a wounded voice. It started low, then the crescendo built into a moan, a weak cry for help.

"Somebody's still alive in there," Celia acknowledged.

"It's not our problem," Sommers blurted, scanning the campsite.

"No, we cannot become involved with rebels or the militia," Ramon concurred. "This is not a good place."

A chill shot up Celia's spine. "Somebody's hurt out there."

"Celia," Sommers began. "We're in Mexico, in the middle of a gun battle. It's not worth--"

"Finally somebody's making sense," Kevin added. "This is crazy. Can we go?"

The wrenching cry floated over to them again. Haunting. Ramon saw the wheels in Sommers' mind turning, canvassing the camp.

Something welled inside Sommers. Something told him Celia was right. *How can I not help? How can I?*

Ramon touched Sommers' shoulder. "This does not concern us, Doctor."

"I was wrong before, with Kevin. I guess human life does concern me."

"You will be putting us in jeopardy if you lend aid. We do not know the full situation."

"Sorry," was all Sommers uttered, crawling away. "I have to help."

"Sommers… Come back! You'll get us all killed."

# 37

## MAMA

Sommers slithered his way inside the perimeter of the brush and stood. He'd never witnessed anything this horrible. This wasn't a multiple car pileup on the freeway or some random gang bang drive-by. This was planned, orchestrated war. The fresh carnage made his stomach sour and it was all he could do to keep moving toward the pleading voice. *God, get me through this,* he prayed.

Stepping over and around lifeless bodies and guns, he finally found the source of the voice. Jorge was still propped against the tree trunk.

Sommers immediately went to him. "Okay, okay..." he began. "Just take it easy."

Right away, he knew Jorge was in trouble. He'd lost too much blood and the abdominal wounds were severe. Reflexively, Jorge tried picking up his gun, but couldn't.

"Easy," Sommers kept repeating. "Just take it easy. I'm a Doctor. El Doctor."

Sommers carefully moved the gun aside and the boy writhed. "Mi Mama," he murmured. "Mi Mama es en Vera Cruz." Jorge pressed the locket with his mother's picture into Sommers' palm.

"Okay, okay; let me help you first."

Sommers opened Jorge's shirt, examining the bullet wounds. He ripped off the boy's sleeves and put pressure on the oozing holes in his chest. Ramon cautiously appeared with the first-aid kit. Sommers gave him a grim smile.

"I need a bandage press," Sommers ordered. "And a ventilator... and a whole boat load of equipment we don't have. He's bleeding to death out here!"

Ramon opened the kit and Jorge's eyes opened wide. His blood soaked hands grabbed Sommers' collar. "Mi... Mama--"

Jorge's back arched and his young body trembled. In that moment, life drifted out of him. Sommers carefully laid him back down, folding his arms on his chest. "He's gone. This place... I didn't have a chance to-- he's only a kid."

"He was dead before you arrived, Sommers. We must go now, before others come."

Sommers damp, blood covered hands, opened the locket and he saw the picture of Jorge with his mother. "What kind of place is this? What kind of country?"

"None of this is our fault or our concern, Doctor. It is time to go."

"Hey, hey, hey," announced Robbie's cheerful voice, grabbing their attention. "Check this out. Come to Dada."

Wiping off the blood, Sommers reluctantly left Jorge, pocketing the locket. He and Ramon walked to Robbie, who was holding a large wrapped bag.

"Can't you keep quiet?" Sommers asked.

"Why should you have all the fun? Look what I found."

Robbie stood next to the Jeep, which had a winch hooked to a pulley that had been erected over the well. He punctured the plastic wrapping and a puff of white powder plumed out. "This isn't baking soda."

He scooped the fine granules on to his fingernail and inhaled. A grin spread across his face, as Celia, Elena and Kevin joined them. "Whoa, I think our little Mexican boys liked partaking in illegal powdered pleasures. It's heroin, people. A lot of it."

"So it was about drugs," Sommers voiced.

"Isn't everything in these coconut countries?"

Ramon touched the bag. "Probably in exchange for the weaponry-- or money."

"Well, obviously someone wasn't happy with the outcome," Kevin cryptically stated.

"We don't need this," Celia uttered. "Can we please just go? This place and all these bodies are giving me the creeps!"

"Wait, wait a minute," Robbie urged. "Do you have any idea what a bag like this is worth on the street, back in the States?!"

"Probably millions, Robbie," Celia angrily replied. "Who cares?! It doesn't matter if you're dead. I want to go now."

"Yes, Ramon. Please," Elena exclaimed. "It is too dangerous to stay here."

Robbie shook his head, laughing. "You two are idiots."

"Shut up, Robbie," threatened Sommers.

"We're Americans-- in Mexico," Celia rationalized. "Who do you think they're going to believe when they see this?"

"You're forgetting; they're all dead. We can--"

"The laws work differently down here," Celia chided.

Kevin was upset and his shoulder hurt. "She's right. You're guilty first-- it's not like at home. We have dead soldiers here. Dead Mexican soldiers!"

They were at a standoff, confused, tired and angry. Then surprisingly, the winch moved, startling everyone. Sommers picked up a dead soldier's rifle and cautiously advanced to the edge of the well. His eyes followed the steel cable down into the murky darkness. "Hey... there's somebody down there!"

Nobody moved.

# 38

## THE WELL

The group quickly encircled the well and tentatively peered down. Dank blackness. A bad odor. Wet echoes.

Ramon pointed his flashlight into the forty foot stone shaft and the beam radiated to the bottom. There was a uniformed arm in the churning water.

"Oh, no. He's dead," Kevin began. "He has to be, hasn't he?"

Sommers climbed up on the well's rim, hung onto the cable, trying for a better look. "What do you think, Ramon?"

"That we should leave. These men, and the ones who will return, will have no regard for us."

Staring down the lighted shaft, Sommers put on his biking gloves.

"What are you doing?" asked Celia.

"We're in this now. We can't just leave somebody to die out here. I don't care who it is."

"It's not your job to save the world," Celia stated.

Robbie smirked. "Go for it. See what else is down there."

Ramon hopped up on the edge. "I will go with you."

"There's nothing you can do until I see if he's alive."

Ramon motioned to the gun Sommers had. "Take off the safety and be careful. Here."

He handed Sommers the flashlight. Sommers checked the line and his balance, and slowly alighted on the cable, using the sides of the wall for leverage. He descended, the well and darkness swallowing him.

Almost immediately the temperature dropped, because of the shade and water. Sommers was at ease, rappelling himself down, his bike gloved hands advancing foot by foot.

Nearing the bottom, he stopped and directed the muted light toward the moving water, but he slipped, his fingers losing their grip.

He plopped into the murky water and became entangled with-- a waterlogged body. His light shined into a bloated face and a lifeless man's eyes. In his controlled panic, Sommers knew he'd been dead awhile... probably one of the first ones.

In the hollow blackness, Sommers wrestled with the corpse and cable, working to get his footing, bearings... air. Escaping the immediate quagmire, he stood in chest deep water, catching his breath, heart racing.

"Sommers...?" drifted Ramon's voice. "Are you all right? What's going on below?"

Sommers set his back against the wall, peered upward. The opening and sky were now pinhole size. "Yeah... the soldier or rebel's dead. It's a mess. I'm coming up."

Gripping the cable, the light flashed around the space and Sommers was surprised to find what appeared to be an opening of some kind. Curious, he swam to its archway, the water becoming deeper, colder, and the current stronger. It was like an underground stream.

"Sommers--" echoed Ramon's apprehensive voice.

"Give me a second. There's something else down here."

# 39

# THE CHAMBER

Fighting the current, Sommers waded to an opening that led into a separate chamber. Cautiously, he hoisted himself into the carved out room.

Sweeping the light, he was amazed, intrigued. Stored inside was an arsenal of damaged wooden crates with guns, ammunition and tightly wrapped plastic bags. "Oh man," he mumbled.

The chamber itself was large and had obviously been excavated by more than rushing water and time. Someone had taken this natural well and historic ruins, and carved out their own storage facility. It was almost perfect. A secret vault, a tomb for storing smuggled contraband. Sommers admired the ulterior motive and its brazen covertness.

The fallen and damaged crates blocked his way from advancing further inside. Getting footing and leverage, he shoved with his body weight, attempting to move one of the wooden boxes. Adjusting his angle to try again, his attention was diverted. Something glistened near his foot in the light. Reaching down, he retrieved two gold coins from the water. Carefully holding them, he read their imprints. "El Governmiento de Mexico – 1891."

He gazed into the chamber and saw some of the fallen crates had dislodged smaller boxes with more coins scattered around them. "And so go the spoils." He pocketed the coins and shouted upward, "I'm ready. Can you hoist me?"

Ramon strode quickly to the Jeep, inspecting the winch and cable. "Elena, start the engine."

Elena hopped in the driver's seat and turned the key. The cold engine sputtered, then kicked over.

"Everyone stand back," Ramon ordered. He hit the winch switch and the cable began reeling in. Everyone helped guide the thin steel strand and grabbed Sommers, as he topped the well's edge. "That's good, good. We have him."

Elena killed the engine, locking the winch. Sommers hopped down.

"Where did you go?" Ramon inquired. "You disappeared. We couldn't see you."

Sommers reached into his pocket. "There's a room, hidden. It's an arsenal down inside the well-- crates of guns, and more bags... like a storage vault, but it's damaged, flooded." He produced the coins. "And there's these. Maybe this is what it's all about."

Elena touched the coins in Sommers hands. "Dios mio, I forgot. I found a coin in the stream, but dropped it when Robbie--"

"Whoa," Robbie interrupted. "How many bags? Are there a lot more?"

Sommers passed the coins around. They looked brand new and everyone held them.

A raindrop hit one, as Ramon examined it more closely. "Excellent condition. Solid gold and old. Antiques. Tell me of the munitions."

"The water's ruined most of them. The room was packed tightly."

Robbie took another hit from the bag and interjected. "So how much of this is down there? I think we're talking new careers here."

"The heroin's protected in plastic bags. I'd guess a dozen or so of them. I don't know-- several pounds I guess."

"Pounds? Are you kidding me?!"

"So someone was using guns and gold to pay for the dope," Celia speculated.

"Very big business," Ramon confirmed. "But ruthless. They were probably trading."

"And it went bad," Sommers reminded. "A dozen bodies worth."

Robbie grabbed one of the coins, scooped more powder with it. "I think everyone is missing the point here. First come, first serve.

The rebels and soldiers are dead. We're not and we have the winning ticket."

"That's stealing," Celia blurted. "We don't know what's down there, and if we take anything, then we're just as bad as them."

"Your thought processes-- take off your lawyer beanie for once, Celia. Look at the other side of the coin. No pun intended. We're doing some good here. We're helping the government-- cutting off criminals' source of income. It's beautiful."

"Oh please, so we can redirect it to your bookie? It's illegal contraband in a foreign country, in which we are not citizens. It doesn't belong to us, and somebody's going to miss it and come looking for it."

"It's a treasure in the end of the world Mexican jungle and belongs to whoever finds it! Equal shares for everybody."

Kevin was tired of the arguing. "We could give the gold to the authorities, tell them about the rest. Probably get a reward."

Robbie angrily shook his head. "A reward in Mexico?! What? Tacos?! Finding gold coins and heroin in the middle of nowhere isn't the kind of thing you report!"

"It's not your choice to decide for us, Robbie," Celia defended.

"She's right," Elena voiced. "Let's leave, Ramon. It's not ours."

"None of you get it!" Robbie screeched. "If these schmucks died over this, those coins are valuable, and so is the heroin. We're here. They aren't."

A flock of birds scattered from the trees and startled them. Upon returning his gaze to the group, Ramon caught Sommers' eyes. "We could make one trip-- remove what could be carried."

The rest looked incredulously at Ramon, especially Celia. "You're kidding, right?! What about the helicopter? It's coming for us-- Kevin's injured. Sick. Remember?"

"Yeah, I am injured. There's also a dozen dead bodies and I don't want to be number thirteen. I say let's head for the chopper."

"Excellent plan," Celia concurred. "There's no point in having money if you're dead."

"Listen, don't take this wrong, Ramon, but you don't seem to care about anything. The boar blood was one thing, but this... let's go," Kevin surmised.

"I don't like it either," Elena stated. "Let's leave. Please."

Sommers walked back to the well, holding one of the coins. He looked at the death filled campsite, then touched the rim of the stone well.

"What is not to like?! Gold is gold. You'll be thanking me by the pool tomorrow," Robbie persuaded. "Look... see that? Sommers is even thinking about it. He gets the picture."

"Don't put me on your team, Robbie."

"Just look at the pros and cons. All of you, come on. Pros-- money. Easy cash and lots of it. Tax free."

"Cons," Celia rebutted. "Death. Dismemberment. Mexican jail for life. Yeah, that's living."

"Only if we're caught."

Sommers surprised them. He spoke, but didn't face them. "We do have the winch."

"No," pleaded Elena. "It's not worth it."

"Only a quick pass, little sister. If there is nothing or it is dangerous, we will certainly leave," Ramon confirmed.

Robbie was elated. "Yes, yes, yes."

"You know we're supposed to be out here riding bikes," Kevin warned.

"Observing nature," Celia stated.

Robbie went to Sommers. "This is about as natural as you can get, Lady."

Celia shook her head. "I don't believe this... Sommers."

"Celia... let's give it a go. Come on. This is an adventure your ex and Misty what's-her-name will never believe."

Celia looked into Sommers' eyes and wanted to trust him, to believe. Every ounce and intuition told her to leave, to jump on one of those bikes and pedal away, find someplace safe far away from there. But she didn't. She stayed, for whatever reasons, shooting Sommers an incredulous look that many opposing attorneys had seen.

"And if it looks bad, we're out of there," Sommers reassured. "I promise."

# *40*

## PASSAGES

On his second trip to the bottom of the well, Sommers was amazed at the basic structure and architecture the Mayan civilization had instigated. Looking closer, he realized everything had been hewn and cut by hand. It was wickedly magnificent.

Digging the hole itself had to have taken weeks, picking away at different soils and through bedrock in order to find life giving water. If the wet substance hadn't been discovered, they probably would have perished, unable to solely rely on the moods of streams and weather.

Sommers was lowered by the winch cable, but this time there would be no surprises. He knew which stones and rocks could hold his weight, and that the hundreds of mortared building blocks would probably be standing another thousand years. He was inspired that he got to witness this forbidden treasure that was definitely not in the brochures.

Landing, he set himself and shined the light on the cavernous, crate filled storage room. The vault. This entity also perplexed him. For some group to conjure this up and create access, again by hand, intrigued him to no end. The rebel causes must be great, he mused. Larger than life to come here and dig this out. Legal or not, moral or not, they had to be given some credit.

An excited Ramon dropped into the well next to him. "You were not kidding, Sommers. I've never seen or heard about anything like this."

"They were intent on hiding whatever they had. I'll give them that. The only thing is I don't think they counted on a rising water table."

"Yes, it could be seasonal though. Perhaps they were off schedule. Maybe they were here to empty the space and got caught by the weather. It happens."

"Perhaps. Come on."

With flashlights in hand, they began moving through the water to the chamber's opening. The water level rose and fell, and the farther they went, the harder it was to keep balanced in the current.

"The coins were here," Sommers pointed, perching himself on an outcropping.

Ramon flashed his light inward. "It would make sense there could be more with the water, pushing everything here. This must have been a bad surprise... discovering their facility underwater."

"Well, you put things in a well--"

Inside, they crawled over and shoved around the crates they could. They soon realized it was very cramped and they were much too large to be working in the space.

"I couldn't get in much past here," Sommers admitted. Who knows what's behind those boxes?"

Robbie's echoing voice was heard. "Hey guys... find anything yet?"

"NO!" Sommers yelled back. "Man, he doesn't quit. We're too big to really get back there."

Ramon touched the slimy stones and wet crates, seeming to listen to them for clues. He stared into the chamber, the water and darkness lapping at his chest. "She does not want to give up her secrets. The coins are here, my friend. I hear them calling. Let us put to use what we have."

Sommers didn't quite understand what he meant, but in the next half-hour Ramon secured a system using the Jeep. He made the winch completely operable for retrieving lodged materials and hopefully, pulling out the crates.

They fed the cable into the chamber. Between he and Sommers inside the well, and the others on top, they began dislodging the boxes and making headway inside. However, even with the technology assisting, it wasn't easy.

They used a steel hook and clasped the cable in an awkward, but effective slipknot. When the winch took up the slack, the crates and boxes were dragged out of the way.

This worked until Ramon overloaded the engine and the winch buckled. Sommers realized he was now intent of finding whatever was down there at any cost. Greed was setting in. Ramon would never quit.

"Pull," Ramon ordered, stretching his body between the well and chamber.

"It's too much weight," Sommers countered.

On top, the winch seized, its Detroit mechanism only able to withstand so much. Smoke from overheated gears rose from its casing. "Shut it down, shut it down," yelled Kevin. "It's too heavy."

The scary part on top was when the Jeep lurched like an angry rodeo bull, escaping its pen. Everyone jumped back and could only watch the smoldering vehicle.

"Maybe we found all the gold and it's time to leave," a rattled Elena stated.

"No," Robbie hissed. "We got this far. Look, we just need to bust through-- get deeper inside. They can do it."

Wiping her brow and still reluctant, Celia voiced her case. "Why don't we come back for it with manpower and the right equipment? It's dangerous."

"And what if we're only one crate away? I don't want to come back to this godforsaken hole! Do you?"

"You're just stoned. I don't really want to be here in the first place, Robbie. It's not your decision, so give it a rest. They tried-- we tried, you know."

"Spare me, Counselor. Who made you God?"

Kevin broke them up. "Stop it. Just stop it!"

Celia wiped her brow again and went to the top of the well, yelling down. "Any more brilliant ideas? Or are we through? We're melting up here."

By her tone, Sommers knew Celia was frustrated. Ramon emerged from the chamber, moving debris. "Use the Jeep. Pull with the Jeep," he yelled.

"I don't believe this," Celia grumbled.

Elena dutifully went to the driver's seat and started the engine. Putting it in gear, she slowly pulled the cable taut.

"Floor it, Elena," Robbie eagerly exclaimed. "Give it all she has."

Elena ignored him, but the Jeep started moving.

Sommers and Ramon watched the progress, then suddenly it stopped, the cable slacking, becoming limp. "Keep it going," Ramon ordered. "What is she doing?!"

The Jeep sputtered and died. Elena tried restarting, pumping and turning the key furiously, until she looked at the gas gauge. "No-- the tank, it is empty."

With the dust settling, Sommers and Ramon assessed the situation. Without the Jeep or winch, they lacked the equipment to proceed. Coughing, Sommers approached the chamber's opening. Off to one side appeared a small passage between the crates, but he wasn't sure. "Now what?" Sommers coughed. "It's still too narrow."

Ramon shimmied back as far as he could, inspecting debris. "Let us work awhile longer-- move the smaller boxes. I have an idea."

# *41*

# THE ONE

Clouds were building in the east, the direction of the ocean. Sommers knew that meant there was probably a low pressure system in the Caribbean, pushing its way north, ready to deposit moisture in its wake. Just what they needed, more rain.

At the moment, they could handle the water, but almost the minute they exited the well, rain had begun to fall accompanied by a light wind. It wasn't uncomfortable, but now they had to work in mud, harder conditions and half of them didn't want to be there anyway. The division of wills was widening.

Ramon tinkered with the Jeep, checking the winch, cable and brace positioned over the well. Although he hadn't explained his plan to anyone, Sommers knew he had an agenda. You could see it in his eyes, as he tightened, adjusted and worked on the crude contraption. This was akin to finding the Genie-in-the-bottle for Ramon and Sommers felt he would do anything to find all of whatever there was.

Walking from the Jeep, Ramon spoke. "The Jeep and cable dislodged some of the debris. Sommers and I can return to the bottom and lift the large crate, then one of us should be able to go in further."

*One of us...* Sommers thought.

"See I knew we would work it out," Robbie cheerfully stated. "We're a team."

"Wait a minute," the judging voice of Kevin blurted. "What do you mean, 'one of us?' I don't need money that badly. This is getting out of hand."

"I'll go," Robbie volunteered. "Let me in there."

"You are too large," Ramon stated.

"There has to be a way-- what about you guys? If one of you lifts the crate-- ?"

"It's too tight," Sommers argued. "You don't know what it's like down there, Robbie."

"Elena, then..."

"Too tall."

"Yeah, okay. No argument there. Then what about Celia?" Robbie asked, arousing their attention. "I bet she could fit. Except maybe for her butt."

"You're such a jerk," Celia retorted, as all of their eyes drifted to her. Even though he was a jerk, he was also right. "Are you out of your mind? You said we'd leave, Sommers. Go meet the helicopter. There's no way I'm going down in that wet hole."

"It figures. You get three feet away from the Holy Grail and bail. No wonder he's divorcing you."

That was the last straw. His words hit Celia like a thunderbolt and she jumped Robbie with no mercy, screaming and clawing at him. "Take it back! Take it back!"

Sommers ran to pull her off Robbie, who stood, feigning helplessness in her attack. "All right, that's enough, Celia. You don't have to do anything you don't want to. Forget about it. Let's take the coins we have and leave for the helicopter. It was a long shot anyway."

She calmed down, regrouped, but then something fired inside her.

"Finally, some sense," Kevin said.

"No-- !" Celia shouted, catching her breath, blood raging behind her eyes. "I can do it. I mean I'll try."

Her comment surprised Sommers. It was the last thing he expected, the willful attorney taking Robbie's bait. "Celia-- " he began.

"I want to, Sommers. You went down. You're okay. I see now."

"That's different."

"Why, because I'm a girl... incompetent? Right. You and Jerk of the Century have talked me into it. Now show me what to do before I change my mind."

Kevin shook his head and looked at Elena. Ramon and Robbie slowly grinned at the prospect, warming to the idea.

"Very well then," Ramon exclaimed, looking past her, toward the well. "Come Celia, time is of the essence."

Celia marched, leading all of them to well's rim and frame, grabbing the winch cable.

"I'll go down, then you follow," Sommers coached, almost feeling guilty at the fact she was going.

"Whatever," came Celia's stoic reply.

Sommers dropped down the cable, alighting and kicking off at key points. He kept an eye on the water and clearances. At the bottom, he scanned the chamber's entrance and his muscles tightened. *Maybe it's too much for her. What are you getting her into, Sommers...?* His reverberating gray matter mused.

"Okay, here I come," the tentative Celia voiced, throwing over a leg and gripping the cable.

Ramon guided her torso. "Hold tight and the cable will take you," he instructed.

"That's what I'm afraid of."

Sommers shined his light toward the surface and Celia descended rhythmically without incident. Grabbing her body, he placed her on some rocks above the swirling water. "Not clausto, are you?" he joked.

"No. It's colder than I thought. Feels nice."

"It's the water. Can you believe this place?"

"Greed. Whomever they are, they're running a lot of money through here."

Ramon alighted next to them. "Hola. Are you ready, Celia?"

"Hey, why not? I've come this far."

Ramon hopped into the water, then directed Celia to the opening.

"It's only about chest deep," Sommers assured, standing in the current.

The water covered Celia to her neck. "I figured there would be some kind of catch." Celia cautiously followed, holding onto outcroppings and Sommers. Pointing with the flashlight, Ramon illuminated the tight passage.

Celia's trepidation masked her wonderment. She knew, treasure or not, gold coins or not, this was a unique find and a once in a lifetime experience regarding the well and covert labor it took to create.

Kevin's voice angled down. "Be careful, Celia."

"You don't have to worry about that," she chirped back.

"Hey, I'll video it as you come out," Kevin said.

"Get it, Celia. Get it all," Robbie's booming voice echoed.

Celia looked into the imposing chamber, chills running up and down her spine. "You know, it's bigger than I thought. Must have taken forever to build."

"It's not perfect," Sommers advised. "See the water lines. The storms caught them. I bet a lot of munitions are ruined. Probably upset whomever was buying them big time."

"Wet guns," Celia kidded.

Ramon's light reflected off his face. "Celia, whatever is left of the debris is jagged. Do not trust any part. There may be room, maybe not. You'll have to gauge that once you are inside."

"Look Celia," Sommers warned. "Just go as far as you can. If anything doesn't feel right, get out. We'll be here."

"When have I heard that?" Celia joked, as Ramon handed her a flashlight, and she positioned herself near the crates at the opening. "Okay. Guess I asked for it. Hey, Kevin... get my good side," she shouted.

Topside, Kevin began filming and zoomed in best he could on the bottom. Ramon and Sommers set themselves across from each other. Using a fulcrum and pieces of scrap lumber, they lifted one of the larger crates.

"Go Celia. Now," Sommers grunted, seeing the passage open wide enough for her to get through.

Celia squirmed underneath and disappeared, wiggling her way into uncharted territory. She strained and maneuvered, bravely inching and contorting her body through the mud and muck, until she reached a bigger crack that allowed her to almost stand. Catching her breath, she deciphered from their markings the crates were military in origin. Probably stolen, she thought.

Sommers' muffled voice broke the tension. "Celia...? Anything?"

"No. It's okay, though. I'm okay."

Rested, she pulled herself over some splintering wood, advancing upward to another crate. They were packed in a way that allowed some movement, if one knew what they were doing. Celia didn't.

The next crate up gave way and collapsed. In the half darkness, Celia tumbled headfirst onto some guns in the water.

"Celia," Sommers shouted. "Are you all right? What's going on?"

Celia sat up, dazed... anxious. She got the light adjusted and angrily shoved the guns and wood away. Getting her bearings, she saw her arm bleeding and yelled back. "I cut myself... Give me a second."

Wiping her arm with her sleeve, she sat up and shined her light around the eerie chamber. Water dripped and the whole place smelled stale. The accidental fall was a wake-up call and reminded her she didn't want to be there. Robbie or not, ego aside, this wasn't a good idea. *Why had she agreed?*

Her adrenaline burned and a pang of fear shot through her system. Maybe she wouldn't get out of this in one piece.

She closed her eyes, inhaling some deep breaths and thinking of happier times and places. She clenched her thigh, remembering reading somewhere, that induced pain takes your mind out of panic mode.

Panic mode... not there yet, but so close. She was scared. *Was her ex correct? Her ego too large?*

Her light flickered and she hit it on a crate. The last thing she wanted, at any cost, was to be in the dark. Flashing it on the rocky wall, she saw what looked like a leather jacket and a cap... a Detroit Tigers baseball cap in almost perfect condition. "Hey," she grinned. "I found something."

Carefully bending over, she scooped up the cap. As she tugged on the jacket, it fell backward and revealed the decomposing remains of a man.

In terror so pure, her vocal cords became nuclear and she screamed for all she was worth, as the eroding corpse fell into a heap a few inches away from her.

"Celia--?" wrenched Sommers' voice.

Almost hyperventilating and unable to deal with the situation, she closed her eyes, hoping it would all disappear... "I found... I found-- there's a body back here! Oh no. Sommers, I can't do this--"

Sommers heard her muffled plea and glared at Ramon. "She's in trouble."

"Give her a moment."

Sommers didn't appreciate Ramon's response. It wasn't in the deal for someone to get hurt. "Celia, can you come out? Can you make it out?"

He listened again. Even in the distorted, watery chamber, he could tell in Celia's voice she was starting to panic.

"He's dead. Oh, it really smells in here. Sommers-- "

"Just take it easy, Celia. You can do it. Retrace your steps in the chamber."

"But I fell."

"Go back the way you came."

Fearfully opening her eyes, Celia listened to Sommers and turned around. "Calm down. Calm down," she chanted to herself. She flashed her light upward, glancing off the crates. Taking a yoga-like cleansing breath in, she exhaled loudly. Frustrated, but determined, she began clawing her way back through the pile of guns and munitions.

Edging closer to her escape, her light reflected off the water, beaming on a partially submerged, crushed metal box. Part of its bottom was cracked, allowing a flow of water to rush through. She hesitated, rubbing her eyes in disbelief... gold coins shimmered everywhere. "Oh my-- wait a minute."

"Come on, Celia. Just keep coming out."

Celia ignored Sommers, instead finding a long piece of wood. Using the stake, she pushed the human remains away and crawled over them to the coins. "I found some-- I found some coins." She picked up a few of the shiny, loose coins and shoved them into her pocket. The supply seemed endless, as she deposited as many as she could. The box was wedged under a crate and wouldn't budge. She began beating on it with the flashlight to no avail. "Come on, you piece of-- "

"Celia, what's that noise?" blurted Sommers muffled voice.

"Just a second." Cramped and sitting with her back to some crates, she began kicking at the box. Her heel glanced off a corner and bent the top back. With that sliver of opening, she was able to bend it further.

Inside were three wooden cases; one was broken open. She saw the bottom boxes were submerged in water, as she scooped out the remaining coins and stuffed them into her pockets. One of the boxes, although submerged, was in perfect condition. The other was broken and allowed some of its coins to be swept away by the water. It was also stuck under the crushed part of the metal box.

Wiggling out the free one, she opened it. The box was full of coins, carefully stacked in golden rows. She ran her fingers over the tops, smiling at their uniform ridges. "I think I love Mexico."

# 42

## GAME CHANGER

Robbie paced anxiously and he wasn't happy about being left out of the loop. The action was inside the well.

The weather wasn't cooperating either, as a light rain fell, forcing both he and Kevin to cover up with their windbreakers.

"Are they waiting on Christmas?" Robbie impatiently probed. "Why is it so quiet down there? Can you hear them Kevin?"

"They'll let us know when they have something. Just chill."

Robbie glared at Kevin, lit a cigarette and tossed the match into the well.

Sommers kept calling for Celia but she did not answer. "Not good. I think one of us should try and get in back there," he told Ramon.

"We will need one of the others-- "

As Ramon was about to yell up to Robbie and Kevin, two crates were pushed out from above and fell in front of them. Celia emerged feet first.

Sommers and Ramon helped her down. She was soaked and muddy, and her arm was bleeding. Sommers saw she had confidence in her eyes and was grinning ear to ear. They helped her down and she held on tightly to the heavy box of coins, like a Christmas present. "I found them… I found them. Look at this!"

She presented the box, a killer trophy, and jingled her pockets. The perfectly aligned coins shined brilliantly, reflecting off their faces.

"Look at that!" an excited Sommers exclaimed.

"It is a fortune." Ramon beamed, handling some of them. "You did very well, Celia."

Sommers shouted upward. "She got them. Celia found the gold!"

Robbie was ecstatic. "I knew it! Bring it up. Way to go, Celia. We're rich, rich, rich!"

"Let me see your arm," Sommers offered.

"It's fine-- I'm fine. It was great. I got all I could... I don't even care about the other box."

The statement bounced into Sommers' and Ramon's skulls simultaneously. *There's more?* Their minds questioned silently, tending to her.

"What did you say?" Ramon asked. "Other box?"

"She has enough... we have enough."

"Could you not secure it?"

"Listen, the other one is stuck-- inside a metal box. It's a mess... being crushed by a crate. I couldn't have carried them all anyway."

Ramon stared into the chamber's blackness. "Inside there... the crates-- what's it like?"

"A nightmare. It's unstable, cramped... smelly, especially with that body. But there's more room than we first thought. Some of those crates are falling apart. You were right about not trusting them. A couple of them caved on me. And you nailed it, Sommers. The whole place is flooded."

She reached into her pocket and retrieved the Detroit Tigers baseball cap. "The dead guy must have been a Tiger's fan."

"Oh people..." blared Robbie's voice. "What're you doing down there? Come on. Let's see the booty."

All three of them gazed up into the lightly falling rain. The higher sides of the well were now wet with trickling water and they noticed Robbie, Kevin and Elena had covered up.

"Just hold on, Robbie," Sommers replied. "There's another box."

"Don't we have enough?" Kevin asked stoically. "We're wasting time. It's raining again."

"Ahhh, what is with you guys?!" Robbie grunted, hitting his hands on the rim. "Celia's done the drill. Send her back inside. Get it all!"

"I'm gonna take him out," Sommers threatened, then looked upward. "Shut up, Robbie!"

"Tell me you all have enough money! 'Gee, Robbie, we don't need any more. Thank you.' The bonus round is ten feet away and you don't care."

"More like twenty-five," Celia quietly voiced, the wind out of her sails. "Sommers-- you said we'd go."

"Come down here and you get stuck, Robbie," Sommers ordered.

"You know, Sommers, I will. We've all just about had it with you and your holier-than-thou attitude."

"We have more than enough. I'm not going back," Celia admitted.

"It's settled then," Sommers resolved. "Good."

Ramon handled the cable, setting it. "Robbie, haul up Celia. I will go in for the rest."

Sommers was surprised. "Ramon-- "

"All right," exclaimed Robbie, dancing again. "All right, Ramon. That's a man taking charge."

Ramon removed his gun belt and took off his shirt. A frightened Elena called down. "No... you promised me! You promised, Ramon."

"Little sister, this is as much for you as it is for me." Ramon handed his shirt to Sommers, smiling upward and waving.

"Look Ramon, she brought out a fortune," Sommers whispered. "You said so yourself. We don't need this. We have enough. Forget it. With the rain and everything, the flooding-- "

"I can go in on top of the crates. She made a path." Producing a knife with attachments, something akin to a Swiss Army knife, Ramon checked a blade and screwdriver/prying device. "It will be worth it, my friend."

"It's not worth it, Ramon," Celia confirmed. "Let's go."

"I will be in and out!"

Sommers and Celia knew they couldn't dissuade him. Ramon stepped up on one of the crates and Sommers handed him a flashlight.

"It's close," Celia reluctantly began. "Straight back, on top, then down. It's kind of dicey about halfway, but keep going. Get past the dead guy and... here." Celia gave him the Tigers cap. "For luck."

"All right, but I'm really a Padres fan."

She plopped the cap on his head and they all smiled at each other. He spun the cap around backward and started climbing up the crates, then disappeared inside. Sommers helped Celia onto the cable. "You did good. That husband of yours really missed out."

"Ex husband. Thanks, Sommers."

Feeling a tug from above, he helped Celia get hoisted from the depths.

# *43*

## GREED

Ramon was much more agile and fearless than Celia. Seeing her original swath, the directions she had given were simple. He quickly found himself in the back of the solitary, lifeless chamber.

Nothing, the dank atmosphere, the rotting wood of the perilous crates, or the smell of death, bothered him. He was as focused as he had ever been in his life. He was on a mission to financial freedom, literally snatching the gold ring from fate, and he wasn't willing to allow anything to stop him.

Crawling along the piled crates, he held the light in his hand and the screwdriver in his mouth. At the rear high point, he found where Celia had fallen and made his controlled descent the few feet to the ground. Soaked munitions sat at the water line.

Carefully stepping on the rotting guns and bracing himself against anything that would hold his weight, he flashed the light until he spied the leather jacket and rotting human remains. Taking a deep breath, he proceeded cautiously, the hair on the back of his neck bristling.

Celia had been correct about the smell and terrible state of the chamber's condition. Ramon wanted out of there, probably as badly as she had, but he was close now, and he knew it. It was eerie in the moist cavern and even though he knew he was alone, he felt a presence. Perhaps it was the ghosts of soldiers and militia he was now trespassing upon. The anonymous ones who hollowed out the well, built the chamber, hid their loot, and then died in vain, never to be heard from again. Maybe they were angry at him or laughing at his folly.

Ramon had left religion behind long ago. He had actually been an altar boy, a favorite student of the priests, but somewhere, as adulthood approached with its worldly temptations, he "outgrew" the incense and wine. Still, maneuvering in that cramped space with death all around, a Bible verse from First Timothy, consumed his mind: *"But those who desire to be rich fall into temptation, into a snare, into many senseless and harmful desires that plunge people into ruin and destruction."* The word 'snare' rolled around his brain confusing him. It didn't feel like a biblical word here, in this makeshift tomb, but no matter, it flew from his head, as quickly as it had penetrated. *But was he being greedy?* He knew God had no place for greed. *No, surely not.* His life had been devoted to taking care of Elena and that's what this was about… security for Elena, not greed.

*Greed,* he kept hearing from within, fighting the sweat and cramped quarters. *Just a little further,* he coerced his mind and body to focus on the job at hand. *It has to be here.*

Passing over the dead man's remains, he saw the metal box, its damaged top calling to him. His demeanor changed to joy. Celia was right. It was real. The coins were real for the taking and he was there. "And so we meet," he asserted, positioning himself. Knowing the task at hand, he shoved his body weight into the crate, once, twice… and toppled it off the box.

Sommers heard the rumbling; the odd sound from within. He was genuinely concerned about Ramon. Somewhere in his mind, he knew they should have left long ago. Drinking beer at the pool and deciding on that evening's "prix fare" menu items at the resort's dining room should have been their biggest concern, not if a house of cards, disguised as munitions, was going to crush them.

"Ramon. Are you all right?" There was no reply, but Sommers figured Ramon was working. He had to give him that; Ramon was determined.

On the surface, the others huddled around Celia and the coins. The outdoor light only made them shine brighter and everyone ran their hands through the polished gold. It was a treasure. The kind you dream about and it was theirs. Robbie was thrilled, mesmerized by the color and sounds of the perfect coins clanking together. The freedoms the coins would bring him

He went to the well and tugged hard on the cable, causing a rise out of Sommers. "Will you quit messing around?" Sommers barked from below, agitated.

"You're like an old woman," Robbie retorted. "You need to see these beauties in the light."

"Just be ready up there. We'll be coming up soon."

"Aye, aye, captain. That's what I wanted to here," a giddy Robbie chirped.

Sommers watched him disappear from the rim and he was glad. He saw Robbie as a festering annoyance. The farther away he was from him, the better, and he didn't like Elena being anywhere near him. "Ramon," Sommers yelled into the blackness. "Can you hear me? What's going on in there?"

Ramon deciphered Sommers' anxiousness and kept working. With the crate out of the way, he could retrieve the broken box easier. He did notice the water was higher than when he first arrived but it wasn't a hindrance. He kept working, inch by inch, using the screwdriver and finding any leverage he could.

Setting himself over the main box, he pried the top and it popped open. A wave of jubilation engulfed him, as another bounty of coins glistened in the light. He knew he'd struck the mother lode and began harvesting the fresh crop of coins.

Seeing more coins underneath, he decided to shift the damaged box in order to retrieve the last few, which were in just inches of water. Ramon repositioned himself and figured the hard work had been done… the disconcerting trek and moving of crates complete.

Placing both hands under the box, he lifted hard and the box emerged easily, almost gracefully, except there was something else… a simple attachment.

A mono-filament wire was fastened to the bottom of the box and as Ramon excitedly pulled, it went taut… the tripwire had been tripped. *The snare.*

To add insult to injury, the perpetrators of the malicious device had devised a minor delay in order to let whomever was in that vulnerable, trapped, key position, know Hell was about to be unleashed into their face in an immediate, final moment of truth.

Ramon froze. His life flashed and memories of Elena flooded his faculties. He remembered Elena when she was a little girl and he helped with her bicycle training wheels. With such promise, she happily rode off down the street away from her proud big brother. *Blink of an eye,* his mind reminded. *That's all anything is anyway…*

The explosion that followed was cataclysmic, imploding the chamber and sending a strong enough ripple through the surface, to knock everyone off their feet. Trash and rubble catapulted from the bowels of the well.

Ramon was killed instantly, obliterated in a TNT, plastique clash that would rival any Marine assault campaign.

Sommers was in the next worst position. He had no warning and saw none of it coming, but the concussion caused a complete breakdown of the well's structure. Whatever architectural integrity had been altered by the chamber's construction now had to pay a price. The water table took over along with gravity, rising incessantly and without mercy.

The bottom of the well flooded with a torrent of water that had been circumvented by the chamber. It immediately wanted to reclaim its original intention and began filling with rubble, debris and flak from the crates.

Sommers was knocked eight feet back into its stony sides and cold, brutal water, quickly covered his head, as the well filled. His mind was hazy, unprepared and wanted to drift, as he was only semi-conscious.

He grappled for anything to hang onto, but found only darkness, swirling and hissing. As the water engulfed his entire being, he tried advancing, but his legs and arms kept tangling in some unseen force, keeping him pinned in watery space. He was in trouble, dire straits, but his body wasn't receiving or acting upon the SOS message his brain was sending.

There was some kind of thickening in his head, blocking all transmission for survival. The neurotransmitters and synapses had taken a coffee break and if they didn't kick in, this would become a permanent vacation. *But the brochures said…*

A piece of timber rammed into his chest, knocking out all his air. The bubbles scrambled for the surface and he opened his eyes. Pain. If he opened his mouth, he knew it would be all over and a section of his brain said it would be all right to do that. *Just let go,* it whispered. *You had a chance at Big Bear on your bike and here's another one. Your lungs are empty, you're beaten and now you can die a hero! What do you want?!*

The words sickened him. Another part of his cerebrum forced him off the bike at Big Bear, to lay it down and bail off, and that had gotten him to this point. *Survival, Baby.*

He had come this far and even in the churning hell of wet blackness that yearned to take his soul, he was alive. But for how much longer?

Sommers reached for the stone mortar above his head and tried to find something, anything, which would help bring his face above water. There was a small, mossy outcropping barely in reach that his hand kept slipping from, until the time it held.

Gripping, he propelled his torso above the water and gasped for air, reclaiming his life. He coughed violently, his lungs burning from the acidic smoke and remains, but he was still alive.

Searching for the steel cable, he cried out and expected to see his friends working, doing everything they could up at the rim to get him out. It was time to vacate, abandon... abort... but in the misting rain, he saw nothing and no one. *Were they killed? Did the explosion's fingers reach that far, or were they at the Jeep, readying the winch for this emergency and his escape?*

He clung to the cable, its grooved, steel twists allowing his fingers to clench and keep his head high above the water. Part of the well wall collapsed, sending in more water and he knew they would have to begin to winch him topside soon. *They will, they will. Just turn it on, kids.*

More debris crashed around him, tossing and turning Sommers like clothes in a washing machine. His biceps burned, as they contracted fully to hold himself on the slippery line. Water covered his head, its wet fingers pulling him back down. Half his body was limp, the fight long gone. *Bodies sink in water and that's all you are... just a helpless body,* his mind reminded.

"Hey!" he shouted, getting each precious word out. "Help me down here! Hey-- somebody!"

Sommers saw the sky in that pinhole of an opening, but still no faces. He attempted climbing, tried forcing his legs to work. They

146

found the sides and he pushed, which allowed his mid-section to rise above the water. It was something positive, as his mind spun and he held on.

He gained another six inches, but the cable buckled, vibrating in his hands. A moment of hope, then confusion, as he looked up just in time to watch the rest of the metallic, snake-like lifeline, cascading down from the surface right for him. It struck him hard and he tumbled into the wet murkiness. The length of cable impacted, sending him completely under the water.

Sommers was back where he started, without the life saving line, this time bleeding from his temple. The blood trickled into his eyes and everything became distorted, blurry, like looking through the bottom of a glass.

He scrambled to stay afloat, dodging munitions and debris, but was pinned again, the water still rising. The well was winning and he knew it.

On the surface, the ground vibrated again, its foundation undermined by poor planning and an incessantly violent, rising water table. Water spewed from the well, the liquid running over the sides.

Then, in one angry movement, wood, guns and a full cache of munitions erupted like a foul, backed up sewer. Barely conscious, Sommers rode the rising, fluid torrent to the surface.

The well expelled him, spitting him out like a seed pit. He flipped over the rim and lay writhing, vomiting water and blood on dry land. He wheezed, sucking in all the air the world had, and felt the grass on his cheeks.

His fists clenched the soil and the little voice that told him to die, to give up, had been silenced.

# 44

## SPARED

After several minutes of lying in the mud, listening to his pounding heart, Sommers regained his senses and pushed himself up to all fours. He scanned the blurry camp, looking for the others. There was supposed to be a group, his group on the coolest vacation. *This couldn't have been a dream...* he wondered. Too much had happened.

Pushing up to his knees, he saw two shapes and focused. It was Celia and Kevin, their backs to each other, bound and gagged tightly. Now he thought he was hallucinating. Something was terribly wrong and the situation seemed to be escalating down into some void.

He rose to his feet and scrambled to them. His battered hands struggled to remove their gags. "What--?" he coughed out his first word.

"Robbie," Celia interrupted. "He did this... pulled a gun. He tied us up, then kidnapped Elena and took the coins."

Together, they helped untie Kevin, who was obviously in pain and not looking well. "I knew we shouldn't have done this," he reminded. "What was everyone thinking?!"

"Where's Ramon?" Celia asked.

"Yeah, what happened down there? The whole place shook."

Sommers had to face them. "There was an explosion... in the back. The whole chamber and well flooded. Ramon... Ramon didn't make it out."

"Oh no!" Celia cried.

"Ramon's dead?!" Kevin anxiously asked. "He can't be. Guys like him don't die in places like this. Are you sure?!"

"Look at me, Kevin. I barely got out. The whole place came down on him. The cable fell in on me-- "

"That means we're out here alone," Celia exclaimed.

"Just take it easy. What happened with Robbie? What do you mean he kidnapped Elena?"

"Our glorious Robbie pulled a gun on us after the explosion. He forced us to stand next to the Jeep while he unhooked the cable and tossed it in on you."

"He was so cavalier. He figured if you weren't dead, you would be."

Sommers angrily spit some blood, trying to process what was being said.

Kevin looked toward the well. "He put the gun to our heads and took our packs. Said a bunch of stuff about you and Elena. I don't know what's happening. This is all too weird. I was just powerless. I'm sorry."

"Forget about it. We'll figure something out, but Celia's right. Without Ramon, we're on our own. First thing, we have to get back to camp. Come on."

Sommers and Celia helped up Kevin and the three started down the hill.

# 45

## BROKEN TRAIL

The jungle canopy acted like a natural tent, causing the trapped humidity to become almost intolerable, suffocating. As Robbie rode, this "greenhouse effect" was inciting him to sweat profusely and chafe. He hated it. Robbie had a hard enough time riding a bike when he didn't have to worry about holding a gun on someone or the constant discomfort and prodding from a hard, narrow bicycle seat.

Elena was proficient and agile, and he had a difficult time following her on the trail.

"Wait for me," he barked, making her slow down.

"Why are you doing this? You know when Ramon gets you-- "

"Yeah, yeah, he'll kill me."

"I want to go back. There's something wrong. They could be hurt."

"I don't want to hurt anyone. Look, cooperate and play along, and I'll send back help. Do you know what we can do with these coins?"

"That's not the point. I didn't see them come out. That's my big brother down there."

"Yeah and he's the most competent of the group. Don't you see what we have here?"

"You shouldn't have left them. People don't do that to other people. I don't care about the coins, Robbie, and I don't care about you."

Robbie sneered and adjusted his seat. "You will. Now, let's keep moving."

Elena cursed at him in Spanish and continued down the narrow trail. She thought about making a break for it. She could certainly out run him, but not the bullets. It would take just one shot and with the way things were going...

When they arrived at the helicopter, the pilot would help her, and they would get back to Ramon somehow. *Two against one,* she thought.

# 46

## SALVATION

Going down the hill from the rebel camp was more difficult, especially since Sommers was battered and Kevin was feeling worse. The three of them pulled together and did the best they could, but they stumbled and tripped at almost every turn. The weather wasn't cooperating either and the hill was now muddy, a natural stickiness that impeded movement and wreaked havoc.

At the bottom of the hill, they crossed the trail, dropped down an embankment and followed the shallow stream until they found their camp. Sommers would never forget what he saw.

Their bikes had been wrecked, broken and thrown into a pile. A symbolic, metal pyre of spinning wheels, demolished frames and unusable technology. The rest of the camp was in shambles, with equipment, tents and gear strewn everywhere. Most of it was smashed and broken as well.

"No..." Celia gasped, realizing the enormity of the situation. "This is unbelievable."

"He left us to die," Kevin sighed, plopping down on the sand.

Sommers went to the pile of bikes, touching them, almost in reverence. "He flattened all the tires. The frames are-- "

"What do we do now, great one?" Kevin asked facetiously.

Sommers grimaced at the rest of the mess. Without supplies, rations... "See if we can find the radio. Collect any usable supplies. Maybe we can salvage... something."

"I'll believe it when I see it," Kevin angrily mandated.

Celia began searching through the remains of gear and packs. Kevin joined her at a slower pace, as Sommers began dismantling the pile of bikes. It came apart in pieces, bike parts falling on the ground.

He knew none of this was good. This was a life changing situation that could go in half a dozen directions and most of them were bad. What Sommers didn't know was exactly where they were and ultimately what they would be up against. That combination troubled him as much as anything.

# 47

## WRONG GUIDE

The awkward grade was taking its toll on Robbie. He was wet with sweat and the seat now rubbed blisters. His body ached and he loathed the process of pedaling, gliding and avoiding obstacles. Elena maneuvered easily and he had a hard time keeping pace. Seeing her fit body in front, operating the machine optimally, was no consolation this time.

He rounded a corner and swerved to miss a low branch. However, his front tire caught a root at an angle, and flipped him over the handlebars.

"Aaaah," he yelped. "Stop... stop, Elena." Robbie was queasy and dehydrated. The liquor and heroin combo hadn't helped and he reluctantly rose to his knees. "Can you believe this? Where are we? How far to the chopper and off this mountain?"

Elena hopped off her bike. "It's not a mountain and I don't know."

"What do you mean, you don't know?! What're you talking about? You're our guide. What are we paying you for?"

"Ramon was your guide. I've never been here in my life. This is my first mountain bike trip this far up."

It wasn't what Robbie wanted to hear. The air evaporated from his lungs and he had a mini panic attack. His face fell and was genuinely afraid. "Don't lie to me, Elena. You have to know where we are." He pointed the gun at her, wanting to force information she didn't have out of her.

"Well, I don't. Wasn't that in your grand plan?" Elena scolded.

"No... Well, the meadow has to be around here somewhere. The helicopter has to land. Show me... why did you pick this trail if you don't know?"

He started for Elena in a rage, but stopped when he heard a rustling in the bushes. He heard more noise. Elena backed away and Robbie gripped the gun, removing the safety.

A bush shook a few yards away from him and he recklessly fired into it.

"Stop shooting, Robbie," Elena exclaimed, covering her ears. "Stop it."

"Come out of there, Pig. Come on… run you little squealer."

More sounds, as the jungle seemed to be coming alive. Robbie didn't know where to turn and began shooting frantically, aimlessly in all directions. Elena ducked at the deafening noise.

Then Robbie's gun was empty, but he kept clicking away, aiming and squeezing the trigger to no avail. "Come on, Pig. Come out of there!"

Machine gun fire strafed at his feet and he reflexively dropped the gun, panicked. He dropped to his knees whimpering, the bully without a stick or stone.

Four men appeared, armed with machine guns. Their leader, Enrique Salerno, confidently stepped forward, his perfect teeth smiling. He was just as curious at them being there, as Elena and Robbie were about him.

"I see fate has brought us tourists," he cockily told his men.

Robbie could barely speak, but got out the words, "I'm an American on vacation."

"Of course. That makes sense. However, our Mexican bullets won't mind that my friend."

"We are on a bicycle tour from the Beach Resort at Vera Cruz," Elena confirmed.

Enrique sensed fear in her eyes, but also saw strength. "I do not believe you are American." He grazed her skin. "No, I do not think so."

"No, I'm not. I… I am one of the guides. We are based in Vera Cruz. The others are nearby."

Enrique studied them, their circumstance. "Mmm, you know what is odd? It is very odd… you two out here alone. A bike tour… if they are close, then where are the rest and where is your other guide?"

# 48

## A CHANCE

The staccato sounds echoed through the jungle, sounding like faint, overhead cloudbursts. "Was that more gunfire?"Celia asked, hoping against hope. "That was more gunfire!"

She and Kevin stopped scouring the camp for gear and supplies, and moved to Sommers, who was frantically trying to salvage a bike, using cannibalized parts from the others. It was extremely frustrating, having all this hi-tech cycling gear and most of it not interchangeable.

The sounds in the distance startled all of them, pumping them with a rush of adrenaline.

"This isn't happening," a frightened Kevin said. "We're going to die out here."

"No, we're not," Sommers retorted.

"They're coming back. You had to know they'd come back for all their crap."

"I didn't know anything, Kevin. Look, right or wrong, whatever happened, we have to keep our heads now."

"Sommers is right," Celia agreed. "We don't know who or what is out there."

"They probably shot Robbie and Elena, and we're next."

"Shut up, Kevin," Sommers ordered. "We're in this together and to get out, we have to stick together. Work as a team."

"Oh no," Celia exclaimed, running to a strewn pile of gear. "No...!"

Celia bent down and retrieved the radio. It was in two large pieces, completely destroyed. She looked at them and started crying. She had mustered all her hope around the radio and now it was gone. "He really did this..." she muttered. "That idiot."

Sommers hurried over, trying to calm her. "Take it easy, Celia. It's not over... not by a long shot. I'm taking this bike and going for the chopper."

"You can't just leave us."

"I'm not leaving you, Kevin. That chopper is our only chance."

"And Robbie?"

"Maybe I can beat some sense into him. I don't have all the answers, all right? But I know if we find the chopper, we go home."

"Sommers..." Celia began.

"We don't have another choice, Celia."

"I was going to say, be careful."

"We don't even know where the thing's going to land. You can't just leave us out here... what're we supposed to do?"

Sommers saw Kevin was panicking. It wasn't the easiest decision, heading into the jungle... leaving them. Sommers also knew Kevin was right on that account.

"We know it's in a meadow," Sommers articulated. "And we know it has to be off this ridge. Robbie and Elena went that way."

"But you don't know that."

"Kevin, I'll find it. You two need to stay here and keep working on the bikes. Here's Ramon's other gun."

"What do I know about guns?" Celia asked.

"Just point and shoot." Sommers checked the clip. "Just push that button to take off the safety."

"I can show her," Kevin assured. "You better make it, Sommers."

"If I'm not back in a few hours it means I didn't."

"Then what?" Celia asked.

"Let's hope we don't have to find out."

Sommers grabbed a canteen and adjusted the bike's seat. He carried the bike to the ridge trail, hopped on and rode off into the jungle, not looking back.

# 49

## LIAR'S POKER

Enrique used a portable gas bottle and made coffee for his men. They sat huddled, as Robbie and Elena kneeled with their backs to each other, hands bound. Robbie was soaked in sweat and shaking. Elena was certainly uncomfortable, but held her own.

Losing patience, Enrique booted Robbie in the stomach, knocking them both over, then jammed his heel into Robbie's cheek. "None of this makes sense, Gringo. Look at it from my perspective and tell me why you are really here." He unholstered his pistol. "Why shouldn't I shoot you now?"

"Okay, okay… a chopper's coming for us."

Enrique's demeanor changed. "The bike tour's helicopter? Where?!" He pressed his heel harder, stretching Robbie's flesh.

"Ow… A clearing… I don't know, all right? Ask the sister."

Enrique left Robbie, helping Elena up. "Such a beautiful girl. Now what clearing does the American speak of?"

"I'm not sure."

Enrique smiled, swigged some coffee, then slapped Elena across the face. She gasped, falling down. "That's not the answer I was expecting."

"I don't know. My brother… Ramon, he's the one with the directions. We were headed down… there's a clearing, a landing place. But I don't know where exactly."

Enrique pierced her eyes with his. He only believed Robbie to a point, but Elena was different. He felt she was telling the truth. "All right then, pretty one. We shall embark on this journey with you. We will find the meadow and helicopter, and everything else Mexico has to offer together."

# *50*

## PUSHING PEDALS

The sun peeked through some high clouds in the north and a choppy head wind kept the moisture at bay. Sommers' whole body hurt, but he rode hard, deliberate, keeping his balance and trying to stay focused. Whatever was happening, he, or they, were in it now.

The bike, his bike, wasn't the same, as the hi-tech frame and tire rims were bent. The derailer stuck and he felt the chain could break at any moment. He only had one brake. Stress fractures streaked the durable, but fragile titanium frame, and he hoped it would stay in one piece. He was riding a crippled horse, pushing it as hard as he could, and he wished he was anyplace but there. Trial court wasn't sounding so bad.

His attorney's voice bounced around in his brain. Wethers' advice at Big Bear about canceling this trip was stinging in his ears. Sommers wished he had canceled. He could've been at Malibu, sunning on the beach, or riding in one of the canyons, certainly without the life threatening baggage he was currently experiencing. He doubted he would come across rebel and militia factions, fighting to the death in sunny California. Wethers' words were haunting.

Never had Sommers been on this end of *life threatening*. It was always the other way around. He was the one rescuing lives from death, snatching them away from the jaws of peril and beginning the healing process. Yet, here he was... a million miles from nowhere in a fast deteriorating situation. *What would be worse, cancer or this? A gunshot wound or this? Burning in a fire?* He didn't know.

Again, he was in the dark, riding, advancing, more on instinct and adrenaline than a true course. He thought it ironic his life so paralleled this moment. Everything going downhill and all he could do was hang on, riding the eye in the center of the universe.

He gripped the handlebars tightly, wanting to get through this, wanting it to end. The jungle had long since stopped being their friend and somewhere in his mind he hoped maybe he could devise some kind of truce with it.

*Let us leave... safely, and we'll never bother you again,* he thought. *We'll haul our lily-white behinds out of here. That was fair. After all, what did they really do?*

In the beginning, coming across the melee, he actually tried to save rebels, the boy and the one in the well. That was a good thing. They didn't bring this mess to the jungle, this horrible event. They were just on a bike trip. *Accidents happen. Does that exploitation of the precious jungle warrant such severe penalties? Does riding through beautiful terrain on a once in a lifetime adventure constitute life threatening trespassing?*

Sommers thought not and he prayed the jungle didn't have a case. Prayed the sounds they had heard before he left weren't gunfire. Prayed all of this was a bad dream and he would awaken at the beach house, maybe late for a lecture or a double shift.

Yet pedaling, forcing his body to respond and nursing his crippled machine along, he knew the reality. What he didn't know was if he could deal with it, as this involved more than just him.

He had abandoned Kevin and Celia, and they were close to hysterical. Right or wrong, black or white, he made the call, and recently, at least in his limited experience, his batting average was down.

Inside, he knew there was nothing else he could do. Obviously getting to the chopper would afford help, but then what? How would they explain... *the courts work differently here,* he thought. Was his action putting them in more jeopardy? Who could they trust? Could what began as an incredible vacation, wind up as a life sentence in a Mexican jail? Frontier justice?

That sent shudders through him. *No,* he told himself. *Get help; take care of your own; then tell the truth.*

Without warning the terrain changed and the trail flattened. It wasn't a clearing and he was still in the jungle, but he felt he was closer. For some reason, that didn't ease his mind either.

160

# *51*

# THE PILOT

Enrique arrived at the clearing and knew from his experience, it was large enough to land a helicopter. He and his men crossed through the tall grass to the other side and hid along the perimeter. From that vantage point, he could see everything and wait patiently.

"You know I don't know if this is the right place," Elena offered. "There could be hundreds of places."

"Yes, pretty one," Enrique responded. "But we are at this one, which is closest to the trail."

"Who cares?"Robbie asked. "Look, why don't you just let us go. What do you say? That's fair."

"My fat friend, the only fair people I know about seem to end up on a bench in a park, feeding birds."

One of Enrique's men held up his hand, cupped his ear and motioned to the blue sky. A moment later, in the distance, the *thwap, thwap* of a helicopter's blades was heard.

"Down everyone," Enrique ordered. "See, I think it's a good bet we are in the right place."

The chopper circled, locating the best landing spot, which was just off center, about a hundred and fifty yards from where they were hidden. It floated down like a feather and cut its engine.

Enrique patiently waited, eyeing the bird, setting his plan. Using hand signals, he sent a man to either side of the craft. They would attack from three sides.

The pilot exited, stretched and was preparing to wait until the bike tour arrived. He opened the cargo doors for the breeze and milled around the engine compartment, checking things. He produced a portable CD player and Neil Diamond began singing, his voice cascading across the meadow, into the hills.

"Couldn't he have brought something else?" Robbie whined.

Enrique angrily nudged Robbie with the butt of his rifle to keep quiet. With his men in place and the pilot complacent, he knew the time was near. He cocked his rifle and pistol.

# 52

## JUNGLE MUSIC

The pop music wafted into the jungle, onto the trail. At first Sommers thought he was hearing things, but as he came closer, he realized the music was real and he grinned. He relaxed. It was something American... something from home.

At the bottom of the trail, still covered by brush, he hopped off the bike. He was about to enter the clearing and call to the pilot, as the sight lifted his spirits. The link to civilization and familiarity was about a hundred yards away.

What he saw next, made him dive for cover and it took an excruciating moment for his brain to register the details.

From the far side, Elena materialized and darted from the brush. She sprinted toward the dormant chopper, screaming, "GET AWAY... WE'VE GOT TO GET OUT."

Hysterical, her arms flailed and she ran in sheer terror. Sommers witnessed it all in a kind of slow motion detail. He watched her muscles ripple, as each running step clawed for advancement. Her eyes radiated some kind of distant energy from within, as if her whole purpose was to protect the pilot... protect his life. Save what was good.

The pilot, caught completely unaware, saw this lithe image of beauty running toward him from the jungle, appearing from nowhere. In his shock, he hesitated, waiting a beat too long, as the machinations of his demise were already in play.

Instead of jumping into the pilot's seat and igniting that big rotor, he gripped the door, confused. *Why was Elena running to him? What could possibly be this wrong? Is she joking?*

His decision was made for him. Enrique and his men appeared, as planned, from the jungle, in a triangular, attack formation. They had him. Target acquired.

Caught on three sides, the pilot's adrenaline fired and he lunged for the cockpit, but was nicked below his shoulder blade by a bullet. The impact threw him crossways into the control panel. With only one good hand and arm, he flipped switches, engaged hydraulics and prayed the electrical would ignite.

Enrique could have easily shot the bird, but he didn't want to damage the machine. The pilot meant nothing to him, as he himself could fly. He needed the helicopter intact, not broken, which meant it couldn't leave the ground.

Enrique tackled Elena, just short of the chopper. She fought hard, but he obviously had the advantage, and together they watched the unfolding horror.

The pilot, now in a semi-conscious state, reeling in pain, didn't have full use of his faculties. The mechanical bird lurched upward.

"The pilot!" Enrique yelled to his running men. "Get him."

The beautiful machine dipped to only a few feet off the ground, its main prop almost catching the earth.

Sommers anticipated the worst and retreated to the jungle. He instantly knew a machine that powerful, turning that fast, could easily catapult hundreds of yards in any direction, chewing everything in its path.

Black smoke plumed from underneath the engine cowling, expelling the horrible smell of burning oil and gas, combined with sweat and blood.

Enrique's men didn't understand. They believed if they could somehow attach themselves to the landing skids and maneuver into the cockpit, they could wrestle the craft to the ground. They were wrong on all accounts.

Sommers watched the naïve patriots grab onto the undercarriage on the same side. This of course put an additional four hundred pounds in a localized spot, on an unbalanced, out of control aircraft. If the pilot didn't already have a fight on his hands with a damaged helicopter and a heavy stick, he now had more than he or his bird could withstand.

In his waning thoughts, the pilot's brain commanded him to "fly level, fly straight." This meant gaining altitude, keeping the rotors far and away from the ground. He revved the engine and maxed out the pitch. The craft spun upward, literally the definition of a whirly-bird in flight.

At a hundred feet, Enrique's two men still hung on, now for their lives, as they realized the end was near. One let go and tumbled onto a rocky cliff. The other, now frozen in fear, with his fingers slipping, gripped tighter, hoping against hope the dizzy spinning would stop. He wished he'd never met Enrique Salerno.

The pilot expired, jamming the joystick forward. For an instant, the helicopter flew straight, but it was short-lived. It ambled over a foliage covered hill, sputtering its last gasps. The big rotor finally connected with a static object, a tree. That was the end.

Sommers remembered that image, of a hulking machine that seemed to implode, wrapping itself helplessly into the trunk. As he lost sight, there was only silence. Nothing. Then came the biggest explosion he had ever heard.

The fireball shot into the sky and he could feel the warmth from the aftermath even at that distance. This was no Phoenix. He knew the chopper had gone down and with it, his sliver of hope. The helicopter was their ticket, out. Now they were really on their own. To make matters worse, they were separated and near panicking. *Who had Elena? Who were the men chasing her and on the chopper? What was happening? Where was Robbie?*

Sommers' mind reeled. For some reason, he'd never thought about finding the helicopter, then losing it. Having it for a moment, then seeing it snatched from his grasp and watching men and the pilot die. That shook him. *But the brochures said...*

He didn't have the answer. He was alone.

# 53

## MULES

Enrique cursed the ground, his men, God... everything he could think of, as he yanked up Elena and dragged her back to the perimeter. He threw her down hard and angrily stood over the whimpering Robbie. "I needed that helicopter and those men's backs. Now yours will have to do."

"Look, we're tourists..."

"Shut up, tourist. Do you think this is some game?"

"No... that's not what I meant. Please..."

Enrique grabbed Robbie's bound wrists, pulling him up, standing face to face. "I feel you are concealing many things from me, American. Now, because of the present circumstances, we're moving on and you're going to aid my cause. Are we clear?"

"Yes," Robbie stammered.

"Very well then." Enrique spoke Spanish to his other men. Elena understood him to say Robbie was to take the heavier gear and they loaded him down accordingly.

Elena was only assigned a pack and she kept her mouth shut. She kept thinking about Ramon and how things would be much better when they met up with him. *He had to be leading some kind of effort to rescue them. He would probably kill Robbie,* she thought. At that moment, that didn't sound that bad to her. In the next, she was ashamed for thinking it.

"I can't carry all this," Robbie whined.

"You can carry it or not," Enrique offered, cocking his gun. "The choice is yours."

Reluctantly Robbie layered on the gear. Enrique led them loaded and packed across the meadow, directly over the spot where the helicopter had sat. Each of them had their own expectations, as they crossed that piece of ground.

Sommers observed them hiking, momentarily relieved to see Robbie was with them. He traced them, as they moved closer to the trail he'd just emerged from. It was the same path, the one that would return them to the rebel camp and the tour's campsite with Celia and Kevin.

In a fleeting moment, Sommers rolled the bike off the pathway and coddled it next to him undercover. He was resolute in his silence, knowing everything had changed.

What could he do? He had a pistol, but they were armed and knew how to use their weapons. They were trained in the ins and outs of shooting, and killing without remorse. They took pride and passion in that. In a perfect world, Sommers would take their handiwork and reverse it. Do the healing. Of course, he was a long way from a perfect world at that moment. This was a parallel universe. The rabbit hole.

As Enrique's group marched closer, parrots squawked in the trees above. Enrique stopped just yards from Sommers, his weaponry at the ready.

Sommers didn't move, he couldn't breathe. For that split second, life left him and his body became a vacant void.

Enrique looked in Sommers' direction, nearly right at him, as hundreds of birds took flight. The group watched them fly away and their attention was diverted. They trudged on.

Sommers heaved a sigh of relief and righted the rickety bike. Tracking them on the trail and hanging back, he walked the machine through the brush and inclined grade. It was harder traveling this way, as he didn't have the luxury of the trail. Funny, he thought, a pathway being a luxury.

Keeping them in earshot, his route was at the mercy of the terrain. He also had the problem of not knowing their exact destination, although he was thinking it was the rebel camp. *Has to be,* he thought. There was no reason to go anywhere else.

However, that didn't preclude them from veering to their campsite or accidentally discovering his friends. They were just over the rise from the massacre. Unaware. What if they heard Celia and Kevin working? *What if…?*

The questions were endless and Sommers concentrated on a plan. If he could pass them, off the trail, he could then be in front of them. At that point, he could ride the bike, instead of lugging it through the jungle, up the hill. The other alternative was to just ditch the bike and run.

Part of the decision was made for him when he slipped in some grass and tumbled into a narrow ravine. The bike broke part of his fall, but he hit hard and lay a moment in the tall, wet grass.

*What am I doing here? He asked himself.* Memories flashed in his brain and he saw everything in just a few seconds. His mind was on overload and there was nothing he could do. In a way, he wished the rebel leader had heard his plight and was coming to kill him. *What a way to go,* he thought. *I would be a legend.*

The other half of his brain confirmed bluntly, *yes, a forgotten, unknown hero. Get out of here!*

Was he now thinking… or just talking to himself? Maybe he had hit the bottom. He wasn't sure. What he did know was he had to stay the course. If they came to their campsite, or heard Celia and Kevin, so be it. But Sommers didn't want to go down without some kind of a fight. He had come too far… this far.

Addressing the facts as a mission, he persevered with the bulky machine, carrying it, balancing it. He slid through the jungle finding a second wind, advancing as stealthily as he could.

At one point, he was above them, seeing the bound Elena and Robbie carrying the load. It sickened him seeing Elena under such duress. They were moving slower and not listening or looking, as vigilantly as Sommers.

At a far enough point ahead, Sommers dropped onto the trail, mounted the broken bicycle and prayed it would hold together for the ascending ride. He had to return to their campsite, now at any cost, warn Kevin and Celia, and hope this group of rebels or militia, or whoever they were, wouldn't catch him.

# 54

## KEEPING IT TOGETHER

Celia couldn't stay focused on working. She and Kevin had rummaged through what remained of the gear and organized it into piles. There were some supplies, usables, but Robbie had definitely either taken or destroyed the lion share.

She had been working to fix the bikes, get them functioning again, so when Sommers did return, they could leave quickly. It was a much easier task said than done. Robbie had smashed the frames, the main structure of the bike. She knew to fix them correctly, one needed a welding torch or soldering gun. Something to bind molten metal together and they didn't have that.

Another concern, and there were plenty, was Kevin. He wasn't acting right. He was lethargic, then had spurts of energy. His eyes appeared glassy, dark, to her, and she felt he wasn't expressing how he really felt. She realized he could be a hindrance if they had to make a run for it.

The sun was setting and the temperature cooling. Should they make a fire or not? Hide with the gear? Move? The questions were daunting... endless.

Celia's mind drifted to her husband. He was probably out wining and dining somewhere with the new love, or lust of his life. *Did she spell her name with an "i" or a "y?"* Sommers' smart-mouth question now plagued her. *The silly things,* she mulled, wishing at the moment, her husband and present marital state was all she had to worry about.

Yes, awkwardly running into them at a favorite restaurant or movie would certainly fare much better than this predicament. She decided if she ever got the chance, she would hug them both and wish them well.

*Ever got the chance...* the words seemed hollow, desperate. But that's what she was. She kept replaying that if she had never mentioned the other box, the last one, Ramon would be with them and they would be long gone, reveling and celebrating the once in a lifetime find along the way. The perfect vacation.

It made her stomach turn. In her mind, she shouldn't have said anything and everything would be different for all of them. Elena would be there, joking with her brother, talking of all the things he was going to buy. Robbie would be talking of sports bets, the point spreads, getting even and having a suite for a month at Caesar's Palace in Vegas. Kevin would just want to heal. The coins probably held more value as collectibles to him. And Sommers... well, she thought. He would brood. He would take the money, use it for debt and fees, and whatever legalese mess he was in.

She felt badly for Sommers. For some reason, fate was angry at him. They were all part of it, but Sommers now had to shoulder the responsibilities and consequences. A combination of separate and exclusive factors had placed them there, but she knew it would fall on him to lead them out. To escape.

Kevin wandered over, eating from a can of peaches. "You okay?" he asked.

"I guess. You know if I hadn't-- "

"It's not your fault, Celia. You were going to say if you hadn't said anything else about that other box, we'd all be back at the resort instead of here."

She was intrigued by his perception, knew he'd been thinking about it as well. "But I didn't have to say anything."

"Don't go there. Robbie had it in for us the moment he touched the coins. It was the drugs working and seemingly easy money. They called to him and he did what he did."

"I'm sorry, Kevin." She hugged him.

"It's okay." Kevin coughed and Celia saw he was pale. "But Sommers has been gone too long."

She felt he was right about that and didn't want to mention it first. It seemed like forever since Sommers had ridden off. "He'll be back. It's probably further than-- "

In the next instant, there was a sound from the jungle, maybe a branch cracking. Celia took charge, grabbing a rifle. She didn't have time to think and just aimed the gun in the direction of the noise.

They huddled near a brush pile and waited. To her, the jungle seemed to be closing in, each branch or vine, a covert tentacle, ready to swoop down and grab them.

Celia had never fired a gun, didn't know if she could even pull the trigger. *Point and shoot,* is what she remembered, but knew it was a lot harder when actually pressed to carry out that action. She hated guns. She worked in an office with keyboards and pens. *This wasn't real, but...*

The sounds stopped and the breeze nipped at the treetops. A branch snapping from behind them echoed and Sommers triumphantly appeared. They were shocked, surprised. He laid down his bike, exhausted. They rushed to him, comforted him with a canteen.

"Sommers--" Celia began.

"How far to the chopper?" Kevin asked, cutting to the chase. "Can we make it?"

Sommers caught his breath, drank some water. Celia sensed something was wrong. His eyes were empty, vacant. She put her hand on his shoulder.

"There's no helicopter-- it crashed!" he bluntly stated, almost staring into space. "Pilot's dead."

"Oh no," Kevin replied. "No, no, no... "

"I don't believe it," Celia blurted, hoping it wasn't true. "What happened out there?"

Sommers got to his feet. "There's three of them, three men, and they have Robbie and Elena. They captured them on the trail somewhere, I don't know. But they're coming this way. They might already be here."

All their faces fell. The trip, the wonderful vacation and jungle, had turned, then stepped on them. "They want what's in the well. It was theirs," Celia warned.

"It's looking like that," Sommers confirmed.

171

"I knew we should have left it alone," Kevin angrily exclaimed. "That's the end. They'll kill us all when they see what happened up there."

"Look Kevin, I don't know the answers, but they have Elena. We have to do something."

"Yeah. Run like crazy the other way and head for the authorities. Do you have any idea how far in over our heads we are, Sommers? Our guide is dead, Robbie went nuts... we-- "

Kevin dropped to the ground, whimpering and panicking, the morphine distorting his faculties. In a way, Sommers wished he could do the same. Just allow the whole situation to overwhelm him and check out. "Get a grip, Kevin," Sommers ordered. "Just take it easy."

Celia gave him some water. "I feel bad for Elena, who wouldn't... but Kevin's right. This has gotten way out of hand. We need-- "

Sommers shot them a knowing look. "I know you two are upset, all right? I am too, believe me, but we can't leave her. You two do realize that don't you?" They looked away, not sure. "Don't you?"

"What're we supposed to do? March in and ask for her back? It won't happen. She and Robbie are probably dead anyway."

"They weren't when I saw them. They're just slaves. Look, we're not leaving her-- or at least I'm not. We owe that much to Ramon."

"Don't bring him into this. If you hadn't wanted to go for the coins, he'd be alive," Kevin accused.

"We all wanted the coins."

"I didn't." Kevin was defiant.

"Stop it," Celia ordered. "It's nobody's fault-- and it's everybody's fault, so stop fighting. We're not splitting up again, so you two need to decide."

Kevin coughed. He was mad at them and the world, the dissipating morphine clouding his judgment. "You saw what happened at the well-- and remember what the soldiers did at the van? Soldiers, rebels-- they'll kill us, end of story. We mean nothing to them."

"Just take it easy, Kevin."

"I'm not going to die out here. I'm not."

"Then we don't get caught."

"Sommers, I'm not saying we shouldn't save her, but don't you think we're outnumbered? And what about us? Kevin's not doing so hot. Maybe we should get some men. Saddle up the good guys."

Sommers knew Celia had a point. They both did. If they were seen or caught, it would be over. "I told you I didn't have the answers. I know we're at a disadvantage, but they're coming and it's getting dark. Let's take what we can and get undercover. We can't go anywhere at night."

"That's your plan?" Kevin admonished.

"One of them."

Sommers began organizing gear and packing.

"We don't have much of a choice, Kevin," Celia said, joining Sommers.

"I figured that out a long time ago," Kevin muttered to himself.

# 55

## MASKS

Darkness enveloped the jungle and their campsite quickly. Sommers took the available supplies and placed them near an area on the edge of the stream, facing the hill. There was nothing left in the open. If the wayward rebels appeared on that trail, nothing would seem out of place. Hopefully, it would be as if the bike group had never made camp, never existed at all.

Sommers, Kevin and Celia hid in the brush, completely out of sight. They had a bird's eye view of the area and Sommers had done an excellent job of camouflage.

Sitting next to each other and eating some trail mix rations, the three huddled, trying to make sense of things and pass the tedious time of just surviving.

The darkness and sounds of the jungle were infectious. Everything seen and unseen took on a whole new dimension, meaning. Treacherous. They knew this time there was something in the blackness to fear. Something was definitely out there that could hurt, if not kill them.

They wanted to stay positive, but they all knew the game and what was at stake... their lives.

Sommers moved more branches and covered them.

"Don't you think we're hidden well enough?" Kevin asked.

"I don't know. Ask me when they find us."

"Will you two be quiet," Celia commanded, her eyes continuously scanning the camp.

"This is nuts." Kevin persisted. "Look, I am in the garment business. I make shirts, one hundred percent cotton, pull-over shirts-- "

174

"Then send me a catalog, but be quiet!"

"I'm on vacation, a vacation... not at war over some stupid coins, drugs and guns, for God knows what. Let the bad guys have them and let's get out of here while we can."

"And Elena, Kevin?" Sommers questioned. "What do you want to do about her?"

"You said you had plans. You did. Well, what are they?"

"If you two are any louder, it won't matter," Celia interrupted. "We might as well send up a flare."

"We wait, see what they do, then follow them," Sommers quietly said.

"That's it?" Kevin snarled. "Anybody could have thought of that. That's just great. They'll hear us, then kill us. They do this for a living!"

Sommers waited until Kevin calmed a bit. "Do you have a better idea?"

"Of course I do. Hawaii. My idea is Hawaii. Kapalua Bay Club with a golf package... and this."

Kevin plunged his fingers into some mud next to him and wiped stripes across his face. "Maybe they'll only hear us and not see us. I'm going to puke now."

Sommers and Celia followed his lead, fingering the mud and rubbing it on their faces, arms and legs. Sommers smiled at Celia and brushed some mud away from her eyes. "I guess I should have taken a cruise."

"Shuffleboard and all you can eat, but there's a two hundred percent markup on liquor and Dramamine."

"What I wouldn't give for a Tootsie Roll," Kevin offered.

Sommers felt for Kevin and knew he was uncomfortable. "I'm sorry there's nothing more for the pain. I don't even know what leaves you could chew on."

Kevin laughed at that, a kind of gallows laughter. "Leaves. It's not your fault, Dr. Death. I'm just scared out of my wits."

Sommers looked at him, knowing they had come far, with a long way to go. "Believe me, so am I."

# 56

## VIOLATIONS

Daybreak exploded on the jungle with heady morning rituals. Plants and animals began their day of watering and foraging, as they had done for millions of years. This was an untouched world, not yet completely spoiled by man; that housed a magnificent ecosystem. Man was the intruder, the spoiler here, but he was in nature's domain and that meant following a different set of rules. Even Enrique knew that… much like the ocean, you couldn't turn your back on the jungle. You had to give it your attention or it would simply rise up and kill you without regard.

As Enrique breached the perimeter of the rebel camp, the smell of death and a gallant battle pierced his nostrils. He could certainly tell from the remains the fight that took place here was one to behold. He envied the dead combatants and a part of him wished he had been there, guns blazing, battling to the death. That was the cowboy in him, what he called the romantic.

Walking through the bodies and carnage, his eyes hardened, becoming angry, as he touched the Jeep. If he had any remorse at seeing the blood bath, he didn't show it. No, that would be the weak thing.

He kept surveying, trudging around men he knew and ones he didn't. He saw Lupe, long dead, eyes open. He had been shot multiple times. He moved on, to the far end, near where Sommers tried to save the De Aguilar boy.

His first thoughts regarded the well. It was obvious something had gone wrong here besides the skirmish. Things weren't as they seemed. No, others had intruded this space after the futile conflict. The pieces were assembling in his head… this destroyed camp, the well and… the bikers, alone in a world they had no business being in.

Enrique's hypothesis was confirmed when leaving the boy. He glanced over and saw the first-aid kit. Opened with supplies strewn about, it carried the bike tour's logo from the Vera Cruz resort. He picked it up and walked to Robbie, proof in his hands.

"You found all the storage, didn't you?" Enrique pointedly asked.

"What-- what are you talking about?" Robbie squirmed.

Just to confirm his point, Enrique strode to the well and looked down the dark shaft. The water had receded, yet he could still hear it rushing below. Obviously, the booby trap had been tripped. "American, I don't think the earth betrayed us on its own." He moved to Elena and lightly brushed her cheek. "Tell me what happened, Little One. I'm sure you know the truth."

Elena's mind raced. She knew her brother had to be close. He had to be. Had they passed by on the trail in the night? But where was he? Why hadn't he found them? "There was an explosion."

"Yes, go on."

"In the well-- "

"It was huge," Robbie interrupted. "Our guide and another biker didn't get out."

"Yes, they did," Elena tearfully countered. "They got out and are looking for us. They have to be."

"Yeah, right. The whole well blew... boom! Place was like a geyser."

Enrique was tired of Robbie's rhetoric. He knew an explosion could only mean whomever had gone inside the chamber, was in very deep. It also meant a person's chance of survival was next to nil.

One of Enrique's men approached, carrying one of the wrapped plastic bags of heroin.

"Hey, we didn't touch any of that," Robbie exclaimed. "No, Sir; no how."

"Ah, then you did find something," Enrique proffered, setting the hook. "That interests me. Where do you suppose the others are in your group?"

"They probably left as quick as they could. I mean, your guess is as good as mine," Robbie chuckled, trying to warm Enrique to his side.

"I don't have the luxury of guessing." Enrique tossed the package back to the man and backhanded Robbie across his face. "We have much to discuss, American."

Standing over Robbie, Enrique barked instructions in Spanish to his men, telling them to rig the winch and start the Jeep. They immediately started to work, rebuilding the scaffolding over the well. They made noise, enough noise to rouse birds and animals, and enough to violate the jungle's serenity.

The intruders had returned.

# 57

## NEGOTIATIONS

Sommers awakened with a start, but didn't move. If anyone was in their camp or near them, he wasn't going to give up their position.

Hearing unnatural sounds from the hills, he nudged Celia and Kevin. "I think our boys have arrived," he whispered.

They listened to what sounded like a distant hammer pounding. It was definitely manmade and ominous. "What do you want to do?" Celia asked.

"Besides ordering room service, we need to carefully go up there. How are you feeling, Kevin?"

Kevin stretched out his legs and both knees popped. "Honestly, I think I'm going to die. My arm and shoulder are throbbing, and my insides feel like they're dead."

"Have some water and we'll help you."

"You're really serious about this, aren't you?" Kevin asked.

"Yeah. Listen, there might be another way."

"And that would be?" Celia nudged.

Sommers scanned the imposing hillside. "You two take the bikes and head for the meadow. From there it can't be that far to the coast and a road. I'll-- "

"We're not splitting up again. I thought that part was already decided."

"Let him finish," Kevin persisted.

"With you two gone, I can see what's going on up there. Maybe make a move to save her."

"No, we stay together." Celia was adamant. "What if something happens to us or if Kevin gets really sick?"

Sommers took a deep breath. "Like I said, I don't have all the answers. You know what I'm going to do, so it's up to you."

Celia's glare pierced Kevin's eyes. He looked at the bikes, the hillside, camp and finally back to them. Every ounce of marrow in his body wanted to leave, abandon everything and ride, walk or run for the ocean and some sense of civilization. If he was healthy, both spiritually and physically, he probably would have done just that, but he heeded Celia's probing hypothesis.

He felt terrible and his wounded shoulder really ached. If they were caught in the wilderness without Sommers, he didn't have enough confidence that Celia had the physical strength to see them through. In his present state, he'd known what his answer was for awhile. He reluctantly spoke. "We stay together. I humbly make this decision under protest to the court, but there aren't any other options."

Celia chuckled, "All right then."

"Tighten the sling on Kevin's arm. Cover up our supplies. We'll worry about them later."

The three went to work, carefully organizing, then hiding what they had with the bikes. Afterward, they began trudging up to the rebel camp, more sounds now emanating from the foliage. They faced the same problems they had before, trying to remain quiet and unseen.

Sommers immediately registered a crippled Kevin was a liability. He couldn't move very fast, and that meant increased odds of exposure. Still, in hopes of unity, he helped him along.

Arriving at the summit, they crawled once again to the edge of the rebel campsite. This time a different picture emerged. Instead of bloody carnage, a small crew was at work. They had rebuilt the scaffolding and the winch was almost operational.

Sommers spied the leader. Sitting in the Jeep, he was smoking, carefully observing his men and his prisoners. He seemed frustrated the vehicle wouldn't start.

They watched him hit the steering wheel, then walk through the dead bodies without concern. Sommers realized he was calculating, formulating a plan. He felt this man was in his element and he would stop at nothing to obtain exactly what he wanted.

180

Sommers, Kevin and Celia bunched up at ground level. A few yards away were Robbie and Elena, bound near the Jeep. They had a clear view and curiously watched the pacing Enrique. Finally, one of his men called to him and he inspected the winch.

Enrique tried starting the Jeep again to no avail. He then pointed to one of his men and spoke Spanish. Enrique wanted him to go inside the well. The man looked over the edge, hanging onto the line, and flatly refused. "No, no voy," he said, definitely not going, backing away.

"Can't anyone take a simple order?" Enrique angrily questioned, drawing his weapon and firing.

Elena screamed, as the man fell dead and Robbie cowered. They were splattered with blood. Sommers, Celia, and Kevin barely kept quiet at the horrific sight, not moving in the brush.

Enrique then jerked Robbie from the ground. "I believe you're up, Dough Boy." He holstered his gun and unsheathed a knife, putting it to Robbie's neck. Robbie was helpless and trembled, as he was forced up on the well's rim.

"He'll never make it," Sommers whispered.

"Is that the man who shot down the chopper?" Celia wanted to know.

"Yes. All the stuff is probably his."

"This can't be happening," Kevin muttered. "I'm really going to be sick."

The two saw Kevin was serious, he was turning paler by the moment. "You have to hold it," Sommers warned. "You can't make a sound!"

Kevin slid backward, into the brush. Celia went with him and Sommers kept a sharp eye on the camp. He listened to Robbie whine, standing on the rim. "We can talk about this... please."

"Are you a negotiator?" Enrique toyed. "Then negotiate for your life Get inside the well."

Robbie broke down, crying.

Watching, Sommers had little remorse. He looked back to the retching Kevin and caught Celia's eyes. *How did they get into this?* he wondered.

"I don't want to die," Robbie pleaded. "I can't do this!"

"Inside now," Enrique threatened, motioning to his other man to prod Robbie with his gun. Robbie gripped the cable, inching closer to the shaft.

With Robbie whimpering, Enrique pulled up Elena and rubbed her shoulders. She cringed at his touch. "You know my wife never understood me either."

"Did you kill her too?"

Enrique adeptly yanked Elena's arm into a painful hammer lock. Sommers started to lunge for them, but Celia had returned and held him back. "This isn't the time," she advised.

He knew Celia was right and backed down.

Enrique released Elena, then caressed her. "Your spirit reminds me of her... when she was alive of course."

Enrique's attention riveted back on Robbie and he produced his pistol. "My patience is growing thin, Gringo. You know one more body here is nothing. Do you understand that?"

"I-- I can't do this."

Enrique cocked his gun, leveled it at the back of Robbie's head. "We are not communicating. I just want what is mine. I am hoping, for your sake, my property is where I left it. If you have conveyed the truth, then we shouldn't have a problem."

Enrique fired the gun, and the bullet struck the winch. Robbie shuddered, sniveling at the ricochet, as Elena struggled with her wristbands. "Please, stop... Robbie has them. He has them all!"

Enrique smiled, lowering the gun. "Of course, back to the negotiator. Why doesn't this surprise me? It's hard confessing, I know. There were three boxes of gold coins-- worth two million American dollars."

"Whoa," Robbie uttered, his face and will falling.

"Quite a temptation I'm sure, for someone like you." Angry and anxious, Enrique jumped on the well's rim and shoved the muzzle under Robbie's chin. Robbie's eyes bulged and he couldn't breathe. "Now, where's my money?"

The whole camp focused on Robbie's answer and his shaking body. Sommers and Celia watched intently, wondering what had happened to coins. Enrique's men moved closer.

"Okay, all right…" Robbie began. "I know where the coins are. You can have them. Just let us go."

Carefully, Robbie showed his hands and reached down. He unclasped his fanny pack, gingerly handing it to Enrique. "Here, they're in here."

"Enterprising," Enrique confirmed. "Especially from such a small mind."

Enrique hopped down and opened the fanny pack. Inside, the gold coins sparkled, and he eagerly ran his hands through them.

"They're all there," Robbie exclaimed. "Except for the ones that blew up."

Enrique closed the pack and looked at Elena. "See, Little One, it is all just business."

With a glimmer in his eye, Enrique pointed the gun at Robbie's head again.

"Hey… wait a minute. You got what you wanted-- "

Enrique pulled the trigger and the hammer on metal clicked. No bullet fired, but Robbie yielded to the shock and nearly fell into the well. The shaky scaffolding caught him, the stressed beams moaning.

"You're sick!" Elena yelled.

"That's correct." Enrique laughed at all of it and produced another gun. "Show me a hero and I'll show you a tragedy."

Sommers and Celia drew deep breaths and slid backward to Kevin, who was obviously in pain.

"Did you see that?" Celia panted.

"You should have seen what he did at the helicopter," Sommers added, making sure their cover was protected. "How are you doing, Kevin?"

"Not great. I heard the commotion. These guys mean business. We're so far down-- "

"I'm not saying we're not, but you saw Elena. What do you think is going to happen to her?"

Kevin didn't have an answer. He just wanted out. "I have to say I really don't care anymore. We're going to die anyway. Just do what you want."

"Kevin-- " Celia started.

"Leave him alone. They'll take off soon. They have what they came for," Sommers lamented.

"You still want to follow them?" Celia asked.

Sommers scanned the brush and could hear Enrique and his men loading and packing. "Yes. Let's get the bikes."

# 58

## SO GO THE SPOILS

Enrique scoured the camp again and again. He couldn't very well take the heavy munitions, so the wrapped bags of heroin and smaller weapons were his only choice. Everything else would have to wait for his return.

They loaded Robbie and Elena to the hilt with the contraband. Leaving, he tossed the fanny pack full of coins to Robbie. "You wanted the gold, Gringo. You can carry it too."

Heading into the jungle, Enrique laughed at his remark and kept a sharp eye trained on Elena. She would be his next prize, one worth the wait.

The main commodity, what everything had been about, was the drugs. As cocaine was the usual "illegal mule product" in South America, smuggled heroin from Asia was a much bigger score. A treat of mega-financial rewards was at stake.

It was unique in these traffic lanes. Not unknown, but certainly on the high end of the monetary scale, heroin could be sold or traded for much more than what cocaine would bring. This of course attracted Enrique from the beginning and why he had trudged into the jungle, nearly losing his life and plane. Its reward was worth the risk.

The gold coins were the bonus he had told Lupe about. Stolen from a Mexico City museum years earlier, the cache of rare coins had meandered north, changing hands in a complex laundering process.

Enrique had been in Houston, finalizing the last transaction for the goods. It was a sweet deal, one that could have ultimately been their largest and perhaps his last.

Enrique just hadn't planned on Lupe's operation being discovered by the militia. Also troubling were these errant mountain bikers on tour. *Was there really this kind of extreme vacation available?* He wondered why tourists would think riding bikes in the jungle was entertaining.

Enrique found it confusing, worrisome. Ruins in the mountains had always provided a safe haven for their activities. This unobserved land route was obviously in jeopardy now. With Lupe dead, an active militia and now tourists encroaching, Enrique was ready to throw in the towel. Houston prostitutes and the American way sounded like an excellent alternative to traipsing around muddy thickets and being targeted from both sides for life risking, all or nothing propositions.

Like anything else, his world was changing, evolving into lower profit margin ratios. He witnessed it every day in other dealings. Seeing the aftermath at the rebel camp only confirmed his brimming fears. People at his level were now doing deals in conference rooms, by the pool or in suites. That was the payoff... not having to be there. He swatted a gnat on his neck.

Racking his brain and trying to comprehend, Enrique's only pleasure at that moment was watching Robbie struggle with the packs. The fat, inconsiderate American in a jam, brought him perverse pleasure.

Prejudiced or not, he hated the fact Americans like Robbie were even allowed in his country. He knew the "Robbies" only came there to drink, carouse and find cheap entertainment. The grand irony was they believed it was owed to them.

He despised his country's economy relied so heavily on the egocentric tourists, invading his home and soiling his nation's fabric. No, for all he cared, the "Robbies" of the world could rot.

On the trail, he touched Elena's hair. "So beautiful... you're even more beautiful when moving."

The comment brought a laugh from Enrique's men. "Yes, we're moving now. Mule and all-- Andele!"

He shoved Elena along, then fired a shot skyward to make them all move faster, but Robbie stumbled and fell. Enrique saw the wallowing sloth, feeling no compassion only annoyance. He drew his gun.

"Please, no-- I'll try harder. Don't shoot me." Robbie shuddered under the muzzle.

"Leave him alone," Elena shouted.

The outburst surprised Enrique, amused him. "Why Little One? He would have certainly left you... or worse."

Tired of the game, Enrique drank from his canteen, then tossed it to Robbie. "Get up. The day escapes us. Elena, walk with me."

Robbie lunged thirstily for the canteen and lifted it to his mouth. It was empty.

# 59

## TRACKS

Sommers, Celia and Kevin followed Enrique's trail. They heard the random shot, wondering if someone, especially one of their own, had been killed. They had a few supplies and two bikes that were barely holding together.

The anxiety was taking a toll on Sommers. Someone like him, educated in the medical profession, didn't like feeling helpless, yet that's where he was. He had no clue what he was doing.

The combination of the Senator's daughter, the dying boy at the rebel camp, the crashing helicopter and witnessing Enrique execute a man in cold blood was too much. The *voices* were nagging at him, tugging at his fragile emotions. "I should've done something," he suddenly blurted to Celia. "I could've done something! All those people didn't have to die."

Celia knew where this was going. "You're doing all you can. This isn't a normal situation."

Sommers stopped, his eyes glassy. "See what happens when you help-- when you don't help."

"You're alive, Sommers. We're alive. Maybe Kevin's right. Maybe we should leave and get the authorities."

All the emotions and feelings of the past few days welled inside Sommers. To go back now would be to fail. "We can't leave Elena."

With that, he rode ahead, not letting either of them respond.

With emotions pent-up, Celia pushed the other bike, allowing Kevin to use it as a makeshift crutch. She was worried about Kevin. The pace and heat were mounting against him.

She thought about heading for the ocean with him, sending help back for Sommers and Elena, but had doubts about surviving.

It took special skills to do that. Ones they didn't teach in law school or courtrooms. They were all caught, like insects in a spider's web, and dependent upon each other. Like it or not, they would have to stay with Sommers.

Disappointed with Sommers and herself, she bit her tongue and helped Kevin. "We have to keep Sommers in sight."

"I can't go any faster. I'm sorry, I'm not a track star, even when I'm not sick." Kevin bent over and stopped to catch his breath. To him, this hellish situation felt like they had been on the trail for days, yet it was only a few hours.

"Rest here. I'll catch Sommers."

Celia touched his shoulder and he took her hand. In one quick breath Kevin summed up everything. "We're not getting out of this are we?"

She didn't have the answer and didn't want to lie. Avoiding his eyes, she smiled, not saying anything, then took off for Sommers on the bike.

Getting away from Kevin allowed her to think. The few moments on the dark trail were hers. Reflecting, she thought she wouldn't have done anything differently. Sommers was right, it was an adventure no one would believe and there was a small part of her that relished being in the thick of things.

It could have been ego or anxious excitement, but the secret adrenaline rush made her grin and ride harder. Somehow, some way, she was fulfilled, and she knew no matter what happened, no one could ever rob her of that moment.

Topping a rise, she came upon Sommers. He was sitting on a boulder, his bike lying next to him. Celia thought it odd. He was holding something... "Sommers-- ?"

He looked up slowly, his eyes red.

"Kevin can't keep up. He's sick... his shoulder is killing him." Celia saw Sommers' gaze return to the shiny, silver object. It was a bracelet, Elena's bracelet, and he was focused on every little facet.

"He'll kill her," Sommers quietly stated. "That's all he wants. He'll use her, then kill her."

"If you know that, really know that, then we're done. Can't you see none of us are cut out for this?!"

Sommers stood, pocketing the bracelet and righting his bike. "We could leave Kevin... come back for him."

"He wouldn't make it alone. You know that."

"I don't even know if we'll make it together."

"You can't be serious."

"Right now, I don't know what I am. Stay on the trail as best you can. They're up there somewhere. I'll watch for you."

"Sommers... please-- "

But he was gone into the brush.

The sublime euphoria Celia felt just a few minutes earlier had long since vanished. Fulfillment turned to fear and reluctantly, she returned to find Kevin.

# *60*

## COKE BOTTLES

The Mexican standing watch near the entrance to Enrique's camp enjoyed Coca-Cola. It was his favorite drink, excluding alcohol, and he always carried a couple of bottles with him when he was on duty.

Enrique wanted his men to be focused on their jobs and he didn't appreciate them drinking on duty. Even the ones who had worked with him before were under scrutiny. This mandate included soft drinks, water... anything that was a distraction.

When Enrique arrived and passed the lone checkpoint, he seemed angry. The guard hid his two Coke bottles and waited for his boss, the other men and the two exhausted prisoners to pass.

When he knew it was safe, he hoisted the large, cane sugared sweet glass bottle, drank it dry and tossed it into the bushes. It made a tinkling sound, the kind glass makes when it hits and shatters against other glass. Satisfied and full, the guard belched and stood his post, letting the day bore out its tedium.

As time wore on, he was curious about the prisoners. The male looked American and the Mexican female was quite pretty. He was also surprised all the men had not returned. However, he knew he would be briefed when he was relieved in a few hours.

Enrique was moody and temperamental, even when things were perfect. He attributed the sullen attitude of the returning group to being weary from the trail.

There was no reason to expect anything out of the ordinary and their operation had been a simple one to this point. They were to find Lupe, warn him of the encroaching militia and tell him to be ready for anything. The Guard felt this must have happened and some of his comrades in arms had probably stayed behind. He would find out about the prisoners later.

Thinking of enjoying his second cold Coca-Cola, he heard something. Slowly reaching for his rifle, he stepped gingerly and parted the underbrush. Moving forward, his boot crunched the glass of a dozen empty coke bottles. A sea of glass.

Thinking some rodent probably had scampered across the refuse pile, he turned and was met with Sommers' bike crashing down on him from nowhere. Absorbing the glancing blow, he was rolled into a heap by the two-wheeler and Sommers, who hit hard.

Attacking first and trying to secure leverage, Sommers thrust his fingers into the Guard's neck, hoping to find a nerve center... a weakness. There was nothing but flesh and thick muscle.

The guard was incredibly strong, agile and now angry. *He did do this for a living.* With the guard taking control, he forced Sommers into a relentless choke hold, taking the advantage.

Sommers groped and jabbed, striving violently to reverse the situation, but there was nothing. His medically trained fingers and hands were useless. This was a brutal war, survival of the fittest... no compromises-- winner takes all.

Sommers weakened from lack of oxygen, as the vice grip became tighter. It wasn't so much the pain, as the cold stillness of the vacuum. It was like his mind and body were in an infinite tunnel, with the diameter closing. This was the first sign. He heard a whooshing sound and Sommers knew he was going to pass out-- *starve the brain of oxygen and... just give in. It's what you wanted.*

The blackness crept, louder static of a fading will. A dark peace and then... a muffled *whack.*

A wielded bicycle seat slammed down on the Guard's head, once... twice... three times, knocking him off Sommers. Celia stood over them, out of breath, ready to hit again. She fell to her knees. "Oh, no. Is he-- ?!"

Sommers gasped for air, static receding... reality and life returning. He crawled over, checked for a pulse. "No, he's okay-- just out."

"I saw him... you. I-- I didn't know what else to do." She started crying, adrenaline fading and emotion taking over. Sommers stood on wobbly legs and comforted her.

"I'm glad you did what you did. He had me."

She wiped her face, angrily pulling away. "I can't do this much longer. Do you understand?! It's crazy. I push papers-- write summations, briefs-- "

"You're okay, Celia."

"I'm so far from being okay... none of this is okay!"

"All right. None of it is fair either, but it's where we are. You did good just now. Thank you."

"You're welcome. I guess."

They smiled at each other, then looked up the trail and saw Kevin limping toward them. They both went over, quietly helping him. "What happened?" he asked, obviously tired and in pain.

"Long story, but the attorney saved me from the death penalty. Celia, help me get that guy tied up. Feeling any better, Kevin?"

"Peachy."

"Can you make it up that ridge?"

Kevin looked upward, rolling his eyes. "Do I have a choice?"

# *61*

## JUST PRESS PLAY

Sommers, Kevin and Celia carefully made their way along the narrow ridge of a box canyon. The topography gave way to a rocky border that had eroded over eons from weathering.

Enrique had made a base camp consisting of a few tents and supplies. It was a safe fortress, protected on three sides by steep, rock walls. The entrance and ridge was to be under the sharp eye of a guard, the one Celia and Sommers had handled.

As Sommers peered downward, he saw Robbie bound to a post in the center of the camp. A couple of tires at his feet and one around his shoulders, helped hold him firmly in place.

Sommers thought it odd, until he realized the simple brutality if the tires were set aflame. Robbie would burn to a crisp, a fiery necklace pyre of sorts.

He kept scanning the camp, hoping not to be seen, searching for Elena. There was movement, the occasional rebel, and he had to keep retreating. "Celia, let me have your video camera."

She handed it to him and he cautiously placed it near the ridge's edge. "What are you doing?" she whispered.

"We can see more with the zoom lens," he said.

Sommers aimed the camera at the camp and blindly recorded slow pans back and forth. Hoping he had captured what he wanted, he retrieved the camera and motioned for them to take refuge into the brush.

Sommers viewed the playback through the camera's screen. He studied every nuance, every frame. "I don't see Elena," he scowled. "What did they do with her?"

"She has to be there," Kevin stated. "Unless they moved on or something."

"They wouldn't leave everything," Celia voiced, taking the camera from Sommers. "Doesn't make sense."

Sommers sidled back to the ridge's edge, forcing another look. "Robbie looks dead."

"Careful, Sommers, they'll see you."

"I don't see anyone now, except Robbie. Nothing."

Kevin and Celia felt Sommers was planning something. They were learning how his mind worked. "What are you thinking?" Kevin reluctantly asked.

"I think we could get in there... or at least one of us could."

"Do you have a death wish?" Kevin blurted, trying to rally support from Celia. "You really are 'death.' You don't know if they're gone or even where Elena is!"

"I know she's not up here with us."

The two couldn't argue with that. The rebel camp was silent, almost hollow, and to Sommers, inviting.

"So who goes?" Celia questioned.

"Me," Sommers immediately volunteered. "That way, at least you two would have a chance."

Celia touched Sommers' shoulder. "You do know he'll kill you in a heartbeat. I think they have their quota of hostages."

"Better me than her." Sommers scanned the camp again, trying to see anything that could help him. He was also mustering courage. Somewhere inside, that voice was cueing him Celia and Kevin were right. *Winner take all, Gringo.*

Celia assertively produced a pistol and some bullets. "Here," she said. "If you're really going, take these."

He took the gun, checked the load. "You keep the extra ammo. If I'm caught and this all goes south, you two will need it."

"More positive waves," Kevin facetiously stated.

Sommers grinned, pocketed the gun and headed across the ridge to a steep path.

# 62

## RAGING LEGS

At the head of the small horseshoe shaped gulch, Enrique's campsite lay about sixty feet below the ridge. Its advantage and disadvantage was the entry and exit points. One either had to walk in at ground level or traverse the rocky walls surrounding the encampment. That meant exposure.

Formed by an errant stream that depended on rainfall at various times of the year, the limestone and caliche base had eroded over time. Sommers chose the only route available, a narrow, stone filled path that was slippery and noisy. He navigated the best he could and prayed he wouldn't be seen or heard.

His footing was precarious at best and because of the steep incline, he walked and slid, grabbing the occasional branch or outcropping.

At one point he slipped, his body giving way to gravity. As if on marbles, he fell, skinning his legs and knees, sliding downward uncontrollably. Finally able to stop, he crouched silently, his heart and mind racing, hoping for anonymity in a completely exposed world.

He slithered behind some brush, almost at ground level, unable to see past ten feet. At some point, he knew he would have to advance completely into the open, take his chances. He was playing an undercover game of give and take with life, his life-- everything at stake.

Calming down, he confirmed the camp was quiet and empty. At least he thought that, as he moved into a partially open area with a better view.

He stayed low, moving silently along the perimeter. It was farther than Celia's video lens represented and his analytical mind told him to remember to write a letter to Sony's camera division. Then he could complain about distance scale ratios and how they appeared differently through playback screens.

Refocusing, he wiped his bloodied leg, then parted some branches. He was advancing with metallic tasting adrenaline rushing through his veins. His labored breathing echoed in his itchy ears, and his heart pounded a mile a minute. Wethers crossed his mind, probably sitting at a desk on the fortieth floor, debating what flavor bagel to have, making dozens of calls and curious to see how short his assistant's skirt was that day. *Was that living? Or was this?*

Sommers was close enough to touch one of the tents. Its fabric was thick, military issue and smelled of sun dried mildew. He angled between two of them and could see most of the camp.

Looking upward, he spied the top of Celia's head. He surmised Kevin was nearby, but couldn't see him. *They're good people, the kind you would want to know when this is over. Have a bar-b-q.* He hoped he would get to see them again.

Retreating to the rear of the tents, he made a decision and maneuvered to the far side of the last tent. Turning around, he saw Elena tied and gagged to a tree. She didn't see him, as she appeared asleep.

He ran as fast as he could to her, kneeling to hide. "Elena... can you hear me? Are you all right?"

She moaned, life returning when she realized it was him. Excited, she tugged at her ropes. "Take it easy. Just be still," a relieved Sommers joyfully stated.

"Sommers-- "

"I know; I know. Just hang on a second. I'm taking you out of here. Celia and Kevin are up on the ridge."

He untied her limp hands and legs. She hugged him tightly, as if she would never let him go. "Did he hurt you?"

"Not really. Where's Ramon? You said Celia and Kevin... "

In that flash moment, Sommers hadn't thought about having to explain where Ramon... or rather, how Ramon wasn't there. His chest tightened, squeezed his being. He didn't have the words then and he sullenly admitted to himself he might never have them.

Looking into her eyes, the ones that only wanted reassurance, he lied. "Ramon's up there... helping with the others."

Sommers didn't analyze it, or think about it again. He had to provide the impetus of propelling them up and out of that camp. He was the captain, and in battle, captains have to make battlefield decisions. "Are you sure you're okay?" he asked again, taking her mind off Ramon.

"Yes, I think so. The rebel leader is named Enrique. They're hiking out soon-- I think they're moving camp."

"Good. Then he'll leave us alone. You're safe now."

Elena's eyes welled up, the emotion coming to the surface. Sommers gently lifted and kissed her. He didn't know why, and didn't want to. "I'm glad you're here. Come on. We have to get back."

"Wait, look through there," she said, nodding toward an opening in the brush.

Sommers carefully crawled forward, parting branches, seeing something that just couldn't be there--

Sitting on wood scaffolding was a thirty foot, semi-submersible submarine being built. Made from fiberglass and carbon fiber, the craft seemed so out of place, yet perfectly placed for what its intent was: smuggle drugs to the United States.

Somers returned to Elena. "Makes sense now. The gold, drugs, this."

"I have heard stories, seen the news about them."

"Not our problem. Let's go."

Moving toward the ridge, he caught the lifeless image of Robbie hanging on the post. He was unconscious, the ominous necklace of tires waiting for ignition, probably set for tonight's entertainment.

It was eerily silent, vacuous, and his doctor brain engaged regarding Robbie and saving lives. Saving the world. But with Elena grasping onto him with both hands, relying on him, he squelched those puritan thoughts. No, he shoved them out of his mind and began trudging through the jungle brush, encouraging Elena up the ridge path.

# 63

## UNFINISHED BUSINESS

Celia was concerned and waited for Sommers, as close as possible to the top of the descending ridge path. She didn't understand it, but there was something comforting about seeing Sommers bringing up Elena. When she saw him, it gave her hope, a feeling of, *hey, we might make it after all.*

Anxious, and assisting them the last few steps to safety, she asked Elena if she was all right. Hugging Celia and welling up, she said, "yes," then immediately asked, "Where's Ramon? I want to see him so badly."

Catching Sommers' eyes, Celia realized he hadn't told Elena the devastating news. Then Elena saw their hollow expressions. It took a moment, but it registered, as she glanced back at Sommers, who shared the grief.

"No," Elena began, falling into shock. "Ramon, quit hiding. I know you put them up to this. Come out."

Like an unweaned puppy, Elena eagerly searched the ridge, avoiding the truth, the reality. "Ramon-- "

"Elena--" Sommers began.

Their eyes met. That trust or bond that had been developing was vanquished and anger filled her stare. She then lunged, out of control, at Sommers and began pounding on his chest.

"NO-- it can't be. It can't!"

The relentless blows slowed and she caved in. Sommers and Celia knew a part of her died then, evaporated. All Sommers could do was hold her.

"You said he was with the others. You lied to me."

There were no words, or actions, or knowledge Sommers could

impart to make it better for her. He had lied. To protect her. They were all alone at that moment and nothing could change it. Exhausted, she collapsed at Sommers' feet, dropping to her knees.

"I'm sorry, Elena. Ramon didn't make it out of the well. He didn't make it."

Celia kneeled, holding her. "I'm so sorry, Elena-- we'll help you through this." She felt her words did nothing, but it was all she had. She was mad at Sommers for not telling Elena, but wondered if she would have done the same. She didn't know.

Elena cried uncontrollably, the full effect hitting her. Sommers huddled with them and was lost. Even though he'd saved her, he felt beaten. Guilty. He was tired, didn't want to be there and knew their journey wasn't over. They weren't safe yet.

In the angst and frustration, Sommers glanced around and saw Kevin retching by a tree. He was flooded with the realization that for Kevin not to be right there with them, he must be severely ill, in pain, or both. He slowly stood, not wanting to disturb Elena.

"I'm sorry again, Elena."

He kissed her on the head and went to Kevin, who looked pasty, eyes glassy. "Good job, Sommers. Getting Elena. Can we go home now?"

Sommers examined Kevin's shoulder and he winced in pain. Celia appeared. "He seems worse," she explained. "He really faltered when you went down there."

"Why do I keep heaving? My whole arm's numb."

"You're in bad shape. Your ribs could have separated... or maybe you tore the shoulder's rotator cuff. There could also be internal damage or you're having some kind of reaction to the boar's blood... dehydration. I honestly don't know, but you need something for the pain." Sommers looked at the camp. "I have to go back down there."

"What are you talking about?" Celia gasped.

"What's left of the medical kit is down there. Somewhere. And that's not all. They're building a submarine for smuggling the drugs, just out of sight."

"That's impossible." Celia's mind raced and she quickly scanned the camp.

"You can't do that," Kevin moaned.

Elena's tear filled eyes pierced Sommers. "There are drugs in Vera Cruz."

"It's too far away. Without something now, he's going to have a tough time. He might not make it."

They were hushed; another crossroads.

"I guess if I was a horse--" Kevin started.

"Right. We'd shoot you."

"It's not worth it, Sommers. I can make it-- I really don't like shots anyway."

Sommers admired Kevin's candor and gallows humor... until he began dry heaving again. He stared at the camp with a grim determination. "My reasoning is this. Let's say we take off and Kevin worsens. We'll be forced to stop, we'll be stuck and they'll be on us on like black on night."

"If they come after us. Why would they do that?" Celia reasoned. "We don't have anything they want anymore."

"I don't know, but if Kevin has something for pain, we can move faster."

"But we will lose the head start of leaving now," Elena exclaimed. "The advantage-- "

"I thought of that too. I want you three to take off now. Use the time and I'll catch you. Start for the ocean."

"Sommers-- "

"I'll catch you. I promise. Elena, did you see anything in the camp... anything that would help me?"

"They were packing. There could be some supplies in the bigger tent. I don't know. Many of the men left. Please come with us."

He saw she was trembling. It was just them, and the angry jungle was snickering. "Go. It's quiet as a church down there."

"It won't be if you're caught," Celia reluctantly volunteered. If there really is a drug sub down there, this is a huge operation.

"If I'm caught, it won't matter."

About to start away, Elena took Sommers' arm. "It will to us." A tear rolled down her cheek and he hugged her. He winked at Celia. "You can do this. Go." He started back down the ridge.

# 64

## BIG DOG BARKS

Elena's eyes kept flashing into Sommers' mind. They were certainly a pleasant image and one that kept him distracted. Unfortunately, the ridge and gravel-laden steep slope, returned him to reality.

Again, he had trouble balancing and keeping quiet. He slid down most of the grade, grasping at outcroppings and loose rocks in a futile effort. It wasn't easier this time and he felt he was being expelled down a ransom chute into Hell.

At the bottom, he caught his breath and at least was familiar with the perimeter. At the far end, one of Enrique's men appeared and milled about, but Sommers reasoned he was too far away to do anything. At least for the moment.

Sommers stealthily proceeded along the edge, staying low. His back hurt and he wondered if it was from the hiking or the biking. He made a mental note to have it looked at when he returned home. Then he chuckled. He couldn't even turn off his brain when his life was at stake.

Burying those inane thoughts, he spotted the large tent and approached silently. All army issue, he surmised. They were well supplied.

Taking a quick look and not seeing anyone, he gauged the distance, crossed into the open for just a moment, then dove inside the tent.

The sunlight illuminated the interior in a kind of yellow hue. It must have been ten or fifteen degrees warmer inside and smelled like the camping section of a sporting goods store. The tent was new, probably stolen, he thought.

Cots lined the walls, but it was empty of supplies. Either they had already been taken or never existed. Then a cloud of doubt enveloped Sommers. Maybe he had bitten off too big a bite this time. Maybe he should have stayed on the beginner trail and not tried for the double black diamond runs.

A time flashed from years earlier when he'd been stranded in some back powder bowl at Mammoth for about four hours. The worst part wasn't being alone or risking the Ski Patrol might not find him. No, it was peeing in his pants about two hours in and having it freeze. Frozen urine in twenty degrees, trapped at a ski resort. *Would he trade that for this if he could...?*

Knowing his options were limited, he peeked outside. The man wasn't around and he didn't know if that was good or bad. There were too many variables without information. *What now...? Well, logic dictated you go to the source.*

Angry and frustrated, his alternatives funneled to one. Robbie. That was a last resort. More variables, combined with the exposure of open running space. Robbie and the exposure.

Sommers' focus led him to another tent... *maybe there*. Then the voice startled him. "Sommers-- " he heard Robbie mutter, almost inaudible, yet distinct.

Looking around the tent flap, into the heart of the camp, the lifeless Robbie moved. Sommers knew they had done a number on him, then abandoned him. The tires though, that was salt in an evil, oozing wound. "Sommers, help me."

The oath flashed. The one that was suffocating him from a thousand miles away and squeezing his ethics less than twenty feet away. The hypocrites and hypocrats. Sommers, the juggler.

He took a bead on the open space, which would put him in the middle of camp. The real question was what was behind the other tents. That he didn't know. He wasn't hearing anything and figured you would hear something before actually seeing it. *Doesn't it work that way... in the jungle? What's the oath say about that? Is it in the abridged version?*

Sommers made up his mind, sprung from the tent and lunged across the open area. There was also a reference in his mind about dealing with the demons you know, versus the ones you don't. *You know them.*

To him, it felt like he only took two steps. The oath. He saw Elena's eyes.

# 65

## SIMPLE PLAN

They watched in dismay, as Sommers handily skirted across the camp. Celia thought it a couple of steps as well. "What's he doing?!" Kevin asked, propped on his knees.

"He's got a plan and we have to rely on that," Celia proffered. "He told us to get moving, so let's go. Can you help me, Elena?"

The two supported Kevin and they headed off the ridge, into the jungle. With Kevin balanced, they both looked back one last time and hoped against hope that Sommers' plan worked.

# 66

## NECKLACE

Sommers arrived at Robbie. Landing and hiding behind the post, he scanned the camp again, but he was safe. There was that instant, where he felt he must be doing something right... *just don't get greedy. Greed... isn't that what got them there?*

He raised his head above the top tire at Robbie's shoulders. "Hey, idiot-- where are the supplies? Which tent?"

"Sommers... you got out! You've got to help me-- this guy will kill me," Robbie breathed.

"I like him already. Which tent?"

"Okay, okay... please don't leave me-- just don't leave. I don't want to die here."

"You forgot. We're here because of you! You owe us. Now where's our stuff, so I can get back to help the others?!"

Robbie squirmed, now fully conscious and aware his pass was three feet away. His mind writhed at the possibilities and fleeting opportunity. "Sommers... if you don't take me, I'll yell and none of us will get out."

"You know you never surprise me. But guess what? I'll shoot you. How do you like that?"

Sommers produced his pistol and pointed the blue gray barrel at Robbie, whose eyes were faltering... end of the bluffing line. "I-- I'm sorry. Just take me with you and do whatever you want. Turn me in. I don't care anymore. I'll help you,... whatever."

Sommers turned it up a notch, pushing the gun into Robbie's cheek. "You're forgetting I have nothing to lose either. I'm tired of it, Robbie. That's why I sent them on ahead."

"You think I like what I did?! Give me a break."

"It's just you, me and the Mexican. If I took you two out, the world would be a much better place. Don't you think-- ?"

Robbie's trembling turned to shaking. Sommers' eyes weren't lying. He'd turned the corner, gone around the bend. The bluff was real.

"Sommers... I owe a ton of money back in the states, all right? I'm totally done there. Those coins... they, they would get me straight, even... give me my life back. Do you know what that would be like?"

Being even, what a concept. The lowest common denominator of a capitalistic economy. Even. You come in, you leave. Even. *But saving a life... or not saving one. And the consequences. The Hippocrates...*

Robbie faced Sommers, tears in both eyes. The blubbering Big Dog was beaten. "Please-- "

*Even...* Sommers lowered the gun. "One mistake... and I will kill you. Do you understand me?"

"Yes. Thank you. Honest to God, thank you."

"Okay, I'm going to loosen the ropes and help you out of the tires."

Sommers slashed Robbie's leg ties and was about to remove them when a noise beyond the tents startled them. "Sit tight, Robbie. Not a word." Sommers scurried near a tent behind the tires, making himself one with the fabric.

Enrique's man sauntered near the middle of camp and Robbie's pole. This time, however, he was drinking tequila and carried a polished .44 magnum. The tequila had taken effect.

Putting down the bottle, he handled the gun, balancing it and playing with it. He spun the bullet chambers and the lubed Smith & Wesson steel clicked in staccato rhythm. He then opened the chamber, loaded two bullets and spun again.

Sneering with alcohol fueled indifference, he put the barrel on the bridge of Robbie's nose, mumbled something in Spanish and pulled the trigger. Click.

This was the funniest thing to the man and he spun around laughing, gun flailing. More tequila and back to the nose.

"Please," Robbie begged. "Don't do it." Click.

Sommers heard the hollow sound, knowing the torment was real and permanent.

Again, the tequila, but this time the pistol went inside Robbie's mouth with the man crouching, wobbling. Peering downward, Robbie saw the bullet, next to the chamber fill. *Which way did it rotate? Clockwise...?!*

Sommers saw Robbie's pants darkening with liquid. It took him a moment to realize Robbie peed on himself.

Click.

Whatever humor existed in the warped moment, it was over. The man, seemingly bored, patted Robbie on the head, grabbed up the tequila bottle, and drunkenly meandered inside the big tent.

Sommers scampered over on all fours, watching. "Nice people. Hope he's a sound sleeper."

"He was going to kill me. He could have killed me," Robbie whimpered.

"I wouldn't try it at home. Get it together, Robbie. Take me to the supplies."

"Enrique's tent is over there."

Sommers carefully removed the tires and moved Robbie out. They put the tires back, so if someone was at a distance, they might think Robbie was still bound.

They were in the open, but it was still quiet. "It looks about forty or fifty feet to Enrique's tent. Can you get over there when I give the word? Can you?"

"Yeah... Yeah."

"Do not mess this up." Sommers reminded him with the pistol. "Roll out. I'm right behind you."

Robbie scrambled from all fours to rubbery legs. He waddled awkwardly with Sommers pushing. Crossing the area this time felt like an eternity to Sommers, with him consciously taking huge steps. The distance seemed to grow and the tent seemed farther.

They manhandled their way inside and dropped to the ground, always wondering if they'd been heard or seen. This tent was different, much smaller, but full of supplies. Sommers reckoned Enrique didn't trust anyone.

"If they see I'm gone, we're dead. The Mexican, Enrique... he's nuts," Robbie blurted. "He's building a submarine out there."

Sommers was barely half-listening. Time was short, but now he had purpose. Somehow, he concluded they had a chance.

"Start looking! We need the medical kit and whatever else we can use."

Sommers searched, keeping an eye and the gun on Robbie. He knew Robbie was winded, but also desperate. He wasn't coming this far for a surprise. "Grab food packets, maps-- anything."

Robbie moved to a tarp and uncovered supplies, their fanny packs. He quickly strapped on two and handed a couple to Sommers. They kept searching, finding batteries, food and different supplies.

Sommers found bullets and saw the wrapped packages of heroin. Underneath one was the medical kit with the Bike Tour's logo. Opening it, Sommers discovered it had been ravaged. "No! They took everything. Can't we catch a break?!"

Dropping it, his eyes rested on a bag of heroin. He gingerly touched it, thinking.

"Thought you weren't into that," Robbie harassed.

"I'm not. Okay, here's the drill. We're going out together, then around the tent and up the ridge."

"Okay, okay."

Sommers stood and stuffed food packets into his shirt, along with the gun. Securing the fanny packs, he grabbed canteens and looked outside. Grabbing Robbie's collar, he nudged him outside and they cautiously left.

Crouching, they crossed over to the edge of the tent. Sommers took one last look. "Now. Move-- Big Dog!"

Running between the tents, Sommers led Robbie to the perimeter, ambled along the edge and up the steep incline. They ran hard, not thinking, just moving. Final shot. Endgame.

At the top, Sommers had a fleeting thought Celia might have stayed, more for moral support than anything else. She was gone.

It really was just them and whatever the jungle and fate had in mind.

Navigating the trail they were on earlier, Sommers questioned if it was the correct one. Was it the one Celia took? How long did she stay on it and how far ahead were they? Too many questions, too much adrenaline and Robbie.

Lounging at the resort, biking at Malibu or just taking a long drive. Anything sounded better than their repetitive footsteps through the brush and the constant breathing, running for their lives.

*Even.*

# *67*

## PALE RIDERS

Celia had found a rhythm. The terrain had leveled and she and Elena had seemed to find a pace to help Kevin and obtain quick mileage. She knew that every step, every second counted.

Sommers crossed her mind, but realized she had to let that go. He had devised a plan, been down there once... *he was smart, tougher than she first thought.* Still, she wished he was there. When he was around events fell into place easier. He cut to the chase, summed up things. Celia opined he would have made a good attorney, if not a doctor.

A doctor... she had nearly forgotten about the irregularity discovered inside her breast... her body. The fight to obliterate it, capture her life back. The battle had consumed almost a year of her life, but she had beaten it. To lose now would be a wicked irony.

But she knew to concentrate on that now was more than even her uniquely trained skill set could handle. She needed to focus on something outside herself... to help someone with her knowledge.

Sommers... Sommers was in legal trouble. Not knowing all the details, Celia felt he had a fairly strong case. She knew of legal precedents where a physician had won, or at least settled amicably with the practitioner, saving face and career. It happened every day, but she surmised something festered deeper with Sommers. It was personal, and in the legal world, that was often a fatal mistake.

She pinned him as an idealist, someone who shouldn't have to pay a price for just doing the job. Of course he wanted to fight, that obviously was his nature. But to be here, in the middle of this mess, Celia found it so ironic. Everyone on the trip was escaping for a few days and now they were running for their lives. She could see the ads: Bike Trips in Mexico, The Ultimate Escape.

"I have to rest," Kevin blurted, faltering between her and Elena. "I don't think I can make it."

"Kevin, we're doing great. Come on now."

"No, really. You two should go. If you made it, you could bring back help, you know."

He lay against a boulder, breathing hard, sweating. He was pasty now, clammy. Elena gave him some water and he drooled.

Celia looked back up the trail. Nothing appeared out of place, just them. "I want to check something. I'll be right back."

She nodded to Elena and backtracked up the trail. She actually just wanted to be alone for a moment. If she could collect her thoughts, then she could think. Weighing Kevin's proposal was in the forefront of her mind. He was astute about him becoming dead weight. A hindrance. But leaving him…

A sound startled her and she looked harder up the trail. It could have been anything, but something bothered her. Instead of returning to Kevin and Elena, she trudged further. For some reason, she wanted to meet it head on. If it was the Mexicans or Army, so be it.

More sounds, but she stood her ground. The noise became rhythmic, repetitive… footsteps. She aimed the rifle, searching and waiting. The safety came off. *So be it…*

Sommers burst through the jungle trail, a wide-eyed, adrenaline rush. He was sweating, out of breath, looking like he had just run a four minute mile. Robbie was a few steps behind, looking worse. Her first thoughts were about Robbie. She didn't loosen the grip on the gun. "You brought him?" were her first words.

"Nice to see you too," Robbie retorted, ever the smart mouth.

Sommers smiled, very glad to see Celia. A friendly face. "We can use him to help with Kevin."

He handed Celia a canteen and she gulped the water, then led them down the trail. "Kevin's worse, especially since we started walking. Did they see you? How many?"

"Believe me, they're going to miss us," Robbie boasted defiantly, sounding almost happy at the prospect.

"Shut up, Robbie. Whose side are you on?" Sommers shoved him. "I don't think they did, Celia. Let's just keep moving."

*Sommers, the stalwart,* Celia thought. She almost smiled.

# *68*

## TREASURE LOST

Enrique had been very close to the camp, but away from the tents. He was working on a vehicle and hauling water from a nearby stream. Focusing on the intricacies of an American made motor passed the time quickly. Exasperated at not being able to start the V-6, his attention turned to what waited for him at camp. Elena.

Rinsing his neck and washing his hands, he made his way across the stream into camp. Almost immediately he sensed something was amiss. A pit hit his stomach and adrenaline rushed. He started running. Even from a distance, he saw Robbie was gone. And if he wasn't there…

Stopping where Elena had been, he cursed and kicked the ground. There was just grass now, a narrowly flattened imprint of where her young body once was.

Returning back to basics and squelching his adrenal rush, he stormed inside his tent, seeing it devastated and cherry picked. A sly grin formed. *Quid Pro Quo,* he thought.

He rifled through the remains, frustrated. Shoving gear aside, he bolted for the large tent, priming his gun along the way. Stopping at the entrance, he took a breath and entered.

# 69

## THE APOTHECARY

Sommers and Robbie hurried along the trail behind Celia. Reaching Elena and Kevin, they found him keeled over, retching again. Elena paused at seeing Robbie and stepped closer to Sommers, as he went to Kevin.

"Any ideas, Doc?" Kevin asked, saliva trickling down his chin.

Sommers examined Kevin's eyes, holding open one of the lids. Resolute, he then ripped open the bag of heroin.

"What are you doing?" Celia asked for all of them.

"With the pain he's in, he's not going to be able to move."

"How could that possibly help him?"

Valid questions all, but Sommers wasn't in the mood. He was in his doctor mode. "It's not my first choice, but the heroin's better than nothing."

Celia kneeled next to them. "This isn't right. You don't know anything about it-- the quality, what it could be laced with. It could kill him."

Kevin looked up, almost alert. "Not from a small amount... right, Sommers?"

"There's a risk, Pal, but we're out of options. Robbie, you said this stuff was good. Did you mean it?"

Robbie towered over them. Everyone's eyes searched him. "Yeah, I guess so. It's not drain cleaner, if that's what you mean."

Sommers pinched a small amount of the powder on a leaf and raised it up to Kevin's face. "I want you to inhale this."

Kevin grinned. "The grand morass."

"It's either going to feel like Heaven or Hell, maybe both."

"Nothing can be worse than this, Sommers."

Kevin faithfully snorted the powder, inhaling it all into his lungs. He sat back, then they all heard the crack of a gunshot in the distance, toward the direction of Enrique's camp. "And then there were none," Kevin gleefully exclaimed, happy at the effect.

"They know now," Sommers offered, standing. "They'll leave us alone. We don't have anything he wants. One bag of dope isn't anything."

"It is on the streets," Robbie gloated.

Before Sommers could respond, Kevin wretched again. Sommers hoped he'd done the right thing; that the drug would work.

# *70*

# GHOSTS

The rest of the day, they struggled along the trail, alternating the shouldering of Kevin. With the numbing from the heroin, he was able to function, move more easily. Still, Sommers was impatient and knew the implications of what was behind them. Seeing the harshness of it firsthand, he kept a sharp eye on their backs, wishing the ocean was just over the next rise.

The afternoon passed and the sky clouded in the east. The moisture, Sommers thought. *More rain... another curve ball.* He didn't verbalize anything, hoped the others wouldn't notice and stay focused on hiking. It didn't take a medical degree to know they were caught between the proverbial rock and hard place, with the weather threatening them and who knew what else.

Toward the end of the day, the rag-tag group topped a small hill. Stretched in front of them was something they would never forget or had planned for. In the eerie stillness, hundreds of graves stood before them in the center of ruins at an ancient village.

Standing structures, buildings and solid foundations littered the grounds before them. The graves were placed in rows, neatly laid out with equal spacings. A creek ran down the east side and the west was protected by hills.

What struck Sommers first was the feeling of abandonment. At a moment in time, this place thrived. It hadn't been built overnight by one person. No, it took hundreds of years to design and construct, possibly centuries, yet it was empty now, a ghost town. *Had they been taken over? Did some disease infest and wipe out everyone? Did the Shamans or elders believe it unholy?*

Sommers had no clue, but it bothered him. *Why did they quit and leave..?*

"That's fitting," Celia volunteered. "Look where we are."

"Every village had a cemetery. They buried their dead, believing their spirits would stay behind to help the living," Elena explained.

"Isn't there anything else in this country besides ruins and jungle?" Robbie asked, plopping on a boulder.

"I think it's what we paid for," Kevin retorted. "What do you want, a Seven-Eleven?"

"A pack of cigarettes would be nice. Menthols."

The wind came up, blowing in their hair and faces. It was that humid, balmy breeze found in the tropics. "I guess they're greeting us, checking us out," Sommers exclaimed.

"Afraid of ghosts, Sommers?" Robbie blatantly asked.

"No, but you should be."

Sommers glared at him and Robbie understood the subtext. He felt if pushed, Sommers might actually kill him. He was wound that tightly. Allaying the tension, Robbie suggested, "Why don't we find some cover in a structure? Make something to eat."

Robbie walked ahead, away from the group. They watched, not happy. "Why did you bring him, Sommers?" Celia probed.

"I thought he could help with Kevin-- "

"Yeah, but-- "

"Look, this Enrique guy would have killed him, especially after we took Elena. I know Robbie's a royal jerk, but I couldn't leave him. It doesn't mean I like him or the situation."

"You did good, Sommers," Kevin offered. "Let's just stay the course."

"You sound like my attorney," Sommers said, walking through graves, into the ruins.

# 71

## MAPS

The late afternoon brought the wind and spitting rain. The group, huddled reluctantly in a rock structure, lit a small fire and used flashlights. They weighted down the map with chipped mortar and studied where they thought they were. It was a big, angry place, as the duration and tedium was catching up with them.

The vacation was over long ago and they needed a break, along with any piece of good news that would instill some kind of hope that a positive end was near. They would have to wait longer.

Sommers traced their route as well as he could. The wind whistled and dust blew aimlessly across the paper. If he'd had his way, he would have bundled it up and thrown it away.

He looked at the folded document, their lifeline of the moment, from a number of angles. He kept running his fingers down a marked line, calculating it to some kind of scale. No matter what he did, what numbers he ran, they were still a long way from where they needed to be and they were on foot.

"If this is right, Sommers," Celia began. "Then we're at least two days from the coast village."

"Two days?" Kevin barked. "Might as well be two years."

"That's on bikes," Sommers stoically reminded. With a marking pen, he suddenly drew a line down the middle, through uncharted territory.

"You know I'm not going to make it," Kevin confessed.

"Don't say that. Straight through is half the distance."

Elena studied his route, tracing her finger across the topography. "Yes, but your route would take us through the 'Valle De Las Almas Perdidas.'"

"Hey, speak English, will you," Robbie ordered.

217

"It means 'valley of the lost souls.' The cemetery and ruins must be the entrance."

"I don't see the problem," Sommers exclaimed. "Sounds like it suits us. Especially if it saves time."

"Wouldn't it be safer to stay on the main route? Where the tour was going?" Celia asked.

Elena held up the map. "There are no marked trails in this area. It would be very easy to become lost. I've heard stories about this place. We need Ramon-- " Tears formed on her face.

They all examined the map. It contained configurations, routes, trails... all drawn by Ramon. The area that Sommers had drawn through contained nothing, just empty space, blank mileage.

"She's right," Celia said. "Who knows what's out there? What if we get halfway and find a swamp or-- "

"I've said all along, I don't have the answers, all right? But I see a shortcut and it looks pretty good. We need to get out of here." Looking again at the map, a level of concern gripped them. "I say we camp here and get a good start tomorrow. We'll each take a watch with the fire inside. Robbie can stay outside."

"Hey, what's that supposed to mean?" Robbie asked, agitated.

"It means we don't want any hassles, and if they are chasing us, they'll get you first."

Nobody argued and Sommers' plan was accepted. They tended to Kevin, making him comfortable. Sommers measured out another portion of heroin for him. Sharing food packets, they stoked the small fire, which was hidden from the outside. It was nightfall and the ruins went to sleep, as they had done for hundreds of years.

Celia drew the first shift. Sommers gave her the handgun and instructed her to wake them if anything caught her eye. She told him to lighten up and get some rest. They needed their leader in top shape.

Celia sat near the entrance, a few yards away from the bundled Robbie. The night was clear, quiet, fairly warm and time passed quickly under the moonlight. To her, it was almost pleasant.

Inside, Sommers did sleep, drifting off almost immediately, near Elena and the medicated Kevin. The fire crackled and the burning wood, and gentle popping embers carried Sommers to a different place.

He was floating in space above their camp. He could see Celia and Robbie and the gentle glow of the fire. They were protected. Without notice, he was walking through the ruins, around the ancient structures.

He inhaled deeply, smelling the ocean, but not seeing it. He trekked further, up a rise where he knew the ocean had to be, but it wasn't. It was just flatlands, the plains, thick with brush. The saltwater air permeated his nostrils and the ocean had to be close. He guessed it was hiding.

Sommers scanned harder, but it was a futile effort. Frustrated, he sat on a bike, a shiny new one, and eased his shoulders over the handlebars. He was tired. Ramon was next to him, also on a bike.

"I see you brought the traitor," Ramon stated, lighting a cigarette.

"I'm a Doctor. I couldn't leave him there."

"I could have... would have."

Sommers now smelled the cigarette, its smoke wafting toward him. Tobacco and salt air. "I came up with a plan."

"Yes, through the valley."

"Is it a good one? Do you think that's the best route?"

"I don't know, Sommers. That will be up to you and the gods. The others, they're depending on you now. Do not trust the traitor. He left us for dead once. A leopard's spots, you know?"

Sommers couldn't see Ramon's face. He saw his bike glimmer in the moonlight and the outline of a frame and figure, but no face. "Something's been bothering me."

"Your conscience probably. A big guilt trip. Do not let it trouble you."

"Would you have still gone for the coins?"

Ramon laughed, smoked his cigarette. "Of course, just maybe not so hastily."

Sommers was about to grin, enjoy the moment, but a breeze blew in his face. He looked for Ramon, but he wasn't there. Neither were the bikes. The wind blew harder.

Startled, Sommers began running down the hill for the camp, but he was back in the jungle, swatting brush, skipping fallen trees. He stopped. He pushed with all his might, running, but his feet wouldn't move. They were stuck. Tugging at his knees to lift them did no good. Dead weight.

From the night sky, a spotlight's beam encircled him. Trying to focus through the haze, he glanced upward. In the trees, he saw the bullet riddled, hanging bodies of the group. Sommers gasped for air, falling backward. Celia, Kevin, Ramon, Elena and Robbie, grotesquely dangled at rope's end. But he didn't see himself. He couldn't breathe. His bodily functions stopped.

Then he felt a presence.

"Gringo--" Sommers heard that chilling voice and was looking down the barrel of Enrique's gun. "You're next-- "

About to yell, a blinding flash of light filled Sommers' eyes, then blackness.

Sommers abruptly awakened to Celia bending over him. "Sommers, Sommers... wake up."

He bolted upright, heaving, his eyes adjusting to her shadowy face. "I had to wake you. You were dreaming."

Sommers caught his breath, clung to her, as he stood.

"You're shaking."

"Good. I'm alive. Nightmare."

"You're okay. It's time for your watch. Robbie's out. He snores loudly."

Sommers nodded, shaking off the sleep, trepidation. "You didn't hear anything or anyone?"

"No. In fact if we weren't in this mess, this is the way I would picture the nights. I almost enjoyed it."

"Right." She handed him the gun and he left the structure, glancing up at the ridge. Celia was right. The night was quiet and peaceful. A billion stars could be seen. He didn't smell the ocean or expect to see Ramon, but he would heed the warning. He cautiously looked at Robbie, then into the jungle.

There were no trees or hanging bodies, but he didn't like any of it and stayed awake the rest of the night.

# 72

## VALLEY OF THE LOST SOULS

Dawn came quickly and Sommers awakened everyone at first light. Robbie was the last to rise, complaining. "I can't believe you made me sleep out here," he bitterly exclaimed. "I was a pin cushion for every bug there is."

"Be thankful they're not bullet holes," Celia admonished.

Kevin made his way into the sunlight, looking pale. He was sore and distraught. "I was thinking last night," he began. "This is a perfect spot to leave me."

"What are you talking about?" Sommers asked.

"Go bring help. There's shelter… I could make it. Leave me some food and water."

"We're going. We agreed last night. We can't stay here. We are not leaving you."

"Why not?"

"We just can't," a hint of desperation leaking out in Sommers' voice. He knew he needed to furnish a better, stronger answer, but he wasn't going to share his dream. They didn't need that.

"You think they're after us, don't you?" Elena asked.

"I didn't say that."

"But it's what you're thinking," Celia confirmed.

"Yes. I don't think we have any time to lose. Going off trail will buy us some. We'll find our way. We've come this far."

Robbie grinned. "So if we die, we can blame it on Sommers. I like that."

"Shut up," Kevin sneered. "What about me?"

"We'll dope you up and take turns being your crutch. This isn't the time to split up."

"It's a mistake," Kevin argued.

"It is what it is."

They listened to Sommers and he organized what gear they had. He gave Kevin some more powder and it began to work. The main thing on his mind was putting distance behind them.

They hiked out of the ruins and slipped off the trail into the "Valley Of The Lost Souls." The terrain changed almost immediately.

Granite bedrock protruded everywhere in large mounds that had chipped and weathered ungracefully forever. It was hilly, and even if they had kept the bikes, it would have made for difficult, if not impossible riding. Sommers could see why it wasn't trail mapped. No one would want to come here, let alone vacation.

He kept a good, forthright pace, every so often checking behind them. He knew Enrique was out there, he could feel it, but he wasn't going to tell the others. *What good would it do?* he thought. *Let them think what they want. Just keep them moving.*

The dream had spooked him. It was just a dream, but the more he thought about it, churned it over and over in his head, the more real it seemed. After what he'd seen Enrique do at the helicopter and the rebel campsite, he could imagine them all hanging in the jungle.

If pushed, he felt they wouldn't have a chance. The reason was simple hesitation. Enrique, a professional soldier, wouldn't hesitate to kill. Everyone in the group, probably including Robbie, would. Simple psychographic background of just growing up in America. The simplicity chilled him, and he wanted out.

*Keep moving,* the little voice echoed. *Keep moving.*

# 73

## DEATH LEADS

The problem wasn't Sommers or his motivations. It was a matter of who was in the best shape. As the day wore on and the sun burned off the humidity, the others, Kevin in particular, couldn't keep up. They waded through a lot of water, but the territory and jungle were merciless.

Sommers tried to ignore their complaints, play down their anguish, but it took its toll. His main concern wasn't so much their physical well being, as it was their state of mind. If their spirits sank deeper... well, he didn't want to think of that. He felt they were the hunted, that it was all engulfing them. They were on the back of the tongue and that was a bad place.

He kept medicating Kevin, in small doses, as their speed and rhythm boiled down to him being able to walk. He was stoned, but to a large degree, pain free. Ambulatory as he may be, his stupefied demeanor became a greater liability.

Passing through another cemetery and some foundations, Kevin fell hard against some rocks. He took down Sommers and Robbie, but it wasn't their fault. He just went down. Everyone was tired, hot, and no one wanted the responsibility.

"Whoa-- " Kevin laughed. "OOPS, I fell."

They all rallied to help. "Are you guys okay?" Celia asked.

"Come on, Sommers, he's high as a kite and just dead weight," Robbie yelled, angrily standing, wiping himself off.

Kevin bled from his head. "We have to let him rest. Look at him," Elena pleaded.

Behind the blood, Kevin was weakening.  His breathing was labored and he was pasty white.

"Can't," Sommers said defiantly. "Just give Kevin some water. Keep going."

Sommers snapped his head back, looked skyward. Out of earshot, a commercial jet flew high overhead. They all gazed at the white, silent vapor trail and wished they were on that plane. A free bird escaping.

"It's headed north," Celia said, shading her eyes, absorbing the view. "Probably a Dreamliner."

"Sign me up," Kevin yelled. "First class, cold champagne."

The mood lightened. Even though it was just a shimmering projectile, five miles up in the sky, people were safely cocooned in the fuselage. A fleeting piece of the real world. Their civilization. Back home.

"Probably to Houston-- " Sommers began, but didn't finish, as Robbie's fist blindsided him.

Sommers toppled, his mind reacting not to the situation, but to swimming gravity. His synapses connected and he felt the grip of the gun he was holding slip away. The impact, pistol... Robbie... the world swirled in a rainbow prism.

For his size, Sommers had always known Robbie was quick, but Celia gamely scrambled for the weapon on the ground. She slid her fingers on top, but *Big Dog* was too fast.

They wrestled a moment and the gun fired in Sommers' direction. He fell backward.

*The anti-Christ-overweight-sea-lion* shoved the attorney into the dirt and Robbie controlled the gun. And the power.

"All right," he maniacally exclaimed. "Showtime. About time."

"You shot, Sommers!" Elena screeched.

"Take it easy, Robbie," Celia asserted, catching her breath on all fours.

"No more orders. That goes for you and the Doc. Is he dead?"

Sommers had difficulty standing and Elena helped him. His biceps was bleeding. "It went through."

"Robbie, what are you doing?" Elena screamed.

"Sommers saved your rancid life," yelled Celia.

Robbie pivoted, riveting the gun on Celia, his animosity for her peaked. He leveled the barrel and whispered, "Bang... "

His laugh echoed, a sick release of sorts. "Bang, bang, bang. Go ahead.  Clean up, Sommers." He looked at Kevin, then walked over and cocked the gun. "We're leaving the baggage and getting out of here. Pronto. I've had it with you people."

"What are you trying to prove, Robbie?" Sommers asked, tearing off his sleeve to make a tourniquet. "What's the point of this?"

"Why? Because you're going to turn me in for Ramon's death. Put the blame on me. Do you think I'm stupid? Plus, I owe lots of money to some very unfriendly people in the hinterland. They care about me just a little less than you do."

"There's been enough killing!" Celia argued. "Ramon wasn't your fault. The place was booby trapped. Who knew that?"

Kevin sobered and he was angry. "Is money all you want? How much? I'll give you whatever you want!"

"Oh that's real easy for you."

"You're right. It is. What-- fifty thousand? A hundred-- what?!"

Robbie hesitated, thinking. "You're just saying that to save yourself. What kind of life do you have... do you have any idea what mine is?"

Kevin took off his watch and tossed it to Robbie. "Here-- if you can read. It's a Rolex.  Gold.  Twelve grand easy. On Ebay. I'll send you the box and papers when we get back."

Robbie studied the gold timepiece. The clear, sapphire crystal showed off perfect time and date. "Right-- you'll have me busted so fast-- "

"Take the stupid watch. It's nothing! It doesn't matter!  Here, take this too." Kevin retrieved a wad of cash and threw it at Robbie.  The bills fluttered around him. A little ocean of Ben Franklins.

Sommers moved to Robbie and he pointed the gun again. "Take the money and put the gun down. Killing Kevin or me won't solve anything."

Robbie was an island and its king with the gun in his hand, the money at his feet and the watch. His eyes began watering and he started trembling. "I... I had to leave Chicago, all right? I'm a dead man at home... following me everywhere, watching me... I don't know what happened. I'm in debt up to my eyes-- gambled it all away on spreads and points, cards-- !"

He faltered a bit, weakened. His admission was as painful on the group, as it was to him. They didn't like Robbie, who would, but they didn't want the reasons, or for the harder ones, the excuses.

Robbie glanced at them, knowing they knew his demons now. Elena held the bleeding Sommers and Celia aided the broken Kevin. He knew he was the source of their trouble. He was at the core of their terrible, finite world.

"Robbie," Kevin whispered. "Come on. Give me the gun."

His hands shaking, Robbie slowly lowered the weapon. He started crying, losing his breath the way children do, when they know they've been caught, accused and tried. Seeing the group, his group, penetrated him. He was tired too. "I'm sorry. I didn't mean for any of this to... Elena, I'm so sorry about Ramon. None of this was supposed to happen... I didn't mean to hurt-- "

A bullet hit Robbie, spinning him around. Wide-eyed, he fell backward, tripping, then landing on a grave marker. His fat body belched, then breathed its last breath. The group stood stunned.

Enrique appeared in front of them. Kevin, fumbling with the pistol, pulled the trigger, only to a hear a numbing, empty 'click.' He pulled again and again, and the gun finally fired, ripping into Enrique's torso, knocking him down.

Sommers lunged for Enrique and kicked his gun away. The wounded rebel sat up, surprised. "And how is everyone?"

Celia ran to the fallen Robbie, checked for a pulse. He was dead and she held up her bloodied hands as proof. "You killed him," she yelled. "You killed him. You're insane!"

"Certifiable." Enrique bled from his upper body. He yanked off his neck kerchief and shoved it on the wound. Sommers regrouped, training the gun on Enrique.

226

"Now," Enrique stated, as if he was in control. "Who has the coins?"

"You do. We don't have them," Sommers voiced.

Enrique smiled, adjusting the bloody kerchief. "That's where the road forks, my friends. They were not in my tent that you so valiantly violated. Maybe your dead, fat friend could assist us. No?"

It dawned on all of them, as they stole a glance at Robbie's corpse. Sommers, keeping an eye on Enrique, reluctantly went to Robbie and lifted up his shirt. Underneath were the two fanny packs, their clip-straps straining in defiance of his girth.

"Open them," Enrique innocently offered. "Open them and find the truth."

Sommers unclasped the packs. Unzipping one, he found supplies, nothing of value. Undoing the second-- the gold coins sparkled. "Robbie-- ."

"I fear greed has reared its ugly head on your vacation."

"Shut up," Sommers barked, realizing all the implications, remembering what Ramon had said. "Just shut up! Celia, help me. We have to get these-- Kevin needs some more-- "

"I don't want any more of that. Just get me out of here."

They began organizing, packing. "What about him?" Elena quietly asked, pointing to Enrique.

"Leave me. I would. Cut your losses now."

"We bring him," Sommers ordered. "And the coins."

"Are you out of your mind?" Celia questioned. "Why?!"

"Because your American consciences are causing you guilt." Enrique laughed.

"Because we don't know how many of his friends are still around. We might have to use him. Collateral."

"You are an idiot... an idiota," Enrique said. "I am worth nothing to anyone."

"He's right," Kevin glumly stated. "He's just more dead weight like me."

"That's fine," Sommers confirmed. "He can tell it all to the authorities in Vera Cruz. The whole story."

Sommers made sure Enrique's hands were bound, then they tended to Robbie. They took his bulky body off the grave marker and laid it out. Unbelievably, he still retained that cocksure facade. It was like he was going to say, "Hey, get me a beer and a pack of Lucky's." But he didn't. Robbie was gone, a victim of maligned circumstance.

"We don't have time to bury him," Sommers surmised.

"There're leaves," Celia pointed out. "We can cover him with that."

Resigned to the task, Sommers and Celia began searching for leaves. Elena didn't move. "I'm not helping," she stated. "He can rot for all I care. He's why we're here and why Ramon--" She dissolved into tears.

They knew it was the truth and didn't question her, allowing her to cry. Sommers quickly gathered a few armfuls of leaves and twigs, which covered Robbie's outline. "The authorities or whoever can do the rest. Let's go."

Without words of prayer or ceremony, they left Robbie and continued on with Enrique under close watch and Kevin in tow. Sommers hoped he'd scaled the map distances correctly, and prayed the ocean was near. His bloody arm throbbed.

# 74

## THE MARAPA

The terrain altered once again to a more lush, tropical environment. They descended from the hills and the high humidity, and dense foliage surrounded them. It was suffocating, endless. Sommers compared it to being inside a rubber glove and it seemed they had to fight for every inch of footing.

Through most of it, Sommers wondered if he'd made the right decision by going off trail. He kept thinking of Celia's comment about the swamp and hoped his next step wasn't into a marshy wasteland or quicksand. *Quicksand? Did that exist down here?* He pictured the headline: "Inept Doctor On Trial, Feared Dead in Mexican Jungle Quagmire."

Any other time he would have laughed, found a sliver of dark humor in the bleak situation. At this moment, however, he was just a few feet away from a known and dangerous killer, and two of his entourage were dead. The whole situation made his head spin and the constant heat wasn't helping.

Celia looked after Kevin, who struggled. Sommers wondered how many other doctors would have done what he did and used the heroin. Maybe the Medical Board was right and he shouldn't be allowed to practice. *Well, you know he administered heroin, at least that's what he thought it was, to a patient in Mexico. Of course the patient survived.* Sommers thought it had to count for something. *Survival first. Rules later.*

They stopped often for water breaks so Kevin could rest. Elena was quiet, probably still in some kind of post shock. She stayed close to Sommers, occasionally holding his hand.

He noticed her affection was more frequent and longer lasting. She clearly didn't have to touch or even come close to him, but she did. Her eyes betrayed the brimming emotion she was trying to conceal. She liked him, trusted him. Sommers didn't mind it either. He knew that in another lifetime... he just wished they could have met under different circumstances, someplace that didn't harbor the baggage of their present predicament.

Enrique moved along silently and it was somewhat surprising at his lack of interest or dialogue. Since they began their trek, he had barely spoken two words and those were just asking for water.

Sommers wondered if perhaps Enrique's gunshot wound had humbled him, or if he had just given in to his fate. Or maybe he was plotting, waiting for a certain moment of weakness to strike.

With such a sinister mind in play, Sommers sensed something happening in Enrique's mind, something deeper, another agenda. That's the last thing Sommers wanted to confront.

A man like Enrique fascinated Sommers in many ways. Here was a character, in the flesh, one usually only gets to read about or see on the news. There was purity, wholeness, and even though it was evil, there was a macabre interest on Sommers' part, wondering how and why a man like Enrique did the things he did.

As the day progressed, the rag-tag group pressed on through parts unknown. Sommers remembered his nightmare and how he was convinced the ocean had to be nearby. All he saw now was thick brush and a dense growth he thought would never end. They swatted bugs, scratched their sweat soaked clothes and stayed the course all because Sommers commanded. He surely didn't want the responsibility, but Ramon in the dream had been right. They were relying on him. It was his show now, his watch.

Arriving at a small clearing, Sommers peered up at the sky and saw more jet vapor trails. What he wouldn't give to be on that flight... a commercial flight with drinks, a processed meal, peanuts and a movie. He fantasized for a moment, watching the white, puffy strip of exhaust fade, until he realized something was different about it this time.

Swigging his canteen and handing it off, he swore he could hear the roaring turbine engines high up and far away. "Hey," he began. "Tell me I'm dreaming, but do you guys hear that?"

They strained and looked skyward, then one by one, the group acknowledged hearing something too.

"It can't be the jets," Kevin scoffed. "No way it's them."

"It's not," Elena said, moving toward the front. "Sommers, come with me."

She motioned and Sommers followed. "Celia, watch him," he ordered, pointing to Enrique and handing her the pistol.

"Done. Be careful."

Elena led Sommers into the thicket. After a few yards, the roaring sound became louder. They parted the vegetation, trekked over some rocks and all at once were at the edge of a hundred foot waterfall. Its thundering cascade fed a wide, rolling river. The view and sound were magnificent.

"Just like the brochures," Sommers spoke loudly, viewing the drop.

"It must be the Marapa. We're going to have to cross."

"I figured," was Sommers' stony reply, still in awe of the untouched beauty.

He started to turn back, but she stopped him. "Sommers... thank you. I never imagined... you'll get us home." She hugged him and for a moment time stopped.

Elena felt good to him, her lithe, tanned body fitting his. Her svelte curves were muscular, toned and warm. It was right and he wanted to stay entangled with her forever, coupled and aroused. *Just leave the others, stay there on that point and forget everything and everyone else. Survival, your survival.* It was a fantasy that had teeth.

"We'll make it," he announced, comforting her.

"I know Ramon's death wasn't your fault. Please don't blame yourself." She kissed him. Not on the mouth, but on the cheek. Glancing into his eyes, just inches apart, he kissed her back, hard, on the mouth. It was desperate... real.

They stayed, clinging to each other, on top of a bluff that overlooked the whole world. Time stood still. He didn't know how long they held each other, but it was long enough to enjoy and escape. A giant release, he happily thought. "I'm glad you're here. Come on, let's get the others."

They followed each other back to the group.

# 75

## SWIMMERS

The Marapa River was a giant artery that fed the ocean from deep in the heart of Mexico. At this point, near its end, its current and width could increase to an alarming rate, depending on rainfall. The spray at the bottom created a colorful rainbow, which masked the violent action of the water, crashing into a rocky riverbed. Because of the rainy weather, hundreds of thousands of gallons of clear, cold liquid now fell each minute and the possible peril it could bring was Sommers' main concern.

Upon arriving at the roaring falls, the group was taken aback as well. Assessing options, Sommers hoped they could find a narrower spot upstream to cross with less of a current.

With new determination and goal, Sommers led the group, each taking a turn with Kevin and alternating, keeping a gun trained on the weakening Enrique.

The jungle bordered the swiftly moving water and smooth, slippery rocks made for a difficult trek. There was no pathway to follow and as usual, as they had come to expect, the jungle wasn't forgiving.

About a half mile above the waterfall, they encountered the remnants of an old, collapsed bridge. Pieces of dangling hemp, along with rotten beams that acted as support, danced and decayed on the rushing surface.

"My people built this," Enrique voiced.

"They could have done a better job," Sommers replied, wading in a bit to examine the remains. Touching one of the foundation posts, he knew what was coming next and dropped his gear.

"What are you doing, Tourist?" Enrique questioned, watching Sommers grab long, shredded rope pieces and tie them together.

"I'm going across. With a line set over there, we can all make it." Sommers tied off one end around his waist and set it tight. He began coiling and tying ends to ends.

Focused on Sommers' actions, none of them saw Enrique quietly position himself and then, animal-like, spring to life. He overpowered Celia and knocked her to the ground. In one swift move he took the gun and it was over before it started. He shoved her to the water's edge and waved the gun, shocking everyone. "My odds will be better if she crosses."

Sommers didn't need to be asked twice. He untied the rope and angrily advanced on Enrique. "She won't make it."

"That is her problem," Enrique retorted, leveling the gun at Sommers. "I think your conscience is bothering you again."

"No, what's bothering me is you."

"I'm growing tired of you, Doctor."

"Then just do it. Pull the trigger!"

"With pleasure and without remorse."

Sommers was at point blank range. Enrique's finger squeezed, as Celia stepped between them. "I can do it... I can, Sommers! Just don't let go of the line." Her eyes radiated a desperate confidence, one that Sommers would have to trust.

"Celia-- "

Enrique trained the gun on Celia's head, the muzzle grazing her temple. "Ever the team. Do anything stupid little girl and they all die."

"I just want to go home. We'll get across and you can have the coins. Whatever you want, just let us go."

"A noble gesture. Sommers, aid the counselor with the rope."

Without another option and at gunpoint, Sommers tied it around Celia with a double knot. They both waded into the river.

"Now or never," Celia gulped, staring at the flowing water.

"Wade as far as you can. Don't fight the current. It'll carry you, but you'll get through it. I'll have you."

Sommers motioned for Elena to help and she planted her feet and set herself behind him. Kevin managed to pull himself in behind her and they all three began feeding out the line. Enrique scoffed at their precision. "I must say you Americans have such a flair for drama."

"We're just trying to protect her," Kevin defended.

"Of course; my apologies."

Celia waded until the water was chest deep. The current sucked at her and the rope went taut. She began swimming through the crosscurrent and made slow headway.

"Keep at it Celia," Sommers yelled, holding a sharp eye on the rope. "Way to go."

"Faster," Enrique yelled. "I don't have all day to wait." He fired a shot, scaring all of them.

"She can't help us if she's dead!"

"Drama and whining. Quiet."

"Always picking on the weakest," an upset Kevin blurted. "Why don't you pick on somebody who can fight back?"

The remark angered Enrique and in one motion, he placed the gun on Kevin's head. "For some reason, I would have expected better from you, American. I think it's time to say good-bye now."

"NO-- don't!" Elena screamed.

"Celia made it!" Sommers yelled, watching the winded attorney drag the rope out on the other side.

His joyous instant was short lived, as he realized the unfolding situation with Kevin. Taking advantage of the moment, Sommers turned and jumped Enrique, tackling him to the muddy shore.

"Mistake, Amigo."

Enrique punched Sommers hard in the face and in one quick move was on top of him. He shoved the pistol's muzzle into Sommers' mouth and cocked it. "The... coins... are... mine, and so are you!"

Sommers remembered Enrique's wide grin and then a loud "crack." Kevin had mustered all his energy and whacked Enrique across the face with the fanny pack of gold. He screamed, "Then take the coins... take them!"

Full of rage, Enrique charged Kevin, shoving them both into the river. He pummeled Kevin, holding his head underwater.

On the other shore, Celia saw what was happening and began coiling the rope. "Hang on, Kevin," she yelled.

With Kevin weakening and squirming in the river, Enrique found footing and stood, placing Sommers in his gun sight. "Time to ante up, Doctor."

Elena stood and cried, "Kevin can't swim!"

The plea took a moment to register with Enrique, but finally got his attention. Kevin held the fanny pack with the coins and was losing consciousness in the river's flow. Enrique had to decide between Sommers and trying to reach the gold.

Violently, Kevin was sucked into the current and swept downstream. Enrique paused. In that flash, Sommers jumped Enrique. As they grappled each other, their bodies flung into the deep water. They, too, were swept into the rushing current.

# 76

## THE OATH

Kevin's spiritless cries were barely audible over the rushing water, as Celia ran along the river looking for the right spot to throw him the line. The river's pace increased and she had a difficult time traversing the rock laden bank. "Kevin-- hang on. I'm over here."

In the river's churning chaos, Enrique kept dunking Sommers and finally pulled away from him, trying to approach Kevin.

Elena ran parallel to them. "Get him, Sommers-- ! He's drowning!"

Sommers gasped for air and tried with all his strength to overtake Enrique and reach Kevin. He knew Kevin was no match for something like this, as he even struggled with the ever present current. He likened it to giant hands squeezing his torso, only to have them release at the right moment and flood his overworked lungs. His arm riveted with pain, but he forced himself to paddle, swim with all his strength. He also knew what was less than a hundred yards away. His waterlogged mind reeled and raced, and began asking, *at what point do you bail... let it go? Where is the point of no return? When do I lay the bike down?*

Celia ran ahead of both groups and jumped on a boulder that extended into the river. From that vantage point, she saw the white water ripples and the encroaching falls. Even with a rock wall cushion, its sound was blatantly loud, unyielding. She knew they were dangerously close and she would only have one chance with the line.

One chance.

She felt the coarseness in her hands and had doubts if she could throw it accurately, even close to them. *What if I miss,* she thought. *What if-- ?*

Enrique reached Kevin, yanking his head from the suffocating liquid. Instinctually, his mouth opened, sucking in air. He'd bought himself more precious seconds of life.

Enrique had a grip, but couldn't get the leverage to obtain the fanny pack, which Kevin's arm held just out of range. Frustrated, he fought and lunged, but couldn't reach the pack.

Seeing the approaching twosome, Celia steeled herself against the boulder and let the line fly. It arched upward and landed directly in front of them. "Yes-- ! The line, Kevin-- grab the line!"

Elena shrieked too, now standing directly across from Celia. She jumped up and down, feeling they were so close. The tether floated on the choppy surface and she wanted to grab it and hand it to them. But there was nothing she could do. Everything rested in fate's hands.

Enrique saw the wispy line and had to release Kevin in order to capture it. He struggled now, the river taking its charge. Seizing the hemp, it tightened, then rifled through his clenched fingers, burning them. He yelped in pain, as bloody skin peeled off and his bared hide became saturated with blood and water. With his other arm stretched out, he barely snatched Kevin, and was now straddled between his drifting body and shore.

Celia worked fiercely, trying to secure the line around a boulder and keep her balance, as the river was still winning and dragging them toward the falls. She wasn't strong enough to haul them in. "Hang on, Kevin," she kept yelling, now competing with the falls' roar.

In the river's swell, Enrique made a calculation. He knew he couldn't hold onto Kevin, the tenuous line and get the coins. There wasn't enough time and he didn't have a strong enough hold. "Roll over," he shouted at the swamped and drowning Kevin.

Kevin flailed, fighting with all his might to stay afloat. If he was going down, he was going down swinging. In the free-for-all, he actually pushed Enrique below the surface and the water gagged him. In the lapse after, Enrique saw Kevin release the fanny pack. "You idiot!" Enrique screeched, finding some hidden force within.

Enrique angrily swam toward them, using Kevin's body as leverage, but torpedo-like, Sommers appeared and grappled him from behind.

Enrique released the line and violently kicked off Sommers. The action propelled him closer to the sinking fanny pack just under the surface and he dove for it.

Helpless in the water, an eddy swirled and shot Kevin laterally toward the shore. His head smashed into an outcropping of boulders. It pinned him against the slippery, moss covered granite, with a tremendous undertow yanking at him. There was nothing he could do, nothing he could grab, and Kevin felt his body being sucked back under, into the main flow.

It was certain death. The watery blackness overtook his body and he closed his eyes, almost welcoming the outcome. Thick fluid filled his ears and the static sounds of death began to rise in his brain, when Sommers miraculously latched onto his shirt, fighting the torrential current.

With his bloodied face underwater, Sommers' airless body hung on and he willed his bleeding, skidding fingertips to find a hold on the rock. They finally gripped something, an indentation, a spur, a lip. Clawing with all his might, he dragged himself and Kevin upward. Celia's hands grabbed them both. With Celia pulling and Sommers pushing, Kevin finally landed on shore. Sommers' exhausted body followed.

"You're okay, you're going to make it," Celia cheered.

"Says you," Sommers replied, spitting water and blood.

Enrique caught the same eddy, a swirling paradox that shoved him further downstream, into some boulders. He was now fighting the river, the rocks and the fanny pack's weight.

Sommers saw the horrible machinations in place and rose to his feet. Celia and a coughing Kevin saw as well, but didn't move.

"You can't be serious about-- " Kevin began.

"I took an oath," Sommers reminded and started for Enrique's boulder. Celia hesitantly followed a few seconds later, not knowing what to expect.

Sommers hopped from the shore to the big boulders, then jumped over to Enrique's. It was an island, the last point of no return, with white rapids all around. Celia also made the jump, stripping off her gear and leaving it on the boulders. She didn't bring the rope and clung to Sommers.

Sommers saw Enrique battling to cling to the boulder and hang onto the fanny pack. He couldn't do both and keep a grip in the violent melee. In a last ditch effort, they all watched the fanny pack slip away from Enrique's grasp. "NO-- " the trapped Enrique bellowed. "I lost them!"

Sommers hung precariously over the tip of the boulder, but still couldn't quite make contact. Enrique kept looking, searching in vain for his coins.

"The gold is gone... we can save you," Sommers breathily voiced. "Reach up."

"Grab his hand," Celia cried out. "Grab it!"

Enrique achieved a sliver of leverage and raised his hand to within inches of Sommers', tips of their fingers almost touching... gripping. Then they locked eyes.

Sommers saw a hollow blackness, a void lacking any kind of compassion. It was like an electrical shock, yet he was intent on saving him. *The oath, his core... what he did...*

In that instant, that nanosecond of harsh reality, Sommers saw a bleak and empty man. A soulless person with nothing redeeming. He almost felt sorry for him, until Enrique spoke.

With Sommers in his sights, he smiled, his capped teeth shining. "Gringos..." was what spewed. A simple, yet effective statement, summing up that moment. It really wasn't a surprise, but Sommers would never forget.

The wry corners of Enrique's mouth spiked up and he slipped away. Water overtook him and the relentless current sucked his body under with a vengeance and out into the massive river.

Sommers and Celia were helpless, as they could do nothing except watch Enrique bob to and fro, and be swept over the crashing falls. He didn't fight. He lost. Sommers knew he had lost it all.

They were both in shock in that moment. Celia helped Sommers back and they lay draped on the rocks, droplets on their skin reflecting the sun breaking through willowy clouds.

"I don't know what to say," Celia said.

"You don't say anything. You don't justify it and you don't worry about it."

239

"Sounds like you speak from experience."

"He chose. I guess we all do."

She put an arm around him and they stood. On shaky legs, they somberly walked over to Kevin. They never looked back at the falls. Enrique was gone... another life lost.

# 77

## FOUND

With the rope now secure on both shores of the river, Sommers returned for Elena. Kevin was breathing hard, sitting up and waiting with Celia. The remaining heroin had been lost in the river and his pain was intensifying. He rationalized he didn't want it anymore anyway.

Sommers checked the rope, and with a final tug, they started back across with Elena in front. Before it got very deep, he stopped her. "I didn't get to tell you that I'm sorry about Ramon. What I said-- "

"You were trying to protect me. It was a bad time. I understand."

Sommers reached into his pocket and produced her bracelet, the one he found on the trail earlier. The gift from Ramon. He slipped it onto her wrist. "Here. I saved this for you. You still know I want a rematch for the bike race."

"I know."

She kissed him and he savored it. A simple kiss in the middle of a river, in the middle of Mexico. Somehow it made up for a lot of things. Beautiful. Deadly.

They waded a bit deeper, adjusting and fighting the increasing cross current, then she stopped and went rigid.

"What's wrong? Don't stop-- " Sommers began.

Glancing up, he saw the reason. A unit of Mexican soldiers stood in front of them on the opposite side. They were armed and looked as if they were questioning Celia and Kevin.

"Soldiers…"

"Tell me they aren't upset at us," Sommers quietly intoned.

A lieutenant waded in a few feet, tugging on the line. Sommers immediately thought if the lieutenant were to cut it, they would be in big trouble. He hoped that wasn't the plan, as he didn't want to go swimming again.

"You have a problem, Señor?" came the lieutenant's question.

"It depends," Sommers answered. "Can you help us?"

This brought a murmur from the other soldiers, their hands poised on their weapons. The lieutenant quieted them and said, "Perhaps you should come ashore."

"Yes, perhaps."

Sommers calmly nudged Elena and they trudged forward. He kept his eyes on the soldiers and the lieutenant, all the while holding onto the rope. His mind reeled at the fact they were entering yet another volatile situation. *Who had he angered so badly?*

Near the other side, part of the unit entered the water and helped them. Sommers thought it conciliatory.

"It is very dangerous for tourists here. May I ask what is your purpose of this visit?"

"We're on a bike tour. Or were. From Vera Cruz. It's a very long story," Sommers expressed.

"Yes, but you are way off the common trails for such a trip. Where are your machines... the bikes? And your guide?"

"Bad map." Sommers hoped the coldness would suffice. Even though the entire trip flashed before his eyes, he didn't want to go into detail, dredge up everything that had happened. At least not yet. "Look, I'm a doctor and we have a seriously injured man-- and I have been shot."

"Yes, I can see."

"I will be more than happy to recount our story, but right now we need your help. Is that satisfactory for you?"

The lieutenant, cautious, but not wanting to be blamed for something later, acquiesced and postured a softer tone. "We will gladly escort you safely to Vera Cruz and its hospital."

"Gracias," the group mumbled in unison, happy at the outcome. "Thank you-- "

"How far?" Sommers pressed.

"Approximately two kilometers."

"Wow, we made it," Kevin coughed, a pressure being lifted. "Who would have guessed?"

Sommers saw Kevin was bloody again. "Hey, you're bleeding."

"So are you." Kevin wiped the blood off his brow and looked downstream, just able to see the falls. He squeezed the blood between his fingers, then nodded gratefully. "I'm alive, baby."

"Who says you can't swim?" Sommers chided, also feeling the monkey off his back, tending to his arm. "Let's get us fixed and go home."

Anxiously they started for the soldiers' Jeeps. It was a welcome sight. Even sitting down would feel good, Sommers thought.

"Wait-- " Celia gasped, looking around. "My cameras. They're on the rocks."

Sommers chuckled. "Now that's a crisis. I'll get them."

He motioned to the lieutenant, taking a mock picture, and headed downstream. However, this time it was different. He actually enjoyed himself, relaxing a bit, seeing the river and jungle for what they were. He gazed around him. The roar of the falls was almost peaceful and he thought it funny how fast life situations can change. The world he was in now seemed like a vacation spot. A beautiful, non-threatening part of the world. *Was the jungle their friend again?*

Spying the outcropping's structure, Sommers saw Celia's gear at the water's edge. He hopped over some rocks and slipped, nearly falling.

Catching his balance on some other stones the river bordered, he saw something... a strap, and then the unmistakable, brightly colored... fanny pack. It had wedged itself underneath a rock in a small pool, just out of the flow. The water gently cascaded over its top, billowing the packed nylon.

Sommers quickly looked around, adrenaline pumping... the jungle... the falls' roar... sunshine... no one else... the fanny pack. It was his. It was over.

He reached for it.

# 78

## TOURISTS

The tired group grew impatient waiting for Sommers. Even Celia and Elena thought he had been gone too long. They shared anxious looks.

The lieutenant, always checking his watch, was about to send someone downstream to check on him, when Sommers appeared, slogging Celia's gear and cameras.

"I think these belong to you," he boasted, handing them off to her.

"What took you so long? Think the whole world revolves around you?" she jokingly asked.

"Slippery rocks." He nodded to the lieutenant. "So, it's two kilometers?"

"Yes. You came very close. You should be proud of yourselves for surviving such a harrowing journey."

"You don't know the half of it."

They piled into the Jeeps. Sommers made sure Kevin was comfortable. Elena rode close, holding his hand, stealing glances.

Sommers didn't know how to feel, or what to say. His mind was in a different place, but he was contented. He could hardly wait for something to ease the pain in his arm.

With the infamous fanny pack strapped on underneath his shirt, he quietly rode into the village, not telling anyone. No, he would save that. The priority now was seeing he and Kevin had some proper medical attention.

The soldier driving took it easy on the rough parts. The tense energy of the jungle lessened and soon they turned onto a paved road. They quickly arrived in the heart of town.

Tourists from a cruise ship in the harbor gawked at everything there and bartered with the locals. Unaware and uncaring, they stood blocking the streets and the Jeep had to maneuver through them to pass. Immaculately clean and suntanned in silly straw hats and loud shirts, most had cold drinks in their hands, as they received their money's worth of Mexican vacation time. Not a care in world. *The brochures…*

The soldier tapped the horn and Sommers remembered the irate faces of the ones forced to move. *Yes, move along two feet, so we can pass,* he thought, knowing they were clueless and half drunk. Subconsciously, he felt he should be part of that group, an innocent cruise tourist, being forced to get out of the way, looking for the next bar and watching the clock, as to not miss the ship leaving port. *Never miss the ship.*

That made him grin and he felt the bulging fanny pack shift, as the Jeep finally pushed through.

# 79

## DOCTOR SOMMERS

The clinic was small and understaffed, but clean. When they arrived, the soldiers helped Kevin, carrying him inside. The lieutenant must have had some pull because they were attended to immediately. Each had a nurse look after them.

A Mexican doctor immediately took Kevin's stats and vitals, and Sommers aided the process. Although hesitant, he explained how he kept Kevin going with the heroin, and that he would have done it again. The doctor reluctantly agreed, started a saline IV and took X-rays. Overall, he was impressed with Sommers' work. Kevin had survived and would live to tell the tale.

However, Kevin seemed uncomfortable with the attention. Maybe he'd heard rumors about the quality of medical care in Mexico, but he did know Sommers had saved his life.

"You did a very good thing, Dr. Sommers," the doctor stated, making notations on Kevin's file. "You overcame immense obstacles and saved your friend's life. After some rest, he will be fine."

"Like a horse," Kevin blurted.

"See Kevin, it was all in your head," Sommers grinned.

About to leave and let the staff work, Kevin grabbed Sommers' hand. His eyes, although now on morphine, conveyed gratitude beyond belief. "The grand morass..." Kevin remembered. "Thanks, man. I owe you my life."

Sommers knew what he meant. It had come down to all or nothing, and because fate had blinked first, they had all walked out of there alive.

He affably watched them wheel Kevin away. Comforted with the knowledge Kevin was safe, Sommers showed the doctor his bullet wound in his upper arm. The good news was the bullet had gone all the way through. The bad news was it tore his biceps muscle and mountain biking would take a hiatus. It didn't take long for the doctor to clean the wound and stitch him up. Another round in the battle had been won.

# *80*

## IN PLAIN SIGHT

The next day Kevin was released at noon. He was still groggy, but completely bandaged with his bad arm in a sling. He didn't care if he ever saw another bike again. He was hungry and Sommers reminded him it was an excellent sign and he would heal quickly.

They found a small cafe on the beach with a view of the docked cruise ship. The sun was out and the water crystal blue. In Sommers' mind it could have been heaven after passing through hell. Drinking beer and eating tacos, they soaked up the atmosphere, now cleaned up and rested.

"I think you were right Sommers," Celia offered. "We should have taken a cruise. That is one pretty ship."

"Maybe, but we would have missed out on some things."

"Yeah, like a life threatening situation with a madman and a trip to the hospital," Kevin confirmed.

"Well that is part of it. The bad part." With that, Sommers produced the weathered fanny pack from underneath his shirt. He dropped it on the table for effect. The group, shocked once more, could only stare in disbelief.

"That's not what I think it-- " Kevin began.

"From the rocks, near Celia's cameras. It must have gotten snagged somehow when El Jerko went over."

The pack had seen better days. The colors were faded, the edges were frayed and it had spots of dried blood. It was bulging from being full and where the fabric had stretched. It listed to one side.

"I think we earned-- " Sommers began, but was interrupted by Celia.

"Sommers... we have company."

In the next instant, the lieutenant appeared. He marched over to them with his captain, a crusty, curious, scowling man in his fifties.

"Just sit tight," Sommers mumbled. "Hola," he greeted the soldiers.

"Hola," the lieutenant responded. "I'm very glad to see you were able to rest. This is my captain. There are questions."

He then spoke Spanish to the captain, who didn't change his dour expression. He kept locking eyes with each of them.

Clearing his throat, the lieutenant spoke. "Enrique Salerno is known to us. A smuggler and a thief; we are still unclear about his intentions and how you came to cross paths."

"His intentions were to kill us," Sommers snapped. "He and his men have two camps in the mountains. At one, around a water well, you will find guns, drugs and I'm afraid... many dead bodies of both soldiers and rebels. The other one is further down where Enrique is, or was, constructing a submarine. Incredible to see, actually."

The lieutenant translated to the captain, as Sommers quietly clenched the fanny pack's straps. The captain wasn't happy and spoke more agitated Spanish.

"A submarine? But your initial contact was-- "

"We accidentally came across their camp on our bike tour at a bad time... after their fight. We took a couple of guns for protection; then Enrique found us. I think he liked killing people."

Another exchange and translation. "What kind of drugs were in the vicinity?"

Ever since the hospital, Sommers feared this would be a touchy issue. He didn't want them to become involved in some kind of drug controversy and thought the best way to handle it would be the truth. "It was heroin. We didn't pursue that, except for a small amount for my friend, who was treated at the hospital. The rebels had obviously smuggled the drugs into your country and I guess were storing them inside the well. Our lives were in danger. Enrique killed our guide and another American on the tour."

After the translation, the captain leaned on the table, actually touching the fanny pack for support. The group was speechless, all eyes glued on his gnarly fingers.

The outline of coins could easily be seen. He then shoved a place mat in front of Sommers and produced a pen. "My captain requests you draw a map showing the camp's exact location. We have been after these men for months."

"I will do that," Elena volunteered, taking the pen and paper, and starting to draw.

Sommers reached inside his pocket and brought out the locket the rebel boy had been holding. It was dented and had traces of blood. "After you ID the bodies, maybe you could return this to the woman inside the locket. She might live here; her son was one of the boys killed."

The lieutenant held the piece of jewelry and his face saddened. He knew there were many young boys involved with the rebels and their causes. Bullets had no prejudice. He had a mother too. "Yes, yes of course. You must realize you are very fortunate to be alive, having associated with such a dangerous man. It could easily be your bodies in the mountains."

"I don't think associated is the right word," Kevin replied, smiling, then sipping his beer.

Elena finished drawing and presented the map to the soldiers. The captain immediately snatched it and mumbled to the lieutenant. They both glared at the group. "Our immediate mission is to find these camps. The rebels have eluded us and their activities are, how do I say-- "

"Are hurting morale?"

"Yes, that is it. We want no further embarrassment. Would you be available in a few days for verification?"

"Lieutenant, there's only one well up in those ruins with dead bodies around it and one sub a few miles away. Look at the map. They're very near marked trails. I hate to say it, but that's probably why they were successful. They hid everything in an obvious place. Don't you think we've been here long enough-- that it's time we all go home?"

The lieutenant told the captain, who raised his hand, shaking his fist. The group's energy fell. They wanted out, but not to be crossways with the military. It was Mexico.

The captain then whispered to the lieutenant, fingering the map. "My captain agrees. You have suffered enough on your vacation. Detainment would not be productive. Please try to enjoy the rest of your stay in Vera Cruz, and please think of returning at a later date for another vacation. Be well."

With that, the soldiers left, the captain leading, holding the map.

Sommers sighed with relief, as did the others. He gently touched the fanny pack. "Robbie asked what they were worth when we first found them. Remember that?"

"It seems so long ago," Elena said, emotion filled.

"Ramon was right about the rites of passage, the bond."

"Living the secrets," Celia admitted. "But we survived."

"You have to fight to survive. Remember? That's the secret."

They focused on the pack, the mood lightening. "Do you know what kind of hero that captain will be when he brings in those kilo bags of heroin and guns? Shows off that submarine? He'll be a god..."

"If he turns them in." Kevin grinned.

That brought a round of laughter, another taste of the absurdity conflicting with reality.

Sommers took Elena's hands. "What would Ramon say to do?"

She thought a moment. A tear formed and ran down her cheek. "He'd want us to keep them. Use them for something good."

"You know I couldn't care less about gold coins that almost got me killed, but we did make it, and that means something," Kevin stated. "They stand for something now, you know."

Sommers put the question to them. "So, are we agreed?"

He thrust out his hand, placed it firmly on the fanny pack. Celia gave him a knowing look, putting hers on top of his. She turned to Kevin, who smiled and placed his next. They all turned to Elena, who grinned through tears of healing, sorrow and happiness. With hers in place, their bond was strong. They toasted Ramon.

"You know we could streak our faces with ketchup," Kevin joked.

"No, no more streaking," Sommers retorted.

"You know, I'm going to check that cruise ship, see if there's any more space," Celia said wistfully.

"You do that," Sommers confirmed. "First class staterooms for four. I can ride the bike in the gym."

Sommers dropped some money on the table and stood up with the fanny pack over his shoulder. He put his arm around Elena and they all started to leave. He glanced at the ocean, the purity of it, and how it contrasted fully with the hokey tourists.

With the sun shining, in a profound silence they welcomingly shared, the four naturally pulled together until they were all walking arm in arm.

Oblivious to the music, tourists and loud activity around them, they slowly disappeared into the safety of the village.

# EPILOGUE

Sommers divided the coins on the last day of the cruise back to the States. They took their shares, said their good-byes and went their separate ways, except for Elena, each taking a flight for home that night. They promised to stay in touch and they did.

Elena addressed her grieving and made the proper arrangements for Ramon. There was a small memorial service and flowers arrived from each of the group and even the lieutenant, who had been promoted after finding and handling the rebel camp.

Celia returned and immediately forced her husband to pay the piper, putting him through the worst divorce proceeding imaginable. She never let up, hiring the best divorce attorneys, challenging him at every hearing and pulling out all the stops. She got what she wanted, him out of her life and a clean start.

Kevin settled with his family regarding the business. His terms of a buyout were accepted and he became the CEO of a multi-national entity his grandfather had begun on a street corner. He made a bold effort and kept his family intact, delegating business matters and spending more time with his kids. He donated most of the coins to a museum, but mounted one in acrylic for his desk. He saw it every day. *Lest we forget.*

Kevin never rode a bike again.

Sommers met with Wethers immediately and filed every document and appeal needed. He then hired a publicist for himself and went on the attack. He took his version to the powers that be and launched his spin.

Public opinion went south for the Senator, and being an election year, he dropped the charges after the Medical Board decided to side with Dr. Sommers. He liked the sound of that. He could practice. He would have a medical career. The payoff.

Weeks later, sitting on his bike in the hazy morning surf at Malibu, he felt absolved, whole again. He held the photo Celia had taken the first day of the trip, next to the helicopter. The group... all smiles. *Do something good,* those words echoed in his head.

"Hey," chimed Elena's perfect voice. "I thought you were taking me for a walk."

Sommers turned, watching Elena walk out of his house toward him. She never looked better. "North or south? The beach is yours."

She giggled, like she had when they first met. The look she had... those eyes. Chemistry. "Mmmm, north. I've seen all the southern beaches I want to see."

"Me too." Grinning, he jogged over, kissed her and they began walking.

He left the bike in the sand.

**THE END**

## About Courtney and Jacquelyn Silberberg

Before committing to writing full time both Courtney and Jacquelyn held various executive positions in the film industry. Courtney was V.P. of Production for Gladden Entertainment (FABULOUS BAKER BOYS, WEEKEND AT BERNIE'S, MANNEQUIN II, MILLENNIUM, SHORT TIME) and Jacquelyn was a freelance DVD producer (Fox, Sony, and Warner Brothers titles). Their short dark comedy, COMMITTED, which they co-wrote, with Courtney directing and Jacquelyn producing, won Best Directorial Debut in the New York International Independent Film Festival. It was screened at several Festivals around the country. Both attained their master's degree from the USC School of Cinematic Arts, Peter Stark Producing Program and have their own company, Mesquite Entertainment®.

As they primarily write feature screenplays, FIERCE THUNDER is their first novel, but they have several others in the wings. Although California residents, they also spend time in Courtney's home town of Dalhart, Texas. Both are avid golfers and met on the golf course. They have six rescue cats and a rescue German Shepherd, who thinks she's a cat.

## Connect with Courtney and Jacquelyn

via Mesquiteentertainment.com or IMDB.com or Pneuma Springs Publishing Featured Authors' page.

Lightning Source UK Ltd.
Milton Keynes UK
UKOW04f2154311015

261818UK00001BA/12/P